W.S.

& Other Lives

By the same author

Fiction
The Eleventh Summer
August in July
Work & Play
Malachy and his Family
Life of a Drum
The Cure

Non-fiction
Driving Through Cuba: An East-West Journey
The Glass Curtain: Inside an Ulster Community

Children's Fiction
The T.V. Genie
The Witch that Wasn't

Carlo Gébler (signature)

CARLO GÉBLER
W.9. & Other Lives

Lagan Press
1996

Acknowledgements

'The Speech of Birds' and 'The Chekhov Student' have been published
previously in *The Literary Review*; 'Puerto Vallarta' in *Foreign Exchange*
and *Departures*; 'The Headscarf' in *Critical Quarterly* and *Best Short Stories
of 1993*; 'Telephone Sex' (under the title 'The Telephone Call') in *Winter's
Tales (New Series Six)*; 'W.9.' in *London Tales*; 'Nuptials' in *New Writing 2*
and *Fortnight*, 'The Fifty Pound Note' and 'Connemara' in the *Irish Times*,
The Fiction Magazine and *The Literary Review*; 'Four Pesos' in *Twenty
Under Thirty-Five*; 'At the Cinema' in the *London Daily News*; 'The Kitten'
in *The Saturday Telegraph* and *The Daily Telegraph Book of Contemporary
Short Stories*; and 'Wesley' (under the title 'The Driver's Story' in *Fortnight*
and *Prospect*.

Published by
Lagan Press
PO Box 110 BT12 4AB, Belfast

Lagan Press gratefully acknowledges the financial assistance
of the Arts Council of Northern Ireland in the production of this book.

The author wishes to acknowledge the financial support of
An Chomhairle Ealaíon/The Arts Council.

ISBN: 1 873687 95 8
Author: Gébler, Carlo
Title: W.9. & Other Lives
Format: Paperback
1996

Cover Photograph: Cowboy (1996) by Leon McAuley
Cover Design: December Publications
Set in Bodoni
Printed by Noel Murphy, Belfast

For John & Sarah, dearest of friends

The mass of men lead lives of quiet desperation.

Walden, Henry David Thoreau

Contents

The Chekhov Student

I

MY NAME IS DOUGLAS Peter. I am a Russian scholar. I am married to a Russian woman and have been for forty years. I am extremely miserable. One of the roots of my unhappiness is Natasha's thriftiness. In the early years of our marriage it was welcome. Times were hard and money was short. But now we have money—not much but some—and life in this area at least should be easier. Yet the business of how much or how little to spend on the housekeeping remains a source of continuous friction between us. Whenever I suggest we spend more, Natasha gets hurt and reminds me how I once praised her for being prudent and economical. "But that was in the past," I reply. "We are rich now, or anyway richer." 'You can lead a horse to water,' the old phrase goes, 'but you cannot make it drink,'—well, that is how it is with us. Our conversations or confrontations about money always end with Natasha getting huffy and taking to her bed for the day. When this happens, an unusually heavy pall of depression descends on the house. It almost drips down the walls like brown water from a cracked pipe. In these circumstances I cannot concentrate on my work. The argument weighs on me and the house is abnormally silent, except for Natasha's sighs and the terrifying squeak our bed makes whenever she turns over ...

If I take the law into my own hands and just buy what I want, Natasha will usually try to humiliate me about it in public. It happened only last week when—which happens rarely—some people came to dinner ...

One of the guests was a shy woman with a glass eye. As she was about to cut a piece of Brie, Natasha pounced on her.

"Do you like that Brie?" she asked.

Our guest was taken aback by the sudden enquiry and did not know what to say. This momentary pause was all Natasha needed.

11

"Aie, it's horrible!" (Here Natasha grimaced.) "Soapy is how I would describe it! And you wouldn't believe what Douglas paid for it. Silly man! But that's men all over, isn't it?—yes!—always taken for a ride, as your English expression says. Poor Douglas, he always pays too much ..."

When Natasha finished she winked at the shy woman. It was a masterstroke. It took all the venom out of her diatribe, and made it seem like the sisterly confidence of one woman to another.

Sitting at the other end of the table, I didn't hear everything but I heard enough. It made me wince. Why does she do it? I thought. How can she talk about money in front of them like this? How can she be so vulgar? We're not in the ghetto living off cabbage soup! We're in London for God's sake. We're in Hampstead Garden bloody suburb.

What I had heard gave me a sour taste at the back of my throat and the rest of the evening was spoilt for me. The food made me nauseous and I could not eat; my head started to throb and I found I could not take in the sense of what was said to me. I felt I was imprisoned in a glass box. I could see everyone's lips moving but I heard nothing.

Later, when Natasha and I were lying side by side in our bed, I asked her why she had talked so disparagingly about the cheese I had bought.

"Oh, but I said nothing," she replied. "You're over-reacting!"

"I am not 'over-reacting'."

"Oh, Douglas, you're such a little boy!"

"I'm not a little boy. Why do you humiliate me in public?"

"I didn't humiliate you. I couldn't humiliate you. I love you! I just joked a little about how much you spend. Come on, don't be cross. Only little boys are allowed to be cross. And old women like me. Only I'm allowed to be cross."

When she finished, Natasha turned round and laid her head on my chest. She laid it in the little hollow where the left arm joins the shoulder—just above my heart.

"Aie, your heart is beating!" she said.

Too bloody right, I thought.

Within a minute Natasha was snoring. Despite her age she has the ability to fall asleep instantly. It was a talent she developed in the camps and she has never lost it. I, on the other hand, who have never known anything more serious than a slight nervous breakdown during my Finals at university, have never found it particularly easy to get to sleep, and after an argument I find it practically impossible. I either lie awake and invent imaginary dialogues in which I perfectly express everything I have felt but failed to say, or else I sink into a cold fury, feel like a stone inside, and become incapable of any thought or action. On this occasion I fell into what I call my 'dead' state, and lay awake listening to the slow drone of Natasha snoring and the distant rumble of railway trucks being shunted in the depot. Curiously enough, the last sound is one of Natasha's earliest memories. When she was three, she and her parents were sent out of Moscow and east into exile. They travelled to Siberia in a cattle wagon. But I am straying from the point. At about four o'clock the dawn chorus started—a sound that strikes terror into an insomniac like no other—and somehow, then, I managed to doze off.

When Natasha does not have the opportunity to humiliate me in public over an extravagance, her revenge is much longer and more drawn out. She will say nothing to begin with. She will just go silent. Days—even weeks will pass—and it will not be mentioned. Our life together will be even worse than usual.

I always begin these wars full of stern resolution. I am determined I will not be the one who breaks the deadlock. But after a while my resolve wavers and eventually collapses. I go to Natasha and I put my arms around her. My mood at this point is always subdued and it is my sincere intention that we make up. I am even prepared to apologise for the offending extravagance. But there is something about Natasha in these circumstances that changes my mood from one of calm to fury. Our last row—we had it a fortnight ago—was typical in this and every other respect. Within seconds, literally, of attempting a reconciliation, I was shouting and Natasha was shouting back. Now when I shout, I go red and then purple, and the veins on my forehead stand up. They look like worms in the ground. I also become incoherent and all sorts of unconnected images and metaphors gush out of my mouth. Natasha, on the other hand, turns cold and white; her thick, red, still-sensuous lips grow thin like wire; and she spits out one perfectly articulated piece of vituperation after another. At the end of this row I was left with only one recourse. I rushed out of the kitchen like a small boy denied his pocket money or an extra half-an-hour of television before going to bed and slammed the door after myself. I often end our arguments by slamming the door and this time I did it so hard, I made all the plates on the dresser shake.

"Aie, Douglas! Don't slam so hard! You'll break all the plates," Natasha shouted after me. "Do you think we're made of money?"

Of course this only infuriated me further.

In order to be alone I locked myself in my study. I tried to work but I was too angry to make any progress with the dictionary. My rage was like an intoxicated stupor. There was nothing else for it. I threw myself down on the sofa and stared up at the ceiling. Hours passed, it grew dark and suddenly I realised—I had been lying there all afternoon.

"Vol—ga boat—men! Vol—ga boat—men!" It was Natasha singing in the kitchen. After each refrain I heard her laughing quietly to herself. She was singing the Glenn Miller version of the song. When she had first arrived in England, it had made her laugh to hear how an American band leader had turned this slow, mournful, Russian melody into a dance number. As I listened to her curious, toneless singing and the hearty, catarrhal laugh that followed each refrain, I thought to myself—as I have God knows how many times before—this can't go on. It's been going on like this for twenty years! Then I dragged myself off the couch and went into the kitchen. I found Natasha sticking some new labels on the spice jars.

"Hello," I said.

"Hello," she replied, as if nothing had happened. "How's the dictionary going?"

"Oh very well. I'm up to Nabokov."

"Well, that's very good. I think we should celebrate!"

From the freezer, Natasha extracted a bottle of vodka and two glasses opaque with cold. Whenever we have a row she always puts a bottle and a couple of glasses in the icebox. It is as established a part of our arguments as is my locking myself in my study. Inside the vodka bottle there was a small green chilli. Natasha spices our vodka in this way, producing a drink of which we are both very fond.

Natasha put the glasses down on the kitchen table and filled them up to the brim.

"Cheers," she said, clinking my glass. This English salutation, as always, sounded strange because of her guttural accent.

"Cheers!" I replied, clinking her glass again.

We both inclined our heads back slowly and a moment later the kitchen was filled with the sound of both of us swallowing.

Another two glasses were poured. There was a moment of silence. In my belly I began to feel warm and at the back of my head I felt something stir, like an uncoiling spring. The attitude of forgiveness was coming.

"I'm sorry," Natasha said.

"I'm sorry too," I replied.

This is how it always is with us. One of us says they're 'sorry' then the other says they're 'sorry'. It does not matter who says it first. We do not make an issue of it. It just so happened it was Natasha. Next time it could be me.

After we had said sorry we started to laugh and cry together, and we held hands. In this way we made up—as we have a hundred times before, and will doubtless a hundred times again.

However, by the following day the euphoria of reconciliation had completely evaporated. We were at war once more and again it was about money. We moved about the house without seeing each other, and when we spoke, it was mechanically. Things have been going on like this since then and will continue in this way for another week, two weeks, who knows? and then we will make up and the cycle will start all over again. Natasha will criticise me for being extravagant; words will be exchanged; I will storm out and slam the door after me. And so we live our lives, vacillating between argument and brief episodes of affection.

Of course it was not always like this. When I married I was full of hope and so was Natasha, and we believed our love would last forever. But over the years life has done something to us—it has defeated us I suppose—and we have become miserable, lifeless and extraordinarily dull. If you asked me to describe this process exactly I would be hard-pressed to explain how it happened and yet I could easily write a book on what it feels like. In such a work—I occasionally dream of writing one— I would begin by describing something that happened once on holiday in Italy. I bought some strong but inexpensive local wine, and by accident I left a glassful on the terrace. Waking thirsty from my siesta, I gulped some down, only to find it had turned bitter in the sun, and that grains of sediment had formed in the bottom. That is how the cup of my life has gone. It never overflowed and now it has turned to vinegar and gall ...

I first met Natasha when I was a postgraduate student. She came to my university faculty shortly after she arrived in England; she came to do a little translating and to earn herself some money. Although only twenty-six, she already had a lifetime's 'experience' behind her. She had spent ten years in labour camps at different times during her life; she had a small new-born son called Misha; and she was a widow. Leo, her husband, the father of her child, was dead and buried in a common grave for political prisoners.

Slowly, over the course of a year, we became acquaintances and then friends. Finally, one afternoon—Natasha and I have always referred to it as our "fateful afternoon"—I invited her to come up the river with me. It was a hot day and the Cambridgeshire fields along the river bank lay green and still in the sunlight. Natasha sat at the front, one arm cradling little Misha, the other dangling over the side and swishing in the water. I stood at the back, working away with the pole, pushing as hard as I could; I was determined to reach the quiet upper stretches where I knew that undergraduates seldom went. It involved too much effort.

As I punted us along, I stared silently at Natasha and she stared back at me, her eyes brown and, as always, seeming to swim with tears. She had put on make-up. Round her eyes she had created dark mysterious shadows. The three moles on her left cheek, arranged in the shape of a triangle, she had painted black. Her lips, which were generous and very beautifully bowed, she had painted a dark red, the colour of fuchsia. When we tied up at a bank and drank the white wine I had bought, her lipstick stained the edge of her glass. Looking at the rim I was amazed to see not only the shape of her lips in lipstick there, but even the little lines that ran across them.

"It's like a fossil," I remember saying.

"Aie," Natasha had said, "Fossils are dead things, and I am an alive woman."

Her reply was both innocent and suggestive. Without thinking about it, I leant forward and kissed her. As her lips parted and I tasted the cosmetic around her mouth, I realised that we had fallen in love with each other, or at least that I had fallen in love with her. I knew too that from that moment on, her lipstick and kissing would be forever associated in my mind. Later, when Misha was asleep, with a sunlit canopy of leaves above us, we made love in the bottom of the boat, without precautions. It was as if we were married already and we both knew we wanted children. At dusk, as we glided homewards across the darkening waters, feeling at once both utterly content and strangely melancholy, I asked Natasha to marry me. Without saying anything, she pulled her husband's wedding ring off her finger and dropped it with a plop in the water. Then she knelt in front of me and took my hand and kissed it as though I were a bishop. I started to cry, I remember, and I nearly lost the pole. That was almost forty years ago.

Happiness followed. Some anyway. Then, slowly, it started to go wrong. Why? Maybe we grew careless. Certainly it had something to do with our being childless. I know I grew indifferent. I stopped making the effort. I ceased being at all interested in what she did, and she likewise became disinterested in what I did. My time was taken up with the university to which I became attached here in London; hers with Misha and the *émigré* association for which she worked. Then, without quite realising when it had happened, I became aware that I was a stranger to Natasha and she was a stranger to me. We started to quarrel and we grew petty with each other. Little things that each of us did became raging sores; the business of money—this was the main canker—or the way I picked my teeth, or the way Natasha spat in the sink. Misha grew up and flew away. We had stayed together—though we had never openly discussed this—for his sake. Now, with him gone, we should have started new lives together, but it was too late for that; and we both lacked the courage to go our separate ways. And so here we are—in our sixties—Natasha closer to her seventies than I—two shrivelled peas rattling around in a pod. And what are we? When I think about it, I think of us as old, cantankerous, boring people, spiteful with each other, totally ineffectual in the real world, and miserable. We live our dreary lives together in this huge, gaunt, suburban house, bought for the children we never had and kept on for God knows what reason? Habit? Fear of change? Hope? The whole business bores me so much I can't think about it any more ...

II

This morning, as I do five days a week, I worked on my dictionary. Then at half-past one I got up to have lunch. In the hall I stopped for a moment in front of the barometer. 'Stormy', it read. I tapped the glass with the end of my pipe. The pipe stem left a trace of saliva on the glass, but the needle did not move. It never does when I perform this ritual. At that moment, Natasha called from the kitchen.

"Douglas, what are you doing?"

As I heard her I felt a twinge of resentment. Why does she eternally ask me what I am doing? She knows what I'm doing! I felt angry but I said nothing of course. I just went into the kitchen and sat down opposite her on the string-backed chair with the frayed yellow cushion, my customary position. Natasha sat on the stool, her neck and back characteristically straight. She is proud of her deportment and often chants at herself, "Straight back, neck like a swan", one of her father's sayings which she remembers from childhood. For lunch I had cheese, a cup of very strong black coffee and two peaches that were slightly bruised. The bruised ones are cheaper and Natasha makes a point of always buying them.

At half-past two I was back at my desk. I tried to work but I couldn't. My thoughts were elsewhere—on our courtship, our marriage, our decline. My little gold retirement clock sat in front of me—just as it sits in front of me now as I write this.

The third quarter struck. It brought me back to the present. How my thoughts had been wandering! I suddenly noticed the room was dark and that rain was falling furiously outside. I got up, turned on the electric light and went over to the window. Looking outside, I saw that water was streaming down from the heavens and that our suburban street was empty except for a Hasidic youth. He was running along in the rain, his side ringlets jumping up and down, one hand on the crown of his hat holding it in place, his long black coat flapping behind him.

It was then that I remembered what the student had said—the student who was coming at three. (Although I am officially retired I still teach.) He had said "I'll come on my push-bike. It won't take me long." Looking out at our privet hedge, which was being pummelled by the rain, and the pavement awash with rainwater, I wondered if he would come?

There was no doubt about it. If the visit aborted I would be disappointed. Douglas, I said to myself, you must be getting old! Why, it's ridiculous, an old scholar like yourself, getting excited about a visit from a student who wants to talk about Chekhov ...

The glass pane against which my face was pressed became hawed up by my breath. Using my index finger, I drew a toy-town house in the condensation. I had not done such a thing for years. Not since Misha was a boy and I had amused him in this way. As I looked at my work, and wondered where I could put the stylised husband and wife I had once been so adept at doodling for my step-son, I saw a figure at the other end of the road on a bicycle with a basket on the front. It was the student, surely? I glanced back at my clock and saw it was five to three. His punctuality was a good sign I decided. (I have a tendency to see omens everywhere.) I wiped away my 'happy families' house with the corner of the yellow curtain, then stepped into the hall to wait for the bell to ring. I did not want the student to see me standing at the window in case he thought I was overly-keen, or worse, lonely.

The student had fifty yards to cover, so I had a little time to wait. Blue hyacinths in wet earth stood beside me on the hall table. They are always watered by Natasha after lunch. As I stood there it struck me that, like certain scents worn by women, the perfume of the flower was registered not so much in the nose, as tasted in the mouth and at the back of the throat. It was a sweet, cold taste, a little like a kiss I thought, and suddenly I was back on the boat with Natasha. Our first kiss, her broad, smooth face, the smell of her lipstick, the cool, lapping water, all came flooding back to me ... and then the bell rang.

III

"I was worried about you getting wet!" was the first thing I said to the student as he came through the door. But as soon as I said this I regretted it. I was fussing again, like a Mother Hen, just as my son Misha says I always do. Misha is right. I treat him—and he's over forty—just as I did when he was a child of four. Mercifully, however, the Chekhov student did not notice my agitation. He just smiled, introduced himself and asked where he could hang his dripping fluorescent cape.

A moment later we were settled in my study. The student took the armchair. It is the only one in the room and it has an antimacassar which is so threadbare and ancient that it positively shines with age. I sat in my wooden swivelling chair with its dark red leather seat. I am sitting in it now. I bought it in Cambridge—it was my wedding gift to myself—and after so many years together, man and chair have grown to resemble one another.

Outside the rain was still pouring, and gusting every now and again against the glass in the windows. "Have you come far?" I asked. "Are you wet? Do you always get around by bicycle?" I put my questions mechanically and I did not take in his replies. I was preoccupied by the fact that I would have to offer him something, and unless he said no (which was highly unlikely), I was then going to have to go into the kitchen. Nothing in itself wrong with that except that Natasha—who had certainly already heard the bell—might be drawn to put in an appearance by the sound of my setting the tea tray, or reaching the biscuit tin from the cupboard. Of course, I had already mentioned to Natasha that I had a student coming to see me. But I had said this in a very off-hand way. And I hadn't mentioned that he was coming to talk about Chekhov.

My motive for being so economical with the truth was that if I had told Natasha everything, I could be certain she would join us. In the past, whenever students came to our house for a literature seminar, she always 'sat in', and these occasions were often disastrous. Natasha's opinions of her country's writers are often harsh and wilful, especially if she believes that the writer had in any sense served the interests of the Soviet state; and to her mind, because Chekhov's plays were so popular with the Soviet regime, the man is somehow suspect.

Now her views are not unremarkable given her experiences (after all, the Soviet state locked Natasha and her family up at various times, sometimes for years at a stretch), but they are unforgiving and inflexible and not everyone automatically agrees with them—which is where the problem begins. Unfortunately, but not unsurprisingly, Natasha is intolerant of ideas which conflict with her own. Disagreement makes her angry, and when she argues her voice becomes ugly and rasping. She also has no scruples in an argument and will shamelessly tell stories about her sufferings in Siberia in order to silence some callow undergraduate who happens to like an author of whom she disapproves.

I, of course, am useless in these situations. I want to say something or do something to dampen anger and put discussion back on the right track, but I cannot get the words out. I become paralysed inside. I become frightened that anything I might say will be rubbish, or that I have forgotten how to speak grammatically. Words and phrases fill my head, growing bigger and bigger, threatening to explode and blow my skull apart, and I feel like I did when I was a small boy and I was teased by my brothers. I used to stand in front of them and long to shout back but I could never get the words out. With Natasha, when she is argumentative—or indeed with any wilful or opinionated person—I become that boy again. What the students made of it all I can only imagine. They probably thought I was a timid academic, a mouse, and that my wife was strident and overbearing ... But I am drifting—I must stick to the point.

What I am trying to say is that this afternoon I wanted to be alone with the student—especially given the punctual (and therefore auspicious) beginning. A trip to the kitchen might draw Natasha's attention to us. But in the circumstances, I thought, what else can I do?

"Would you like something?" I asked. "Tea?"

"Yes," replied the student, and then he asked tentatively, "Do you ever use a samovar?"

"Sometimes," I said rather abruptly , "although my wife thinks all samovar-users are pretentious types who imagine they're living in a nineteenth-century Russian novel," and with that I hurried off.

I was nervous and I wanted to get in and out of the kitchen as quickly as possible. But as soon as I got out into the hall, I regretted my brusqueness. He probably thinks I'm aloof, I thought. First I had made an idiot of myself fussing at the door, and then I had topped that by being rude. What might have been a wonderful afternoon suddenly seemed headed for disaster.

I went into the kitchen and plugged in the kettle. As I stood and waited I heard a noise upstairs. I heard our wardrobe door creaking open, the sound of coat-hangers scratching on the rail and the soft sound of clothes being thrown on to the bed. I remembered Natasha had mentioned something about sorting out some very old clothes which she wanted to give to her *émigré* charity. I found myself hoping that this was the afternoon she had chosen to do this. That would mean there would be less chance of her sitting in with us. I began to feel more relaxed. When the kettle boiled, I made the student his tea in a glass and added a twist of lemon, which I thought was a nice Russian touch.

Ten minutes later, whilst the student sipped his tea and I was holding forth on Chekhov's marriage, my study door opened and Natasha came in.

"You must be the student!" said Natasha as she grasped his hand. As soon as she sat down, Natasha began.

"I heard just now Douglas talking about Chekhov's marriage. What a disaster! What an egotistical woman that cannibal wife of his was. Cared for nothing but herself. So vain! And, apart from herself, the only thing that stupid woman cared anything about was the theatre ..."

As I listened I began to feel sick and irritated. I longed to say something to deflect or curtail her but as soon as I opened my mouth I became unable to speak. I felt like the spout of a kettle, so furred up it no longer pours. It's happening again! I thought. Oh, my God! was there any end to it? I looked across at the student. I would like to be able to say that he was shrinking and sinking too. But as far as I could tell he was not. As he sat, listening patiently to Natasha, he did not seem to be either bored or irritated.

Experience has taught me that when Natasha is holding forth, the only thing to do is to sit and wait. She tires herself out eventually. So I sat and I waited and it was at this point—although she had been in the room for several minutes—that I actually looked at her.

Natasha usually goes around our house in slippers, a dark tweed skirt and a shapeless jersey. But this afternoon I saw she was dressed quite differently. She was wearing make-up and had put on her blue dress. She had also dabbed on some perfume. Of all her clothes, the blue dress is her favourite. I bought it for her thirty or more years ago. Having been out of fashion its style is now back in fashion, which pleases Natasha greatly, for it justifies her hoarding of it. We saw it one night when we were walking home, in the window of a large department store in Kingston. We had just moved to London; I was a minor academic at the start of my career; we had no money. It was very expensive and we could not afford it.

But a few weeks after the Sales started. I went to the store and queued and, to my great delight, I was able to buy it. I brought the dress home in a box with red and white stripes and a big velvet bow which I had got the salesgirl to tie on. The most wonderful night followed: a 'red letter night', and this afternoon, as I looked at Natasha in the same blue dress, memories came flooding back to me; Natasha in our bed, naked, her hair in a single plait snaking down her back, the small, blue elasticated tie at the bottom, the shape of her body, its warmth and her smell, which was and still is a little like dry sherry and beaten egg-white mixed together.

When we first married and in the early years, we often talked about growing old. We looked forward to it; we had plans and schemes. We were going to do things together. We were going to love each other. Our physical life was going to continue as passionately as ever. No separate beds or separate rooms for us on retirement. We were going to sleep together as man and wife and enjoy the fruits of each other to the end. So much for dreams. Today we share a room and a bed. That much of our plan has been carried out. But the rest—it doesn't bear thinking about!

A scratching noise brought me back to the present. It was Natasha crunching up the remains of the humbug she had been sucking when she had come in. As she consumes a great number of boiled sweets, this is a sound with which I am intimately familiar. After spitting in the sink, I find this her most irritating habit.

I looked over at the student. What can he be thinking? I wondered. Again I tried to make out if he was bored and again I decided he was not. His face still wore the same earnest expression as he listened to Natasha's headlong, impetuous monologue.

"Chekhov was a very funny man, you know," she said. "Very humorous. Very typically Russian in his humour. But his humour is always something else too. A little sad. Humanistic. So it is puzzling why the Soviets embraced him as they did. Humour was never their forte. However, they did and he became their stooge ..."

I stopped listening to what Natasha said and fell into the stupor of rage with which I am so familiar. The chief characteristic of this state is that it renders me oblivious of what is going on around me. Hours can pass and I do not notice them. The telephone can ring and I will not hear it. People will speak to me and I cannot remember afterwards what they have said. I was in this sort of a state this afternoon when suddenly I became aware that Natasha was speaking to me in Russian.

"Where is Ludwig's telephone number?" she asked.

"What?" I also spoke in Russian.

"Ludwig's telephone number! I think this young man ought to talk to Ludwig in connection with his Chekhov studies ..."

Why is she asking me for Ludwig's telephone number? I wondered. It's in the bloody book of course! Where else would it be? The afternoon was destroyed and now, to top it all, there was this absurd enquiry!

"For God's sake," I exploded in Russian, "it's in the bloody address book under L for Ludwig, as it has been for the last twenty years."

Natasha was shocked; here I was, angry and lucid at the same time. She looked at me, her eyes full of hurt, and raised her eyebrows in the direction of the student. She clearly thought this display in front of a stranger was immodest and humiliating. Natasha is a stickler for protocol. But I was past caring. It did not even matter to me whether or not the student spoke Russian—although his question about the samovar suggested he could not.

For the first time in my life—and this is a ridiculous statement coming from a man of well over sixty—I was expressing what I felt without thinking about it. My words had emerged clean and true, and this was a far cry from the gibberish I usually trot out. It was an exhilarating feeling, and like champagne it went straight to my head. Then, through the mists of my intoxication, I became aware that Natasha was asking me something.

"Can I borrow your glasses?" she asked. I saw her hand was stretched out towards me.

She wants to borrow my glasses, I thought. Why does she want to borrow my glasses? Everything was a dreamy blur and I could not make sense of what was going on. Then I remembered. Natasha always uses my glasses if hers are not to hand. Typically, famously, our eyes have reached an identical state of long-sightedness.

I took the glasses out of my breast pocket and handed them over and, as Natasha took them, the Chekhov student caught my eye. Our eye contact only lasted a fraction of a second, but in that moment something of immense importance was signalled to me. It was not exactly complicity. It was more that he had understood the difficulties of my situation. It was one of those rare moments when a stranger, having been afforded a privileged glimpse into another's life, communicates their absolute sympathy without the use of words.

Natasha did not see the look which the student gave me, not that I would have cared. She just took my glasses without saying a word, settled them on her nose and started to thumb through our address book. As I sat and waited I looked out of the window. The student did the same. We were embarrassed to meet each other's gazes again. We wanted to return to our old guises, to be strangers, both unknown to each other and unknowing of each other.

Outside it was still raining. I could hear water flowing along the gutters and pouring into the drains in the street. There was a dog barking and

I heard a door slam. A sort of trance descended on me and my thoughts turned to the afternoon and evening ahead. There would be more talk of Chekhov, refreshments, and my outburst would be forgotten. It would melt away like a sugar lump in our forthcoming cups of tea. The tutorial would draw to a close, the student would leave, and then Natasha and I would have the most monumental row. Oh God! It was hours away but I could predict its course already. Natasha would accuse me of betraying and humiliating her in front of a stranger. I would counter that a shout in Russian hardly constitutes humiliation—or something like that. Natasha would say it did. I would say it did not. The impasse reached, we would raise our voices, there being no other recourse except to shout louder. Then it would all come out, everything that had been building up inside Natasha. All the resentments, the slights, the hurts. And of course some recent financial recklessness on my part would be mentioned ... As I thought about the row I felt sick, though not to the same degree that I usually do. The sympathy the student had shown gave me a sort of strength I would say; the courage to face the future storm with a little more resolution than is customary.

IV

After the student left, Natasha and I quarrelled of course. If our arguments can be described with a medical metaphor, then this was not so much like the lancing of a boil, as the excavation of a cancer! Which is quite something given how much we do fight. Its course was much as I had predicted except in one significant respect; I did not feel as constricted inwardly as I usually do. I would not say that I was articulate or that I said everything that I felt. But I said a good deal more than normal. It unnerved Natasha, and her usually well-aimed barbs lacked their characteristic accuracy.

After two hours of shouting we were hoarse and had run out of energy. I heated up a tin of soup and we sat in the kitchen together and drank it from mugs. Not a word was spoken. Afterwards, I came in here to my study and sat down to work. I heard Natasha moving around the kitchen and then going upstairs. She went without saying goodnight. As I listened to her feet above my head, padding across the landing and into the bathroom, I wondered if I should call out to her. But I did not. There'll be tomorrow, I said to myself, or the next day. Relations have soured so badly I am indifferent, it seems, to our reconciliation.

After I heard Natasha climb into bed, I went over to the window of my study and looked out into the street. It was a melancholy spring evening, and the surface of the road was like wet black rubber under the street lamps. In the distance an aeroplane moved across the night sky, green and yellow lights flashing on the stern and tips of the wings. Suddenly, I found myself thinking about the people sitting inside this metal cylinder and staring out through the portholes at the city below. For a moment I imagined what they must be seeing; the white lights of travelling cars, ribbons of yellow street lamps, perhaps the dark curve of the Thames. After our rows I can rarely think of anything. I am usually like a stone. But this evening was different and I wondered if I hadn't finally begun the painful process of separating myself from the paralysed little boy who stood in front of his teasing elder brothers unable to speak, and whether this hadn't something to do with the look the student had given me? He had let it be known that he understood and he sympathised, and his insight was a rare gift. Even writing about it hours later, I can feel an inner warmth on account of it ...

It is now three o'clock in the morning. My clock has just struck. I can hear Natasha turning in our bed upstairs. I cannot remember when I last stayed up writing like this. Not since I first fell in love with Natasha and scribbled verse to her all night. So why have I written all this? To tell you the truth I do not know. I entertain the vague fantasy that it might be Exhibit A in a Coroner's Court following my suicide. Another fantasy I have is that these papers will be found after my death. Misha will find them—or perhaps Natasha if she outlives me. As they read what I have written, my wife and my stepson will see me completely differently. They will see me from my point of view. They will see my suffering and they will perhaps understand it. Like the suicide, this fantasy is also unlikely to come true. No, if my back were to the wall, I think I would have to say that the motive behind my writing all this is quite banal. It is simply that I want to fix on paper what happened. I need to describe the troubles of my life—and my God aren't they everybody's?—and the enormous significance to me of another's insight into them ...

I think I shall have some cocoa now and go to bed. Tomorrow or the next day I will read over what I have written. It will lift my spirits and to the Chekhov student I will offer my thanks and my appreciation ... Is that why I have written all this? Perhaps the answer is more serious? Today, this evening, I have begun to make sense not just of this afternoon but of my life. I have started to put it down in an orderly fashion. And why should I do that, unless perhaps—and I do not know it yet—unless perhaps, I am dying ...?

The Headscarf

I

MICHAEL WENT OUT THE back door, then turned and waved goodbye to her through the window. Margaret heard his shoes scuffing on the concrete, and a moment later his van moved off. Then silence, and now the day was hers.

Margaret picked up the newspaper and rearranged the pages. Michael always turned to the sport's section first, but she liked to read through methodically, starting at the front.

The paper re-organised, she scanned the front page. A soldier injured by a sniper; a nail bomb defused; a tit-for-tat killing at a Belfast traffic lights. Margaret felt weary, and unmoved; she had read it all before.

Suddenly, Margaret remembered her appointment and looked up. The clock on the kitchen wall said half-past eight. She had only forty minutes to get ready. Then she immediately registered the fizzy, popping feeling, which was the first sign of anxiety. It was almost like the tonic, in a G&T, pricking the back of her throat.

Margaret folded the paper and began to clear the table. The crockery was white—a soft-white, not clinical—with a blue band around the edges. The bacon fat on her husband Michael's plate was white as well.

Margaret stacked the crockery. The bubbling sensation that was her anxiety was becoming stronger, painful almost, and she found herself wondering whether she would encounter a checkpoint this morning on the way into town?

After years of struggle against this wily adversary, Margaret knew that activity was the best defence. She stood up and took hold of the pile of plates and crockery she had made. For two years before her daughter Amanda was born, Margaret had worked as a waitress in Lavery's Hotel in town, and in her mind's eye, she saw herself now as she had been twenty-five years ago, decked out in her smart black uniform and white apron, rather fetching in a way, running in and out of the kitchens through the green baize doors with trays of food. Oh yes, she had enjoyed those days when she was young and adventurous and capable.

Suddenly, Margaret felt a sharp draught of air on the back of her neck. She turned to see where it was coming from, her movement abrupt and jerky. A cup flew off her pile of breakfast things and crashed to the floor. The other dishes wobbled in her arms and, fearing they would topple, she pulled them against her breast. A moment after, she noticed, there was a brown tea stain down the front of her white dressing gown, and round her feet lay the broken pieces of the cup. They looked like lumps of snow.

Margaret squinted through her kitchen door, along the hall, and out into the village street. Michael, she realised, had forgotten to close the front door when he had come back from the Spar shop, earlier that morning, with the newspaper. Now, standing there, Margaret suddenly felt rather stupid, and she wondered if anyone had been passing, and had seen her drop the cup?

The plates still in her arms, Margaret scuttled down the hall. She shut the door with her foot, then peered out the front window into the street.

Mercifully, there was no one on the forecourt of McSpirit's Garage opposite, while on the pavement immediately outside her house, there was just the wee girl, Nellie, absorbed in riding her bicycle.

Margaret went back to the kitchen, put the plates into the basin in the sink, and turned on the taps. She loved where she lived, she thought, squirting *Squeezy* into the water and watching the bubbles froth up, except for the lack of privacy.

Everyone in Derrybawn village had known about her breakdown after her brother Paddy's death, and her not being able to eat or sleep, and the quite uncharacteristic quarrels she had had with friends and neighbours over the most trivial of matters, and the crying fits that followed the rows, when she had wallowed in self-disgust.

And everyone in Derrybawn had also known that she had gone to see Dr. Armstrong in the end, and that the pills he had prescribed had done the trick, and restored her to her old self. But what they didn't know, what she had not dared let anyone know, not even her husband Michael, was that one symptom of her collapse still remained: an uncontrollable fear of the roving vehicle checkpoints.

When she travelled with Michael, she could keep the fear under control; it only took her over when she travelled alone—perhaps, she thought, because Paddy had been alone at his end. Before solo outings, Margaret would sometimes spend hours with the map, choosing the route she thought was the one least likely to have such a checkpoint, and sometimes, Margaret felt so anxious, she cancelled her arrangements altogether, rather than go out.

Washing the first plate, Margaret now gave thanks; as this was an early morning appointment, there just wasn't enough time for the fear and terror to really get its claws into her. A small mercy that.

II

A few minutes later, wearing her grey summer dress, (she believed the dress was lucky), Margaret made her way down the yard to her car and climbed in. The picnic blanket—it lay on the back window ledge—gave off a familiar and comforting smell of sand and sea which filled the whole inside of the car. The blanket had acquired its smell on the innumerable excursions to Donegal which she and Michael had made over the years.

Margaret nudged the car out of the yard and turned on to the village main street. She drove on, passed the primary school, several houses, and finally, (which she regarded as the village boundary), the old forge, with its collapsed roof and scorched gable, the marks still plainly visible despite fifty years of Irish rain.

Beyond the windscreen, she saw that the sky was clear and blue. In the fields, a silvery dust of frost coated the grass, and sheep were huddling in the sheltered hollows along the hedgerows.

Hackett's Hill now came into view. A tractor had obviously driven across the grass earlier that morning. She saw the tractor wheels had made two parallel lines in the frost, their curving shape like a vapour trail in the sky left by a passing jet.

She drove on. She watched the blue-black road unfurl under the car bonnet, and maintained an empty state of mind. If she could keep it that way, the anxiety would trickle away. Margaret had managed this trick once or twice in the past. The key to success was to concentrate on the outside world …

The old sawmill loomed ahead, a big stone building, long abandoned, with gaping, empty windows, and a chimney which lent over at a slight angle, and which, amazingly, had an ash tree, of all things, growing on the top of it. Some of the wilder local elements used the tree to fly the Union Flag on the Twelfth. But as Margaret always stayed indoors, or went south during the Twelfth, she only knew about this by repute.

The road bent round to the right as it passed the mill. A magpie flapped on the verge. "One for sorrow," Margaret said to herself, and the words were no sooner out, than she wished she hadn't said them.

Then she straightened the wheel and, with a sinking heart, she told herself she shouldn't have spoken, for a hundred yards away she could see that there were men in the road, and she could see that they were wearing the unmistakable dark green uniforms of the police. Margaret's heart began to pound and her hands began to sweat.

She looked in the mirror. There was nothing behind, just the tilting chimney and the empty road bending out of sight.

Next thing—although it was way too early to do so—her foot went automatically on to the brake, and the car started to slow. It was the same pattern every time. Margaret understood the mechanics of her fear as plainly as she saw the checkpoint ahead; her difficulty, of course, was that for all that she comprehended, she was not able to control herself.

This had all started with Paddy. It had been her brother's misfortune to arrive at a checkpoint at precisely the wrong time; he had no sooner pulled up, than the mortars had fired. And what she feared, quite simply, was that, like Paddy, she too was going to arrive at the wrong moment.

With fifty yards still to go, the speed of the car was now down to less than five miles per hour. It was not only way too slow, and so must have seemed highly suspicious to the police; it was also—and she realised this—utterly illogical; for crawling along like this could just as easily bring her to the checkpoint at the wrong time, as maintaining her speed.

However, as she liked to put it whenever she interrogated herself on this matter, she preferred to dawdle towards her Maker, rather than rushing into His arms.

Peering ahead now, and ignoring the part of herself that was somehow above events, looking down on her and hooting with derision, Margaret saw there were two policemen in the road; a soldier behind them in a helmet with foliage looped through the netting, and boot polish on his face; and more figures in the field beyond the hedge, with rifles raised.

Finally, she rolled to a halt beside the tripod with the sign, *Stop Checkpoint*. The taller of the policemen came over. She recognised him as Quinlan; he was from the barracks in town. He had often stopped her on the roads before.

They said good morning to one another. She was quite calm. From the outside, she knew, nothing showed.

Then he asked, "Do you have any identification, Mrs. Maguire?"

It was all she could do to stop herself shouting, "Well, as you know

29

exactly who I am, why don't you let me through," and drive off; but she didn't, and instead she handed the policeman her driving licence.

While Quinlan studied it, Margaret stared up at him. He had a spot of blood on his chin and a tiny trace of shaving cream in his ear. Yes, it was amazing how observant she was in these situations—impending death, no doubt, concentrating her mind. Margaret felt a longing to play with the catch of her handbag coming over her, and as a precaution, she slipped her hands under her legs.

She looked back at the policeman and noticed that he had grey sideburns, and rather long and luxuriant sideburns at that.

Ordinarily she hated body hair, (indeed she was on her way to have some of her own removed), and she absolutely forbade her husband to have either a beard or a moustache. And so it surprised her, now, that she should find Quinlan's facial hair attractive. But then, which was even more surprising, she next found herself wondering if she and the policeman were the same age? Early fifties, she guessed. Good God! What was she thinking, she rebuked herself. She was a married woman.

Yes, it was amazing, she thought again, what went on while her heart was fluttering fearfully against her ribs.

"Thank you very much, Mrs. Maguire."

She took the licence back.

"Are you going into town?" he asked, clearly bored, clearly wanting to get the conversation going.

"I am," she replied. She smiled at him; she felt expansive. Any second now she'd be off, and the ordeal would be over. "I'm going to the hairdressers," she continued. "A woman's treat, you know."

He smiled and she drove away, glancing into the rear view mirror now and then, where of course she caught sight of Quinlan staring after her, gradually growing smaller and smaller. After she rounded the next corner he disappeared, and then there was just the empty road behind.

She felt a wave of relief and a modest sense of her own ridiculousness; a grown woman getting into a state like that. She even managed a half-smile, and then it hit her.

"Oh Christ!" she said aloud, startling herself with the sound of her own voice. Why on earth had she said she was going to the bloody hairdressers? Yes, technically, it was true, she was going to one in Omagh, but it was not to get her hair done. She was going to have her eyebrows plucked and her legs waxed and then, and only then, was she going back to her own village, to Derrybawn, for her weekly shampoo and set at Mrs. Cassidy's, at eleven-thirty.

She put a hand up to her head. Her hair was greasy. She was bound to meet Quinlan on her way back, and men being so damned literal, he was sure to be deeply suspicious when he saw her unwashed, unlovely head of hair; which would lead, of course, to questions, to being detained, to being kept hanging around the checkpoint for hours and hours ...

Margaret braked abruptly and pulled over. Didn't she have a headscarf? she thought desperately. She opened the handbag and tipped everything on to the seat. Keys, purse, Michael's paying-in book, two brochures from the travel agents, two biros and an *Ulsterbus* ticket. Damn, damn! she thought.

III

The beauty salon of *Cut 'n' Curl* hairdressers in Omagh, was at the rear of the premises, and overlooked a tyre store. The walls were covered with photographs of beautifully made-up models. The room smelt of lacquer, shampoo and nail varnish.

Ordinarily, Margaret enjoyed lying on the couch, and on top of the length of coarse paper with which it was covered. This came from a big roll at the foot of the couch; the paper was changed with each new customer. It was the crinkle it made when she moved, that she liked.

And ordinarily, she also enjoyed the feel of the wax tightening, while she half-listened to Patsy, the beautician, and half-listened to the radio, permanently tuned to Radio 2. Each time the tweezers pulled an eyebrow hair (Patsy plucked while the wax on her legs set), Margaret felt a twinge of pain of course, but she was able to ignore it by letting herself grow drowsy in the warm air which wafted from the heater that was always on, and by revelling in the touch of another.

This appointment, however, she got no pleasure. The wax seemed too hot, and she was tormented as she lay there by the thought that the skin beneath was wrinkling and reddening, and that when the time came to pull it off, a layer of her skin would rip away with it, and her legs would be left raw and untouchable.

Meanwhile, as these fears were fermenting and the wax was setting, Patsy was plucking away and, understandably, Margaret found her eyes watering, her whole body tense with pain.

Patsy sensed it too, and the more Margaret winced, the more firmly Patsy gripped her head, which in turn caused Margaret to feel more trapped, more tied down.

Margaret started to swallow and tried to think of other things. She counted to ten, told herself to forget about the wax, told herself to concentrate on listening to Jimmy Young on the radio, to concentrate on letting herself grow drowsy. Once she was relaxed, Patsy would soon follow and not hold her so hard.

But the more she tried, the firmer grew the conviction that there really was something wrong with the temperature of the wax. It really wasn't her imagination; it really did feel too hot. Patsy had made a mistake and put it on when it was boiling, and with every passing second, the damage was growing worse.

It was imperative that she say something, she thought, but then she mocked herself. There was nothing wrong. Patsy did not make mistakes.

As she argued with herself, Margaret's head spun and she felt herself growing breathless; then, suddenly, she sat up, pulled at the neck of the nylon smock, and asked for a glass of water.

"The wax is too hot," she said, as Patsy handed her the glass.

"Oh."

Patsy lifted a corner of the rubbery coat on her left leg, and Margaret saw the skin below was unharmed, just slightly redder than usual, as it always was after a wax.

"All looks normal to me," said Patsy, emphatically.

"Yes," Margaret agreed, and returned the empty glass.

IV

When the depilation was completed, Margaret left *Cut 'n' Curl* so hastily, she forgot to leave her customary tip. She only remembered in the street, and then she thought, Oh what the hell! She had better things to do and Patsy could wait until the next time.

She rushed over the road to *Dorothy Perkins*, ran through the door, and hurried past the clothes racks to the area where accessories were sold. And here, among the lace gloves and bangles, suspender belts and evening bags, she found what she was looking for, the largest headscarf she had ever seen.

"Don't put it in a bag," she said, as the girl at the till reached for one. "I want to wear it straight away. It seems it's going to rain."

"The forecast said fine," the salesgirl said firmly, a remark Margaret decided to ignore.

With the headscarf thrown right over her head and knotted tightly under her chin, Margaret drove towards home. Her heart was beating, her palms were moist. Quinlan would not stop her, she assured herself ferociously. He would not see her hair through the headscarf. She would sail through. Her thoughts were ceaseless and frantic.

Then she recognised the stretch of road where the checkpoint had been, for she saw the chimney of the sawmill in the distance with the ash tree growing out of the top of it, and she saw that the police were gone. The empty tarmac glistened in the sun, while the mill with its blank windows looked down on her as she approached. She rounded the corner and emerged on the far side. The tractor marks on the hill had vanished as well. The frost had melted. She pulled the headscarf off and laughed loudly to herself.

She was early for her hair appointment. Mrs. Cassidy gave her a cup of coffee while she was waiting. Just after eleven, she was called to the washing area. As Margaret lowered her neck into the cold porcelain 'U' of the sink, she saw Mrs. Cassidy's upside-down face looking at her curiously.

"You look a bit pale, Margaret. Are you alright?" said the hairdresser.

Mrs. Cassidy was testing the water on the back of her hand, then making minute adjustments to the tap.

"Oh, yes," she murmured.

Margaret felt the first jet of warm water on her scalp and, with a nod, she indicated that the temperature was right. The hose was held over her head and she felt the water running into her ears, then down over her neck.

Any moment now, she thought, she was going to feel the delicious prick of cold shampoo in the middle of her head. She closed her eyes, she moved her neck against the china edge of the sink that held her fast, and she readied herself for what would shortly follow—Mrs. Cassidy's big, strong hands soaping and massaging her head.

The Speech of Birds

I

CONNOR WOKE UP AND lay quite still in his bed. What had he been dreaming? Could he remember? Yes, he could. He'd been given a task. He had to get something for his brother. But he hadn't gone to the shops to get it. He'd dug it up in the garden of the Dublin house. It was a small cuckoo clock. But, he thought, it was not like his father's cuckoo clock at home in Dublin. It had no face, no hands, and it was edible. This was unusual because, as far as he knew, cuckoo clocks were not edible.

Connor was now fully awake. But he remained as he was, quite still and taking everything in. He could smell bacon frying, and he could hear hens clucking out on the lawn and the rattle of a metal bucket. This, he knew, was his granny, on her way down to the hens with their meal. "Come on, come on," he heard her calling. In his mind's eye he saw the scene below, saw the enamel bucket cracked around the rim which his granny carried, and the yellow meal in the bucket that was the hen's feed; saw the old tyres scattered round the hen-house which, cut in half, served as troughs; saw then his grandmother bending over, pouring into the tyres the yellow meal mixed with the previous day's rancid milk, and then the hens running about everywhere and falling ravenously on their food. He had often stood behind his grandmother, watched the scene and marvelled at her tenderness with her hens, and also her legs, the white thighs of which always sprang into view when she bent over and her dress rode upwards. The purple veins in her legs which then showed were what particularly interested him. These, he knew, were varicose veins. Well, he knew the name. But what exactly were varicose veins? They made granny tired. She had told him that often enough. But what were they ...?

No, it was a fruitless line of thought, so he gave it up and looked across the room instead at the picture of Christ that hung over the fire-place.

34

The picture showed Christ nailed to the cross, his crown of thorns jammed savagely on his head. A sponge on the end of a pike was being put to his lips. This, Connor knew, was Christ being offered vinegar for his thirst, and his granny often said it was but the least of the many indignities He suffered that day.

Then suddenly it came to Connor—a disagreeable feeling. Today, he suddenly recalled, today was the day of the outing to the seaside, to Lahinch. But he was not going, only his brother was going, and the day before his granny had explained to him why. Sean was younger and more sensitive, she had said, and as there was only room for one child, it had been decided it should be Sean who should go because Connor, being older, would understand that Sean, (whom everyone called the 'baby') couldn't be left behind.

This interview had taken place in the breakfast room with its big table covered as usual with a white cloth, the *Johnnie Walker* whisky statuette over the mantelpiece, and the velvet lined cupboard full of glasses which smelt of oranges and chocolate. On the wall beside the breakfast room door there hung three porcelain ducks of ascending size. As Connor listened to his granny calmly and patiently explaining why he wasn't going to the seaside, Connor looked at these closely, and as he looked he believed he would never forget them.

Then, while he was still staring at the ducks, he became aware that his granny was asking him if he had understood. "I have, yes," he had said, knowing that his agreement and understanding would please her. "I have, yes," he repeated, but as he said 'Yes,' outwardly, inwardly he said 'No.' No, it was not alright, and no, he did not understand. Why should his brother have a morning of sand and sea, followed by a big lunch in the hotel where he'd be given fresh fish and as much lemonade as he wanted, followed by an afternoon playing on the billiard table in the bar, a privilege which was always granted by the hotel proprietor who was a family friend. It wasn't fair! Moreover, what was his in return but an interminable day cooped up in the house with his grandfather? For lunch, mutton chops fried for an hour under a sheet of newspaper and indigestible. His grandfather's afternoon sleep would follow then, during which Connor would have to be immaculately quiet lest he woke him. Then, towards four, his granny being away, Connor would have to bring his grandfather his tea, and woe betide if it wasn't stewed to the right strength.

Then there'd be the walk up to the Calf Park, where his grandfather would count the cattle, water them, and then perhaps move them to a

35

different field. This last task was always a nightmare, for his grandfather would invariably insist on his helping with the moving of the cattle. And no matter what his grandfather said to the contrary, Connor was frightened of the huge bullocks, and he disbelieved what his grandfather said regarding their timidity and docility.

They were so big for a start and they moved so fast. Furthermore, which added to Connor's fears, Eamon, the farm-hand, had told him that the vet who'd done the castrations had been drunk at the time he did them. It seemed many of the bullocks weren't properly castrated, and some, evidently, were not even castrated at all, whatever that meant.

Connor's particular nightmare was that his thin, etiolated grandfather, waving his walking stick like a lunatic, would step into the middle of a huddle of recalcitrant bullocks, just as he did in real life, and that the beasts would then suddenly change before Connor's eyes into bulls. Then they would knock grandfather to the ground, gore him with their horns, and grandfather's blood would spurt out of his wounds and mix with the mud and the grass.

All this Connor would watch with terror, unable to move because he would be rooted to the spot with fear. Then, when grandfather was at last dead, the bulls would swivel about and fix him with their dark black eyes. This would be so frightening it would startle Connor out of his paralysis and he would start to run. The bulls would hasten after him. Connor would run and run, and behind his back he would hear their hooves thundering on the ground, sense them getting closer and closer and closer, until at last he would feel the hot breath of the animal at the front of the pack on the back of his head ...

When it reached this point, the daydream would always stop, and he would be unable to prevent himself going back to the beginning again, and if he was particularly unlucky, the fantasy might repeat itself two or three times before he could shake it off. In fact, lying now in his bed, he didn't doubt that as the four o'clock departure for the Calf Park with his grandfather approached, these images would try to force themselves before his mind's eye. He was going to have to be particularly cunning and resilient if he wanted to avoid them.

However, and he emphatically reminded himself of this now (because he knew he had to fight this anxiety with every means at his disposal), it was indisputable that after the Calf Park things would improve. Grandfather and he would saunter back to the farmhouse together, and his grandfather would then very likely give him a fig-roll, or maybe even a slice of ice-cream from the block which Connor knew was in the icebox in the larder; and with the ice-cream held between wafers, he would run as fast as he could across the flag, climb the railings into Dan Egan's field, and then dive into the middle of the sacred rhododendron bush that grew there. And there he would then sit in the green darkness, eating the ice-cream, listening to the bell of the chapel tolling across the fields, and watching—in the far distance—the local greyhound fanciers striding their dogs up the mountain road.

However, despite this happy ending which he could predict with some certainty, was it fair that he should be deprived of the seaside and what went with it? For instance, there was the shop on the seafront of Lahinch which he badly wanted to visit, where they sold soap that oozed ink, catapults made of thin wire which threw a stone with devastating accuracy, and comics with the most beautiful, radiant colours printed on paper that gave off a most tantalising and evocative smell. Like chewing gum it was. No, it was not fair ...

Now, as he lay in bed, thinking all this, Connor felt a little stab in his chest. It was the asthma, or at least the first signs of it. Whenever he was distressed it would descend on him. Years of wary antagonism had taught him there was only one way to cope with it. That was to go numb. To sweep away what ever thought was distressing and move on, thinking of nothing. That was the way. So, very slowly, Connor lifted back the bedding. Easy, unhurried movements were another key factor in the battle against wheezing. Then, gently, Connor took off his pyjamas and got dressed, while downstairs he could hear his granny making his breakfast and, he supposed, talking to his brother.

II

The hire car stood on the drive outside the house. It was a big black car with four doors and a gleaming silver bumper. This was the car that would convey everyone to the seaside. In the village it was rumoured that Mr. Mac, the owner of the car, actually had four others like it, and whenever anything went wrong with this—his main car—he would cannibalise one of the others for the necessary spares. This was thought locally to be rather extravagant, or at least this was what Connor believed everyone thought. The truth of the matter was that he couldn't really get hold of the real meaning of these stories which he heard the grown-ups speaking of to one another.

"Connor!" someone suddenly called. It was Mrs. Flynn, one of the occupants of the car. Connor slowly wandered over to her. "Did you get them?" asked Mrs. Flynn. She pulled on a cigarette and exhaled a cloud of blue smoke.

From under his arm, Connor produced the small box of chocolates she had sent him to fetch from the village shop. He put his head and shoulders in through the window and handed Mrs. Flynn the package.

"You didn't get them wrapped," she said immediately. Suddenly, Connor remembered her asking him to do this. He'd forgotten but what could he say? Adults never really believed you when you said 'Sorry'. At least this was his impression.

So, without acknowledging even that he had forgotten, Connor asked abruptly, "Can I have the paper bag the chocolates are in?"

"You're not to blow it up and pop it in here," said Mrs. Flynn. The coarse brown bag was on her lap and it rustled as she smoothed it with the flat of her hand.

While he was waiting for Mrs. Flynn to finish with the bag, Connor looked at the two elderly women sitting beside her. They were distant relatives of Connor's, and they were staring straight ahead and not acknowledging his presence. In Connor's eyes, all three women now looked like shop mannequins, and emphasising this effect was the fact that all three were wearing huge hats which—it seemed to him—filled the entire back of the car. Then Connor remembered his brother, and he looked for him but couldn't see Sean. He wondered if his brother had not perhaps fallen down the crack at the back of the leather seat, a wide space down which money sometimes rolled.

Now Connor turned and looked into the front of the hire car. It was empty—Mr. Mac was in with his grandfather—but there, lying upside down on the seat beneath the steering wheel, was Mr. Mac's peaked chauffeur's cap, its rim greasy from years and years of use. The only other thing in the car that was as greasy and worn was the St. Christopher's medal stuck to the dashboard, and it was only like this, as Connor knew, because Mr. Mac touched it for reassurance all the time when he was driving. The front of the car seemed cavernous compared to the back filled with the women and their hats, and seeing this brought it all back to Connor now, all the old resentments ...

There was plenty of room for him in the front. He and his brother could squash up; his granny could fit in; and Mr. Mac would still have plenty of room to steer and make his gear changes. It was unfair! Unfair he wasn't going! And why wasn't he? he now asked himself grimly. To his mind, it hadn't anything to do with the lack of space in the car. No, he wasn't going, he believed, because for some reason that he couldn't possibly grasp, his brother was preferred to him. As Connor saw it, adults preferred Sean's company to his. They liked Sean more. Of course they said they loved both brothers equally—adults always said that sort of thing, but there was something about the way they made their protestations that left Connor absolutely certain that what they said was false. They did not love both brothers equally, and at the very moment this thought rushed into the centre of Connor's mind, he heard a voice saying, "Mind Connor, mind". It was Mrs. Flynn, and he realised she wanted to give him the bag and then to throw her cigarette out of the window through which his head and shoulders were sticking in to the car.

Connor took the brown paper bag from Mrs. Flynn and withdrew; then he watched as her cigarette butt fell to the gravel and smouldered there. There was lipstick on the tip, bright and red. This intrigued Connor, and he knew that even after a week of incessant rain, incessant rain that would turn the butt first a light brown colour, and then a bleached white colour, the trace of red lipstick would still be discernible. This was a mystery he could not penetrate.

Connor wandered off a little, stopped, blew up the bag and popped it. The bang, because he was out of doors, was not as loud as it would have been had he popped the bag indoors, as was customary. This disappointed him, but only for a moment. For then, all of a sudden, he remembered what he had been dreaming that morning, before he had woken up ...

In the dream he had been back home in Dublin and, for some reason, he had to find the gooseberry bush under which, as an infant, he had slept in his pram; and which was the same gooseberry bush under which he had then lost something important when he was three, on the day his brother was born. But, try as he might, he could not find the gooseberry bush in his dream, and he knew that that meant only one thing; he would never be able to find whatever it was that he had lost under the bush. But what was it he had lost? Was it a gold coin? Or a silver pirate's pistol? Or a black wand with white tips? No, try as he might, he could neither remember what he had lost, nor could he find the gooseberry bush.

Then, in his dream, Connor saw a river flowing at the end of the garden where in real life there was only a fence separating their garden from their neighbour's. He abandoned his search for the bush, walked down to the bank and gazed out across the water. It's wide, wider than the Amazon, he thought, for he could not see the opposite bank. Then, all of a sudden, in a moment of stillness, he heard the cry of birdsong and it sounded so particular to him, so lucid. He had never heard birdsong sound like this before. It was eloquent beyond speech. "The birds can speak to one another," said Connor to himself in the dream, and a moment after this he woke up ...

Standing on the gravel in front of his granny's house, the crumpled and torn brown paper bag he had just popped in his hand, Connor remembered all this, and the remembering of it was of great significance to him. Yes, the birds can speak, he thought, and suddenly he understood, but not in a way he could put into words, exactly what it was that he had to do. He had to learn to listen for what he had never been able to hear before and, if he did that, then the fact of being liked or disliked wouldn't matter anymore. He would be like birdsong, bright and enduring.

Puerto Vallarta

I

I WAS SEVENTEEN AND Laura was eighteen when our parents sent us to Mexico. This was the time of their divorce and they were trying to atone in the way they always did, which was by giving us something.

Laura is actually my half-sister, and her surname, until she married, was Henson. My surname is Greene. We have the same mother, different fathers. It was always complicated being introduced to strangers when we were children. That Mexican summer, as I like to think of it, it was my parents—the Greenes—who were separating, Laura's father being long dead.

The man we were sent to stay with in Mexico was Laura's grandfather. He was a rich old American who had started a small passenger airline in the 1940s, and then sold it on to TWA twenty-five years later.

I can clearly remember his visits to our house in Richmond when I was a child. He was a very tall man, with a long face, and rather small eyes set close together. He smoked cigars, and he carried a cigar-cutter on a gold chain which he kept in his waistcoat pocket. I was always intrigued by the lengths of ash he tipped from the ends of his Havanas; they were like pumice stone to my childish way of seeing things.

He was a generous man, and he always treated me on equal terms with Laura, although we were not blood relations; he was her grandfather, not mine. However, I was not particularly friendly with him either. None of us were. He was not 'family' you see. His son—who was Laura's father and my mother's first husband—committed suicide only a couple of months after the wedding, and so there had never really been enough time for proper family links to develop. We never called him grandfather. He was always simply Old Man Henson.

41

We arrived in Puerto Vallarta in the afternoon. Los Angeles, where we had stayed overnight on the way, had been hot, but nothing could have prepared me for my first encounter with tropical heat. When I stepped through the door and out on to the stairway, it was like plunging into a molten sea.

We went to the baggage room. All the suitcases from our flight were being thrown through a hole in the wall. The porters were picking these up and slamming them on to metal counters. Laura feared that the bottle of perfume in the middle of her hold-all would break. An official wearing a large gold badge chalked X's on our bags. Through a side door I noticed a woman. I guessed she was about fifty or so. I'd never seen her before, but she was staring at us closely. Then she smiled, in that neutral way that strangers meeting strangers so often manage to achieve.

"You must be Johnnie and Laura?" she said.

She introduced herself as Mary Hughes. She was Old Man Henson's secretary. "I'm afraid he couldn't come in person," she apologised. "Something rather unfortunate has happened."

We shook hands. Her face was creased and her eyes were rimmed red. She had been crying.

Outside the airport, we crammed into her tiny Fiat and began to bump towards the town. Fields stretched on either side, green like spinach. The earth was terracotta. Cork trees towered everywhere; they looked like giant mushrooms.

"What was it that happened?" I asked.

She sighed.

"Two of our workmen were on the roof," she began. "Somehow they touched one of the wires that bring in the town's electricity. They're all over town—just above the rooftops. The voltage was so high, and of course it was a bloody metal ladder they were carrying, all their flesh was burnt away where the ladder touched, right down to the bone. The local hospital here wouldn't take them. They didn't have insurance. We flew them to Guadaljara. The hospitals there wouldn't take them either. Oh Christ! Twelve hours we were in an ambulance in this boiling heat. Finally, the Red Cross took them, but it was too late. We buried what was left of them yesterday."

The indicator flashed; we pulled into a garage and stopped in front of a grimy pump. We had been followed into the garage by an army jeep, but instead of waiting behind, it overtook and pulled up sharply in front of us. Four soldiers with shiny boots were sitting in the back of the jeep. The pump attendant, who was poised to fill our tank, straightened up and immediately walked over to the jeep.

"But we were first," Laura protested.

"No," said Mary quietly. "In Mexico, the National Guard are always first. That's the first lesson you learn here."

We arrived in Puerto Vallarta proper. My memory is of peeling walls and crowded buses with workers clinging to the sides. Suddenly, Mary began to accelerate towards a blind corner.

"Let's hope we don't meet anything coming the other way," she muttered.

Oh God! I thought, as we rounded the corner with the engine of the *Cinquocento* screaming. I opened my eyes. Now we were climbing an extremely steep hill—it must have been one in six—with a pit in the middle large enough to have swallowed a car. We swerved past this hazard, reached the top and turned on to a flat cobbled road.

"That's the only way to do it," Mary exclaimed. "Go for it blind."

We pulled up before a large white villa. The two boys playing on the steps—we would later discover they were from Juarez's shop on the corner—darted away like shy animals. This was to be our home for the next month.

I got out of the tiny car and, without thinking what I was doing, I looked straight up. A thick metal cable stretched above me, attached by wooden arms to the houses as it ran down the street. Standing on any roof top I could have easily reached out and grasped it, the town's electricity supply.

"Do people electrocute themselves all the time?" I wondered.

"All the time, honey," said Mary, "Welcome to Mexico."

A man came out who was introduced to us as Luiz, the caretaker, the cleaner and the cook. He was small like a jockey, wiry and capable. Between us we took the luggage and went into the hall. There was a life-size statue of Saint Francis of Assisi in the corner. We followed Mary up a ramp on one side, and emerged at the top onto an enormous floor which was kitchen and living-room all in one.

We found Old Man Henson sitting on the balcony. He was staring at the jungle-covered hills which ringed the town.

Mary called softly, "Leo."

He turned in his seat and looked at us blankly. I suddenly felt I had blundered into a house of mourning. I wished I could have tiptoed out. Then his face changed like a slowly developing picture.

43

"Well, well, well," he said, the words rising and falling.

Old Man Henson rose from his creaking cane chair and came forward wheezing slightly.

"How do you do," he said. "So, Laura a woman, and you Johnnie, a man. Honey," he called out coaxingly, "come and meet our guests."

From the other side of the floor a woman emerged from a bedroom; she was a Mexican and wife number three. She was a youngish woman with a dark brown dog at her side. She was small with a wide face. The dog was snub-nosed and enormous.

"This is my wife," said Henson, "the dearest thing I've ever known."

Mrs. Henson's bracelets jingled as she shook our hands. The dog was watching us.

"What kind of a breed is he?" I asked.

"Rottweiler, German, bred for sledging I believe. Marvellously loyal."

Henson took the dog by the ears.

"Once they bite they don't let go," he continued. "The last one we had took six bullets but he still held on. The guy in question lost three fingers. He's not much good for breaking into houses any more."

"What's the dog called?"

"Prince—and he's a prince among canines, aren't you Prince?"

"Hey Prince," I called, slapping my legs.

Prince bristled and curled his lips.

"Don't call him, Johnnie," said Henson quietly, dropping ice into a tumbler. "Don't call him. Just let him be." He screwed the top off a gin bottle. "He'll come when he's good and ready, and not before."

"And meantime," added Mrs. Henson, "don't run when he's around, and never touch him. Never! He's not used to strangers, but he's quite safe when we're here."

Laura and I must have looked anxious for she continued: "But he won't trouble you, don't worry, he lives in the basement with Luiz. Now I'll show you to your rooms."

We followed Mrs. Henson back towards the ramp. I was happy to leave Prince behind with his master.

"This house is like a ship," Mrs. Henson announced. "You will live up here on the deck, but your bunks where you will sleep are below."

My bedroom was the one closest to the bottom of the ramp. I went in and shut the door quickly. I wanted to get something solid between me and Prince, now lying upstairs I imagined, at Henson's feet, his chest rising and falling as the old man twirled the ice-cubes in the bottom of his gin glass.

44

My bed was on a dais, a battered fan overhead. I found the switch and the cream-coloured blades started to turn, slowly at first, then faster and faster.

Beyond the bed was a door of wicker which opened onto another balcony. I went out. A patchwork of tiled roofs stretched away as far as the eye could see. The tiles were all a reddy-yellow colour, except around the chimney holes where they were black with soot. I heard Laura singing in the next bedroom along the balcony. I burst in on her baying like a hound.

"You little horror," she screamed. "Did you see the way that horrible dog was watching us?"

"I did."

"He's got the most horrible eyes. I hope they keep him locked up."

"Me too."

I tried to bite her arm and we went back out onto the balcony, laughing. After a few minutes it began to get dark, and then it was dark. It was as if a curtain had suddenly fallen. Cars flitted in distant streets, their head-lamps throwing out tunnels of light. The roof-tops of the town all merged into a single shape. A mariachi trumpet sounded sadly in the distance, and Laura put her arm through mine.

"It's so nice to be in paradise with my kid brother," she said, and kissed me chastely on the temple.

My first night in the tropics, I fell asleep to the sound of Prince moaning in the basement. He sounded like wind howling down a chimney flue.

III

The next morning after breakfast, we put some belongings into a string bag, and set off on our first excursion. The streets outside were hot and still. We photographed each other in front of a tattered election poster. A mule clattered by without a rider, a gleaming machete hanging from the filthy grey saddle. We descended by a set of buckled steps with a cock tethered halfway down, his red comb shivering. At the bottom stood a hearse filled with bright plastic flowers. A funeral service amplified over loudspeakers boomed from the nearby church. A man sat fanning himself, sweat marks under the arms of his brown shirt.

We wandered through the town. We passed the post office with a blind man sitting outside. He was blowing tunelessly into a kazoo while a sickly-faced girl in a filthy dress held a cup out to passers-by. We dropped some coins in and she smiled to reveal purple gums with no teeth. We crossed a bridge over a river. Young boys cavorted in the water, their brown skins shining with wet. Women were washing clothes on the bank sides, and islands of suds slipped away from them. The sun was high. We were growing irritable. We would never get to it, we thought, and then suddenly there it was in front of us.

"Our first taste of the Pacific," said Laura. She hummed the music of strip-tease as she took off her shift.

"Last one in the water is a cissy," she said.

She trod painfully across the hot sand of the empty beach and stopped at the ocean's edge. She was wearing a bikini and I could see the outline of her body.

"It's lovely and warm," she called, splashing her arms.

"Go on then," I shouted.

I knew the facts of life, but knowledge was no substitute for experience. If anything, it sharpened my sense of non-achievement. Then, suddenly, I felt annoyed on account of my ignorance, and a little morose.

IV

On the morning we had agreed to play tennis, Mary appeared in the kitchen, immaculate in a set of whites.

"O.K., guys. Get your things." She was bursting with desperate energy.

We picked up the tennis rackets which Luiz had dug out for us—they had strings of slack yellow gut—and trudged down the ramp. At the bottom, Mary put her head over the stairs leading to the basement.

"Princey," she called down. "Where are you?"

There was a scampering sound and, a moment later, the enormous vicious shape of Prince bounded into the hall on legs as thick as bannister rails. Prince was holding his play-bone in his mouth. This was a piece of thick leather knotted at either end. It was about the same size as my forearm.

"Would little Prince like to come for a ride this morning?" she asked, stroking his dark cranium. He arched his back and dropped the saliva-covered play bone to the floor where it lay like a cannibal's relic.

"I didn't know Prince played tennis," said Laura.

"Now, now. Don't be a spoil-sport, Laura," said Mary. "Poor Prince. Cooped up in the house all day. He likes to be taken out, just like you do. Don't you Prince?"

Mary tried to move his head from side to side but Prince didn't budge. Her skirt had ridden up and we saw that her knickers had Snoopy on the back of them.

"Come on then. The court's booked for eleven." She strutted towards the door, Prince going with her.

We followed nervously, our tennis rackets held protectively in front of our bare legs.

Outside, the Fiat stood in the boiling sun, its two doors hanging open. Laura and I climbed in the back, Mary and Prince in the front. The *Cinquocento* squeaked and bumped as we lurched away. Then we turned down the hill and passed the pit.

"Are they ever going to mend that hole?" I asked stupidly.

"Oh, some time in the next century," said Mary blithely, and she swung into a side street and pulled up in front of a chemist's shop.

"Hang on, kids," she said. "Won't be a mo," and before we could say a word she was gone and we were left alone with Prince.

"This is unbelievable," murmured Laura.

"My heart's beating so much it's going to burst," I said.

"Do you think he knows us enough not to attack?"

Prince sat on his haunches, and stared into the sunny street.

"Remember what father says—'If you see a mad dog don't panic. Just remain absolutely calm and still.'" My voice trembled.

"I'm going to vomit," said Laura.

Prince yawned and lay down.

"Good Prince," I said soothingly, and gently I began to push the seat forward. If I was able to tip him off the seat and get him down on to the floor where the front passenger's feet went, then perhaps I could open the passenger-side door, and then Laura and I could escape.

However, before any of this came to pass, I heard a low growl and Prince lifted his head. We stared at one another over the top of the seat. His lips curled to reveal strong, white teeth.

"Don't move," hissed Laura. "Follow your own bloody advice and stay still."

I shrank back into my seat. Prince growled again and lowered his head. Sweat trickled over my ribs. Laura took my hand. I looked out of the window. Two men struggled by with a swordfish, its skin the colour of gun-metal. I noticed a young boy sitting on a string backed chair in front of a doorway. In the room behind him I saw furnaces, and a few seconds later, when my eyes had adjusted, a conveyor belt with tortillas on it. They moved in the darkness like small round moons. Then, finally,

I saw the tortilla-makers inside the room, poking in dark ovens with long wooden spatulas.

At last, Mary returned with a small white package. Prince heaved himself on to his haunches and she climbed into her seat.

"Sorry to hold you up," she said lightly. We said nothing.

We drove through the town and turned onto a highway. Rusting Buicks and Chevrolets hurtled by, filled with staring faces. After a few miles a buckled sign appeared with the words 'Tennis Club'. We turned through a gate and pulled up under the shade of a pine tree.

"Our tennis club—toast of the province," exclaimed Mary, tipping her seat back. Laura and I scrambled out of her car as fast as we were able.

"Now, you stay here, Prince," continued Mary, "and mind the car." She slammed the door. "This way for the courts, gang. Follow me."

Laura took my arm.

"You know when you said, in the car, what father said about staying still?" she whispered.

I nodded.

"When you said it, I thought, 'This dog would kill a tree if he didn't like it,' and I wanted to laugh only I thought, 'If I laugh, he'll eat me.'"

We passed through reception and emerged under a verandah, the roof made of palm fronds. In front of us, several empty courts stretched towards the sea.

"Come and meet my partner, Midge," called Mary. She had donned the wrist-bands of a professional tennis player.

We went over and shook hands. Midge was not alone. Her husband and two sons had come along. The boys had silver braces on their white teeth, and Bob, the husband, was huge and tanned.

We stepped on to the court. The tarmac was sizzling, and the white tramlines were dancing in the sun.

"This is a nightmare," whispered Laura.

Mary and Midge were on the other side of the net. They were hunched forward, ready for action. They both had steel rackets in their hands, and sun visors on their foreheads. These cast a pallid green shadow over their faces. It was like a scene from an old-fashioned comic book. They were the toffs who had all the money, and we were the townies who had nothing.

We gritted our teeth, knocked up, then started to play. What followed was exhausting but not too humiliating. As Mary and Midge discovered, our lack of skill spoilt their game.

At one set each, Laura suggested that we rest.

"Yes, siree," agreed Midge.

We fled to the verandah.

"I bet it sure is hot out there," observed Bob. His boys smirked.

I noticed an old-fashioned cooler cabinet—the type you open from the top—with the glorious words *Coca-Cola* written on the side.

"But, if you think this is hot," Bob continued eagerly, "you should be here in August. Oh boy, I'm telling you, August is a killer."

I lifted the freezer lid. An unpleasant smell of old rubber drifted up. The bottles inside were lying submerged in brown murky water, and floating in the corner, belly upwards, was a large, dead lizard.

"Yuck," said Mary beside me. "Listen, honey, I bought some cold drinks for us. They're in the lunch box under the front passenger seat. Lime juice and guava. Would you be a love and get them for me?"

"What about Prince?" I said.

"Don't mind Prince. You've been around him for long enough. He knows you."

Back at the Fiat, I found Prince stretched across the front seats, fast asleep.

"Hello, Prince." He raised his head. "You speak English?" I said. "I'm just getting the lunch box."

Suddenly, Prince rose up on his haunches like a monster coming out of the sea.

"No-speaka-da-English? Come on Prince. Stop being such a dickhead. Let me open the door."

The hairs on his neck began to bristle.

I retraced my steps to the verandah.

"No lunch box. I'm disappointed," said Mary.

"Prince wasn't very friendly, wouldn't let me into the car!"

"And I don't think Prince likes us," added Laura. "When you left him in the car this morning, he was awfully funny with us."

"You're making a mountain out of a molehill. He's just not used to you," replied Mary.

I followed her back to the car park. Prince was sitting at the open window, staring out. As Mary approached he growled. "Prince," said Mary. "Remember me?" His growling dropped to a low rumble and his lips slipped back over his teeth. Mary pushed him over onto the driver's seat and pulled out the lunch box.

"Now you be a good guard dog," she said and slammed the door.

I took the lunch box from her as we walked away.

"You know," she said, "sometimes, that Prince worries me."

Then she told me a long story ... Prince as a puppy, tormented by children. Prince coming to the Henson's, and having great trouble making friends with anyone. Prince going to dog training school in Arizona where, according to the dog trainers, he was found to be too temperamental, too wilful to be trained. After three days, the dog trainers sent Prince home from Arizona.

"You'll probably think this is ridiculous," she continued, "but after the accident with the electrical cable, I had to bring the police up to the roof. And this is what worries me. Prince was up there. There was blood and bits of clothing and I don't know, skin, I guess, and Prince was snuffling and licking everywhere, and frankly, I think he ate the bits stuck on the ladder."

When I handed Laura her lime and guava a few minutes later, she looked at me and said, "You've gone as white as a sheet."

V

The town ran out of water and the sewage plant closed. Excrement began to float in from the sea. From a distance it looked like shoals of corks, but close up there was no mistaking it. There was talk of dysentery.

At the end of the street where the Hensons lived, there stood two detached villas, joined by a bridge. Each house was owned by an American film star—they were not in town—and the villas came with a swimming pool. Mrs. Henson bribed the caretaker, then told us to skip the beaches and swim there. So off we went.

The pool was surrounded by vegetation with thick rubbery leaves, and the water was cold and chlorinated, like in England. After swimming, we found a watering can, wrote the names of the two film stars in water on the sun dried pool side, and took each other's photographs.

Then a huge iguana appeared, four foot long with skin like stone. Its tongue snaked deftly through the air as it watched us.

Although it was harmless, it made us uneasy. We wandered back through the shuttered rooms where the furniture was shrouded with white sheets, calling for the caretaker.

At last we found him, asleep at the kitchen table, a plate of rice and aubergine in front of him, and flies buzzing around. He woke with a start and began to apologise in Spanish.

It did not matter, we assured him. He brought us to the front door, showed us out and closed it after us.

"God! De-press-ing," said Laura.

A group of tourists in a nearby jeep were pointing their cameras at the bridge above and clicking away furiously.

"This is the famous love crossing," the guide explained. "When Richard and Elizabeth want to see each other, they don't have to come out into the sun here in the street, and walk to the other's front door. No, with this bridge ..."

As usual, the two boys from Juarez's shop on the corner were sitting on the steps of the Henson's house, and today they were playing with a scrawny kitten. Their heads were shaved and their bodies were dusted with white disinfectant powder, protection against infection from bad water.

We skirted past them and found Luiz in the hall. He was watering the plants from a bucket. We were buying clean water from the water truck. The tank in the kitchen was full of it.

I went into my bedroom. Then I heard the Juarez boys calling unhappily in their piping voices. I went out to see. The little kitten had run into the middle of the hall. Luiz was gone. Suddenly, I saw Prince at the top of the basement stairs. I shouted at the boy, "*Vamos*". The child panicked and scuttled towards the kitten. The dog leapt forward, opened his vast mouth, then snapped his jaw shut over one side of the boy's head. The boy fell, and screamed. The kitten screeched as Prince trod it underfoot. I picked up a large potted plant and threw it across the hall. It hit Prince on the ribs, bounced away and smashed on the marble floor. Luiz ran down the ramp with a dripping pail and threw the water in it with all his might at Prince. The dog let go and Luiz grabbed him by his collar. The other Juarez boy was screaming in the doorway. The victim was on the floor, howling, covered with wet red earth. There was blood everywhere.

The Juarez boy needed fifty-six stitches.

During the conversations in the house that followed, we learnt that Prince had managed to slip through the rope by which he was normally secured. His attack, the Hensons agreed, yes, it was regrettable, but also, it was only natural. As a guard dog, of course he would bite any stranger in the house ...

And Mexico, they continued, Mexico was a violent place. Gangs of thieves descended nightly on the houses of the rich. Prince was the best protection the Hensons had.

In the late afternoon, I went for a walk. At the bottom of the steps I found the church was open—the one where we had seen the funeral on our first day. I put money in the collection box, lit a candle, and asked God, please, to take Prince away.

VI

The hostess of the party opened the door to us. She was a middle-aged Mexican in a halter dress of bright colours.

"Come in, darlings, come in," she said. In the hallway, we told her the Hensons couldn't come.

"Oh, that was a terrible business with the dog and the little boy," observed the woman, whose name was Maria-Teresa. "Mrs. Henson—as you know she's my best friend—she was in the beauty salon just the next day—red eyes—bad skin—looking terrible. I said to her, 'You've really got to look after yourself, you know! You can't take these things to heart,' I said. But let's not think of sad things. This is a party."

She led us into a big room filled with people. A wall of glass looked down to the sea. The ocean shone silver and a pale moon hung in the sky.

Maria-Teresa introduced me to her husband, a large American called Fred who wore a blue shirt and red Bermuda shorts.

As soon as his wife left us, Fred began to tell me about Rosicrucianism. He was making a serious study, he said, of this ancient and important philosophy.

I nodded mechanically. Then, mercifully, Laura came over and dragged me away through a door.

I found myself in a bedroom. Maria-Teresa was sitting on the bed rolling dry, browny grass, and tobacco.

"Was my husband talking about Rosicrucianism?" she asked.

"Yes."

"Thought so."

She lit the end of the joint and handed it on.

"You know," she said, "I'd like to retire to a desert island and smoke my head off for the rest of my life."

I inhaled deeply. The smoke scorched the back of my throat. Through the open windows drifted the sound of the sea. The night was warm and still.

"Listen," she continued, "I've got a party to attend to. Enjoy yourselves but don't bring the dope outside, O.K.? You never know who's got a line to the cops," and she went out the door.

"Have you seen the three Mexican beauties?" asked Laura.

"No."

52

All I could remember was Fred and Rosicrucianism.

"They've seen you. They want to meet."

Ten minutes later I was back at the party. The girls Laura had spoken of were on a sofa, sitting in a demure row, like in a dance hall. They had bare knees and glowing shins. I liked the one in the middle the most.

I was just about to go over when Mary cut across my path. She was wearing a purple cheese-cloth dress. Her eyes were shining and she was slopping her glass of Scotch.

"Come and meet someone," she said.

"Can I meet them later?"

"WHAT! No way, you're going to meet Sherri, NOW! She's dynamite." Mary squeezed my arm conspiratorially.

Sherri was a tanned American clutching a bottle of Marqués de Riscal.

"Would you like some?" she asked. "It's French wine."

Mary downed her Scotch, then swigged from the bottle.

"Listen, you guys …" began Sherri. "I have a problem. Maybe you can help me."

"Anything," slurred Mary, winking lasciviously at me.

"I'm in the swimwear business. I need a name. So I just want you to tell me, right off the top of your head, what you think. O.K.? Here it is. Live Wire."

"What?" asked Mary.

"Live Wire," repeated Sherri emphatically. "You know like for electricity … Pylons … Live wires … That's our image. Wear one of our swim-suits and you're like … A shock … Are you all right?"

"I wish you hadn't said that." Mary started to cry and heads turned. "I wish you hadn't. You've just touched on something, very, very upsetting …"

"What did I say wrong?" Sherri tugged my arm.

"Nothing at all," I assured her blandly.

I took Mary into the bedroom I had just left. It was still filled with the sweet smell of marijuana. I found Mary a tissue. She finished crying, and we came back out to the party.

I went straight to the sofa where the girls had been sitting, but now it was empty. I didn't want to feel disappointed, so I decided to be active. I went over to the buffet. I would eat. Pink and yellow tropical flowers floated in great bowls. A flashbulb lit up the room for a second. Somebody laughed. I picked up a plate.

"Hello," said a voice at my side.

It was the girl who had been sitting in the middle—the one I liked. We went outside and I met her friends. She told me her name was Angela-Maria. We all talked quickly and excitedly, and the starched white table napkins they were each holding, crinkled and crackled as they spread them on their laps.

I fell into my bed later under the clanging fan. Prince was moaning eerily, as per normal. I closed my eyes and a picture of Angela-Maria immediately sprung into my mind. For the first time on that holiday, as I drifted to sleep, I did not once find myself listening involuntarily to Prince.

VII

The following day, the town's water supply was back on. Laura and I went to the beach. Shiny bluebottles buzzed around our heads all day. We left the beach early, and went back to the house. I went to my room, and fell into a depressed sleep.

In the early evening Laura woke me. The Hensons were playing bridge in someone's house.

"We have to go out and eat," she said.

I got dressed and we wandered into town. Every time I saw a girl, I thought it was Angela-Maria. Laura must have sensed it but said nothing.

We found a small restaurant. It was filled with middle-aged American women and young Mexican men. Every year, I had gathered from the Hensons, professional American women used to flood south across the Mexican border in search of the masculine that was banished from their everyday, correct American lives; and in Puerto Vallarta, they found it, for the price of a shirt, or a cigarette lighter.

It was hot, so Laura and I sat outside, under the awning. We ordered pizzas, but all we were able to eat was the mozzarella topping. The air was sticky and heavy. We drank a couple of tequilas and felt slightly light headed. Suddenly, everywhere was still, like a forest after gunfire. Thunder rumbled in the distance, and then the rain started needling on the awning over head. Within seconds the noise above was deafening and waterfalls of water were sheeting down around us. We ran inside. The electric lights wavered, everyone went "Oh," and then we plunged into darkness. Candles were lit and the proprietor gave everyone free drinks. A man ran in with a newspaper over his head which disintegrated when he lifted it away. Laura and I drank more tequilas. The water pouring over the edge of the awning diminished to a trickle. The storm—at least for the time being—was apparently over. We paid our bill and left.

Outside, the streets were flooded with two feet of rainwater. It was dark and swiftly flowing. A dwarf was standing in the middle of the torrent, chest deep. The power cut was absolute. There was no light to be seen anywhere.

We began to make our way home along the cobbled pavements, wet and slippery. Now we understood why the roads were a couple of feet lower. When it flooded, like tonight, they became the course along which the floodwater ran.

At last we turned up the hill for home. Fallen telegraph poles and palm trees lay across our path. Roof tiles, planks, and pieces of guttering were scattered everywhere, and sticking out of the pit was a crashed Chevrolet, its tail fins pointing up in to the air. Thunder started to boom again. That was the way with Mexican storms. They came, they went, and then they came back again ...

Laura and I began to run as the raindrops started falling. They were as big as the old two-and-sixes. At the front door we got the key into the lock, and rushed in laughing. Then we stopped laughing. The hall was pitch dark. We tried the switch. Nothing. We called out for Luiz. Again, nothing. Blackout.

"There's matches and a candle on the hall table," whispered Laura.

We found them, and by the tiny flame of a waxy Mexican match, we lit the wick. The front door closed in a gust of wind, and upstairs there was an ominous banging.

"I think there's something up there," said Laura. We linked arms and tiptoed up the ramp. At the top, we came into the kitchen. Sheet lightning flared and, for a moment, everything was vividly clear: the enormous American refrigerator with its rounded edges, the refrigerator door hanging open, food from the refrigerator on the floor; the magnetic knife rack with half-a-dozen knifes stuck to it; and two potted plants with monstrous, rubber leaves. Then everything went black again.

"Is there anybody there?" we called into the darkness, our voices rolling around the room where we had found Henson sitting on the day we arrived, and across to the far side where the Hensons slept.

"Hello ..."

We crept by the linen chest with the striped Mexican blanket, then under the huge, sinister painting of an Indian holding a lily. We came into the seating area. A gust of rain spattered into our faces. The flame of the candle wavered but did not go out. We stumbled on rubble and debris. We looked up. A huge hole gaped above. It ran along the whole of that side of the house. The roof had collapsed in the storm. Sheet lightning rolled across the sky again, and that was when we saw him. Prince was lying on the sodden master bed, surrounded by tiles and splintered rafters, a length of metal gutter beside him stretching up into the darkness. We stood transfixed with terror for what seemed like several minutes, us watching him and him watching us. At last there was a lull in the storm and it was then that we realised from his absolute stillness, that it was not Prince we were looking at, but his corpse.

We retreated to the kitchen. There was Scotch in the cupboard and we drank in the darkness, huddled over our candle. The liquor tasted musty. Neither of us spoke. Outside, the storm raged and finally, died.

After a while we heard Luiz calling. He appeared at the top of the ramp. He carried an enormous flash lamp.

"There's been an accident, Luiz," we said, and solemnly we led him to the master bedroom.

By the beam of the torch we saw everything. Prince's eyes were wide open, and his big red tongue was covered with a froth that was like egg-white. The carcass of a chicken—he had obviously taken this from the refrigerator—lay nearby. It was covered with tile dust. The fur and flesh of his massive left shoulder had been stripped away to the bone.

We climbed onto the roof and there the picture became clearer. The electricity cable had blown off its wooden arms and got wrapped around the gutter. The two had welded together. When the roof collapsed, the gutter went through the hole. It hit Prince on the bed below. He had died of a massive electric shock.

On adjacent roofs, all around us, there were figures speaking in Spanish. The roof of every single house in the town, it seemed, had been damaged in the storm. Luiz called out to the house nearest. I did not understand what he said, but I caught the word "Prince". The reply from the neighbour was a whoop of joy, and it was soon echoed by other whoops, on other roofs, the whoops spreading away from us, like ripples on a pond.

VIII

Next morning I went out early on to my balcony. It was still covered with puddles of cold rainwater from the night before. I looked down into the garden below. Luiz was digging a hole in the corner.

When the hole was finished, Luiz went back into the basement where he lived. With the sun rising, I noticed the puddles of rainwater on my balcony were beginning to steam. Luiz and some Mexicans I did not recognise, now struggled into view. They were carrying the corpse of Prince on a door.

Old Man Henson and his wife were behind; he, tall and stooping in a white linen suit; she, small and hard, in a tight, black dress. The Mexicans tipped Prince into the hole. He landed on his back with his feet pointing upwards. Mrs. Henson covered her eyes with her hands and began to cry.

The men set to, spading in the earth quickly until a ruddy-brown mound replaced the hole. A crude wooden cross was put at the head.

"Don't worry, honey," I heard Henson comforting his wife. "We'll get another, and he'll be just as great as the mighty Prince."

I slipped out of the front door and began to wander down the cobbled street. The fish-man was coming the other way, prickly red mullet dangling from a piece of scaffolding stretched across his shoulders. To bring the women out of the houses, he repeatedly struck the scaffolding pole with a metal bar. This produced a sound that was both exquisitely sweet and melancholy.

I passed Juarez's shop where Prince's victim watched me with his good eye. The other half of his face was covered with an enormous, lumpy, white dressing.

I arrived at the steps which led to the town. Looking down, I saw the girl from the party was climbing up. I stopped to wait for her, excitement mounting. She reached the last step, breathless. She banged her chest and we shook hands.

"I have come," she began shyly, "to invite your sister and yourself to come out with my friends and I, tonight."

After that, I saw Angela-Maria every day, and of course, I fell in love.

IX

On the last day of the holiday, I met Angela-Maria in a small square. It was filled with shoe-shine boys; they all had blue-black hair and brown skins; the customers were all policemen, wearing boots with Cuban heels; the policemen's uniforms were all shabby, their carbines were all shiney. I kissed Angela-Maria without thinking. The shoe-shine boys whistled, the policemen scowled.

That night she came to the Henson's house. I led her to my bedroom. No one knew she was there. We drank beer. Then I peeled off the bathing costume she had worn at the beach where we had spent the afternoon. Her skin tasted of salt, and the fan clanged over head.

57

The next morning, we said goodbye. She went off to work and I caught a flight back to England, with Laura.

X

A few weeks ago, I went to a party given by Laura. She is married now, and she lives in a ground floor flat in a stucco mansion near Regents Park. I didn't know many of the guests, and I'm not good at starting conversations with strangers, so I spent much of my time looking around. There was a large wooden propeller hanging over the mantel-piece, and a life-sized female figure, her whole body swathed in bandages apart from her breasts and groin.

I sought Laura out in the kitchen.

"Do you remember Me-hi-co?" I said.

She was extracting baked potatoes from the oven.

"Oh yes, where you first did it, didn't you?"

It was not meant maliciously. It was just somehow Laura's way to come out with such statements.

Later, in the early hours, I asked her the question again. She told me that she remembered swimming in the film stars' pool, the iguana, and the nightmare tennis match. That was the sum of it. "Oh, and Prince," she added. "I remember Prince. Night—mare! Fancy a line of coke? I could murder one myself."

It was getting light when I walked home through the park. The sky overhead was like mother-of-pearl, and in the chestnut trees with their vivid green leaves, the birds were beginning their dawn chorus.

Laura and I had talked through the night—mainly memories and recollections—and I couldn't remember us ever having talked in quite this way before. Now, as the dawn grew brighter, I realised what had happened.

Every life is made up of discreet demarcations, when we cross from one state of existence to another, and this night, just gone, had been one of those. As we had talked, (admittedly fuelled by the cocaine), Laura and I had passed on from the way we had been when we were younger—snappy, garrulous, brittle—to a new way of being with one another, a way that was like that of older people, and particularly our parents. Yes, that was it. I was older. She was older. We were older. Our youth was over.

At St. John's Wood roundabout, I bought all the Sunday newspapers, and turned towards home.

Nuptials

As Damian walked along the Belfast street, little bits of grit blew into his face.

Damian had to stop and blink. On one side he was aware of a man chasing after his tam-o-shanter as it bowled along the gutter, while on the other he glimpsed, through watering eyes, a young girl wrestling with an inside-out umbrella. Somewhere, Damian heard a tile shattering on the ground.

When the secretary from Queen's University had telephoned him, this was the day before at his home in Dublin, she had warned him of autumn storms.

"Awful weather we're having in Belfast these days," she had said. "Raining cats and dogs you know." Then she had added, "The peace dividend," and laughed.

Walking on now, eyes narrowed, Damian remembered first the conversation and then the lines of Jonathan Swift:

Drown'd Puppies, stinking Sprats, all drench'd in Mud,
Dead Cats and Turnip-Tops, came tumbling down the Flood.

He had decided that the theme of his, as yet unwritten lecture, was to be how the differing traditions of Ireland—English and Irish, Scots-Ulster and Gaelic—nourished one another. So could he start with raining cats and dogs and Swift? he wondered. But however he began, he knew that his conclusion was that the people on the island of Ireland now had more in common, uniting them, than they had separating them.

Damian had agreed to speak at a forthcoming conference on 'Nationalisms and the Nation State', and it was to meet the organisers that he had come to Belfast. But before he met anybody, he was first going to call in at the second-hand bookshops which he always visited whenever he was in the city, and which, conveniently, were on the way to the university buildings.

Damian bent down and pulled up one of his socks; it was cotton, with a black and red pattern, like a Malevich painting. He had bought them in Stockholm where he had spoken at a conference on 'Regional Variation and the European Union'. Clothes were his only frivolous pleasure.

Just then, Damian heard cries. He turned and saw—on the other side of the street—a girl being dragged out of a photocopying shop and pulled towards a lamp-post. She was shouting and possibly laughing—he couldn't be quite sure—and the group pulling her along were also shouting. A Rag Week stunt, he thought. Damian stood up, put the briefcase under his arm, and walked into the first book shop.

As the door clanged shut, Damian sniffed the unmistakable bookish odour of dust, old paper and cloth. This was a good moment and one he was able to summon at will when he was alone at his desk at home.

Damian turned to the section nearest him: 'Literature—Unsorted—Various'. Outside, the shouting went on. He lifted down an edition of Aldous Huxley's *Eyeless in Gaza*. It was a book he had not read before and, as he always did on a first encounter, he turned straight to the end and read the last line:

> He put a couple of eggs on to boil, and sat down meanwhile to bread and cheese. Dispassionately, and with a serene lucidity, he thought of what was in store for him. Whatever it might be, he knew now that all would be well.

Yes, interesting, but there was no price marked inside the cover. Damian looked up and saw the owners of the shop—he knew them vaguely—standing at the shop window.

Damian walked towards the pair. The woman was in her fifties with red hennaed hair. Her name was Isadora. Daniel, her husband, was a thick-set man in a blue jersey bearing the insignia of a well known Belfast rugby club.

"Excuse me," began Damian.

Isadora assumed a face of disgust as she made room for Damian at the window.

"Cutting up a bit rough over there, aren't they!" said Daniel.

Damian looked across the road; the girl who he had seen being dragged from the shop had been stripped to blouse and slip and strapped to a lamp-post with brown tape. The crowd had started around her shoulders, and in one continuous spiralling motion had wound their way down her body, trapping her hands by the side of her hips. Her feet were bare and her slip was caught up in the tape, exposing her white knickers.

The crowd now formed a circle around the girl. A bucket was produced from somewhere, lifted up and tipped over the girl's head. It was water and Damian knew immediately how cold it was: he could tell from the way the girl's body went rigid and the way the thin blouse stuck to her. A cheer went up. Damian felt sick.

"So what do you think of Belfast?" growled Daniel.

Damian sighed, shook his head ambiguously and watched as a girl in a tight, short suit began to apply make-up aggressively to the victim's face, while a second emptied the vile yellow liquid contents of a silver carry out tray onto her head.

"Nice people, aren't we," continued Daniel, "and they say our 'Troubles' are over."

"Well, perhaps not yet," said Damian.

The girl with the make-up box stepped back, and someone produced a plastic red nose and forced it on to the girl's face. The victim shook her head violently. This only improved the entertainment for those around her. The girl herself had long since stopped laughing, that is, if she had ever been laughing to begin with.

"Any good book shops for sale in Dublin?" muttered Isadora.

The owners moved away from the window, but Damian, although he didn't want to, nonetheless found himself continuing to watch.

Now eggs were broken on the girl's head and shoulders and breasts, and then a bag of flour was tipped over her. The flour stuck to the egg, and suddenly the girl was transformed from something abused but recognisably human, into something furred and white and primeval. The girl sensed it, and dropped her head forward, as if she were ashamed.

Damian returned the Huxley to its shelf, put the briefcase under his arm, and marched through the door.

Outside, two policemen, backs to the wind, rifles cradled in their arms, were resolutely ignoring the scene. Damian looked across at the girl and he saw the crowd was gone.

He began to cross the road carefully. There were big puddles on the tarmac, and he worried momentarily about wetting his new Milanese leather button boots.

Stepping up on to the far kerb, Damian saw the girl's feet were bare. He also saw that her tormentors, with unexpected consideration, had slipped a piece of cardboard under them. The girl's toe-nails were varnished red. There were egg shells and flour on the pavement, and a strong smell of curry. Her legs were bare and white, with a bruise the colour of a plum showing on one thigh between two brown bands of tape. Her bare arms, where the skin showed through the flour, were goose pimpled. She was also very small, which Damian hadn't taken in from the other side of the road. Her hair was smeared with egg, flour and curry, and hung down in rat's tails. Her face was wide and angular and probably quite pretty, he thought, but with her lips now crudely daubed with red lipstick, her eyelids coated with green mascara, and the false red nose, she looked both pathetic and surreal. She couldn't have been much older than eighteen.

"My God, it's cold," she said, quite normally.

"What's going on?" Damian asked, coming closer.

"I'm getting married on Tuesday, and this is what some like to do here." He saw that she realised he was appalled. She looked away.

"Does this always happen to everyone?" Damian asked. He had never come across anything like this before.

"No."

"Will this happen to your fiancé?"

"I don't expect so. He hasn't told anyone at work he's getting married."

Damian shifted uneasily from one foot to the other and swopped his briefcase to the other arm.

"What time is it?" she asked suddenly.

"I'm sorry, my watch packed up on the train," he apologised, and to prove it, he showed her the watch.

"Are you up from Dublin?" the girl asked, noting his accent. But then, not waiting for a reply she sighed, "My God! How much longer?" The door of the photocopying shop banged open and up came the girl who had applied the make-up. There was a gold cross hanging from her neck, and from her thin wrist dangled a black camera.

"Come on, Aoife, give us a smile?" said the girl, lifting the camera. "One for Seamus."

"Fuck off," shouted Aoife, as the girl who was tied to the lamp-post was evidently called; at the same time she turned her head away.

"Come on now," Damian heard the girl with the camera calling, playfully, teasingly.

"Let me go," said Aoife reasonably, "I'm cold. Come on Colette, you've had your fun." Aoife was getting angry now.

"Ah no, didn't we say two-thirty?" Colette was enjoying her power.

Damian looked again at her gold cross. Judging by their names he presumed both girls were Catholics, like himself.

"Would you like this done to you?" he asked Colette, as she folded away her camera.

"Next time round I'll not let anyone know I'm getting married," she laughed, "but I had this—worse actually—last year." Then she added, "Anyway, it's only a bit of fun."

"Colette, I'm fucking cold," said Aoife.

"Let her go," said Damian calmly. "Go on, let her go."

He aimed to sound persuasive but he sounded like a schoolmaster.

"No," said Colette curtly, and turning on high heels, she clipped back into the shop.

"Cut me loose, will you, mister?" said Aoife. Her teeth were chattering.

Damian had a small penknife which he used for scraping the bowl of his pipe. He unbuttoned his green felt hunting coat, undid his tweed jacket, reached a finger into the top left pocket of his waistcoat, and pulled out the knife. The silver handle was shaped like a fish.

Damian opened out the short blade and went behind the lamp-post. He started to saw the tape which held Aoife's shoulders. Nothing happened. The tape had too many layers, and his blade was blunt. Why hadn't he got a Swiss Army knife? Damian wondered angrily. Everyone else in the world bloody had.

He jabbed the knife at the middle of the taut tape, and to his delight it went through with a pop. Damian made another stab, then a third and a fourth. Hurrah.

Then he heard the door of the photocopying shop open and shut as someone came out.

"What are you doing?" said a young male voice sharply. It unnerved Damian.

Without looking up, Damian stabbed violently with the blade at the tape. The knife went through easily but then carried on, struck the lamp-post and snapped in two. The blade tumbled down inside the tape, and landed on the pavement at Aiofe's feet with ping.

"I said, what do you think you're doing?" repeated the male voice.

Damian started to bite at the tape. He felt frustrated. Damian was also fearful and on the verge of panic. He was also aware that more people had emerged from the shop.

"You'd better stop," Aoife whispered to him.

Damian straightened up and he saw that they had all come out. He counted eight, which close to seemed like a large crowd. One was a

63

middle-aged woman in her fifties and that surprised him. He hadn't noticed her before.

"She's a bit cold," said Damian quietly and, he hoped, unthreateningly.

The faces stared back at him. Damian could not tell whether they agreed with him or not.

With the toe of one of his boots Damian moved the broken blade of the knife towards himself, and then, looking sideways, he caught a glimpse of himself in the shop window. He looked ridiculous and foppish in his elegant clothes, his briefcase between his feet. He also looked weak, a pushover.

Three youths stepped forward. They all had short, aggressive haircuts and pimply faces. Damian noticed their huge trainers.

"Why don't you just piss off, mister," one of them said.

"Leave him alone, William," called the middle-aged woman, "he's a stranger, and he doesn't know what he's about."

"I'm not here to argue with you," said Damian, defensively.

"All right, fuck off then," shouted another, and smirking he added, "Paddy."

Beside him Damian heard Aoife whisper, "Go, mister, get away." Behind the make-up her expression was apprehensive and fearful. That was when it struck him. The fur of flour was supposed to make Aoife look like a grotesque bride in a grotesque dress. "Go on," Aoife whispered, "it's only a bit of fun." What a bizarre and hateful welcome to marriage, he thought.

Damian started to walk slowly away. He could hear them chanting "Wanker, wanker," and he knew that whatever happened, he must not show his fear.

He slipped his hand into his jacket pocket and found his fountain pen. He took off the top and then held the pen by its stem, nib upwards. If anyone came up behind him, Damian would plunge it backwards, striking the forehead or, if he was lucky, even the eye of the assailant. But no one ran up and Damian walked on without incident, all the way to the safety of the university gates, his pen pointing sky-wards, the nib gleaming like a dagger.

Telephone Sex

THE HARROD'S COSMETICS HALL was hushed and scented when Mark called in to buy his wife a lipstick. Samantha, his wife, who liked to be called Sam, always wore pink lipstick which he detested, so Mark chose the same pillar box shade of red as the salesgirl was wearing.

"I don't hold out much hope my wife'll wear it," he said.

"She might," said the salesgirl. The name on the shining name tag on her breast was Agatha.

They fell into conversation. Mark invited her to lunch. Agatha accepted, as long as it was only for an hour.

He took her to the Brasserie on the Brompton road. When they sat down, he saw she wore no blouse under her uniform. Between the lapels there was a lovely triangle of bumpy, freckled skin. He wanted to put his cheek there and feel it.

After weeks of wooing, Mark got his way. One Friday afternoon, his wife Sam decided suddenly to go to her mother's in the country. She took the children with her.

At closing time, he went to Harrod's and told Agatha he had a surprise for her.

He brought her home. Agatha thought it strange to be in the house, where signs of the wife were everywhere, but she said nothing.

Mark gave her a *Guide to the Hotels of England and Wales* and told her to chose somewhere for the weekend. Next thing, her uniform was off. In bed, he said her skin was like a shark's. As soon as they had finished making love, Agatha asked to use the telephone. Agatha lived with her mother, and she didn't want her mother worrying where she was.

"I can't talk exactly. I'm going away for the weekend." She spoke quietly into the receiver.

Agatha's mother, at the other end of the line, took the hint. "How nice for you," she said.

In the end, Mark and Agatha didn't go away at all, but stayed where they were in the house in Primrose Hill, in the bed which he had made up in the guest room. They only got up to eat.

When they talked, he told Agatha about his miserable marriage. Fifteen years of relentless hostility, Mark said, and yet he had always lacked the courage to break free.

Agatha had been married once herself, she told him. It had all happened when she had been very young—a short marriage, which ended unhappily. She had a child. The boy lived with her in-laws in Scotland.

She omitted to tell him that she had once suspected her husband of an infidelity. In fact it was only a friendship, at least at first. In the end, her jealousy drove him to do what she most feared. It drove him away and into her rival's arms. The experience had taught Agatha a bitter lesson. Leave well alone and matters sort themselves out; drag them into the light, and they only worsen.

She was thirty now, and tired of being alone. Who knew where this might lead? Even when she saw Mark change the bed linen on Sunday morning and thought, He could have waited 'til I'd gone, Agatha said nothing. He has to, she reproved herself, the sheets smell of us, and he must get them out of the way before his wife comes back home.

In the afternoon, they went for a walk in Regents Park. After thirty-six hours of nakedness, Agatha found it strange to be in her clothes. She had washed her underwear, and felt damp around her middle.

They went into a playground near the mosque. Arab matrons, in yashmaks, sat around on benches, while their children played in the pale autumn sunshine.

Mark held her hand. She saw the time on his wrist-watch. He would be bringing her home soon. Agatha imagined sitting in his car outside the flat in Streatham. She imagined him saying, "When will I see you again?" in an insincere way.

In the event, when he got her home, Mark asked if he could come in. Her mother gave them tea in the front room. It was rarely used and smelt of apples. Her mother had the good sense not to ask how the weekend had gone.

After a year of furtive meetings, Mark told Agatha he was going to leave his wife and that she had given him the strength to do so. Agatha was thrilled but held her breath.

He left Sam, as he said he would, and rented a flat in a mansion block at the bottom of Ladbroke Grove. There were scenes and outrages. His children were distraught. His wife issued dire threats, and once she made a feeble attempt to take her life with twenty disprins.

Agatha saw him rarely. He had said that would be wisest during this period of transition, and she saw the sense in that.

When they did meet, he talked and fulminated while she listened and nodded sagely. She never said anything unpleasant about Sam. Ever.

After six months of vile solicitor's letters and increasing unpleasantness from his wife, Mark's patience broke and he said, "Oh, to hell with it." Agatha moved in with him, bringing two suitcases and a doll with a porcelain face. She had won this at a fairground when she was ten. Since then, she and the doll had been inseparable.

Shortly after moving in, Agatha met Mark's children for the first time. When Jason and Jennifer talked about their mother, as was inevitable, Agatha showed no emotion.

"God! you coped with that marvellously," Mark observed at last, after they had dropped the children home to Sam. It wasn't until they were in bed together that Agatha expressed, through her passion, everything she had been waiting to say all day.

Agatha was again the perfect partner when she met Mark's friends; when she met his family; even when Sam came upon the two of them by chance in a restaurant.

As the outraged and clearly drunk wife weaved towards them, Agatha steeled herself. As Sam screeched into her face, "You whore, you husband-stealer, you whose brain is in your cunt ..." Agatha remained perfectly poised in her chair.

When the wine hit her face, all Agatha thought was that it was warmer than she had expected. She felt it run down her bare neck and on to her breasts under her blouse. She saw a restaurant of people looking on with that painful English mixture of disgust, fascination and disdain.

She picked up the white starched table napkin and began to wipe herself. She heard weeping. She looked and saw it was Sam. The screaming harridan was now wet-eyed and puffy cheeked, deflated, ashamed, humiliated.

Two waiters began to lead Sam away. Sam was shouting incoherently. Sam stumbled at the door and was gone.

Agatha dabbed at her neck. Everyone was eating again. Conversation had restarted. She had outfaced the enemy with her silence, and she had won.

"You were brilliant," said Mark. She squeezed his hand in reply. In bed, later, she asked him to make love to her twice.

Having flung the glass of wine into Agatha's face, Sam decided to throw in the towel. This was either because she had made a fool of herself, or because the action had drawn her anger. Agatha couldn't gauge which, but whatever the cause, the change was like a turn on a pinhead. Sam now agreed to a divorce. Sam now agreed the house in Regent's Park could be sold and the money divided. Mark and Agatha began to look for a place of their own to buy.

One Saturday, Mark and Agatha drove to Tufnell Park. It was a grey, muggy, June morning. Rain seemed about to fall but it never came. On the radio there was a programme on separation. They heard a Radio Four voice saying, "Divorce invariably involves a drop in living standards". Without saying a word, Agatha reached for the dial and retuned to Capital Gold.

The flat they went to see was a conversion in a Victorian house. It overlooked a railway line. There was only one bedroom.

"Divorce always means a drop in living standards," whispered Mark, as they stood in the tiny kitchen. "Where am I going to put the kids when they come for the weekend?"

"We'll sleep in the living room," said Agatha, "it'll be an adventure."

She put her arm through his, and the next moment a train whistled past outside. They stood listening as it rattled away down the line.

The train clinched it, and they decided to buy. Once it was theirs, Agatha took charge of the decoration. She painted the kitchen marigold yellow; the hallway Russian blue; the bedroom was apple green; and the tiny front room with the marble fireplace, she painted a lovely off-white.

They planned to marry when the divorce came through. Agatha found a new job in an art gallery. The children came every other weekend. They often talked about their mother but, when they did, Agatha only smiled and said the nicest things.

"You handle them so skillfully," Mark would often praise her on Sunday evenings. Agatha's only reply would be to squeeze her arms around his back until he called out, "Steady on."

Then Mark's work took him abroad for a week.

At one o'clock in the middle of the second night he was away, the telephone rang.

"Who's that?" asked Agatha sleepily.

"I'm Val." Her voice was a husky parody of a seductress.

"Who?"

"Tell Mark that Val loved lunch, and is available for him any time, any where, any place."

The dialling tone sounded. Agatha was awake now. She rattled the bar pointlessly as characters did in films. Who the hell was Val?

"But I don't know any Vals," said Mark, when he got back. "Let's hope she rings tonight."

She did. Agatha answered and motioned Mark to pick up the receiver in the hall.

"Hi. Val speaking. Is Mark there?"

"I'm so pleased you called," said Agatha, "please keep talking. The police are recording everything you say."

Val slammed the phone down, and then rang back immediately.

"You're a big fat hooker," she shouted, and hung up.

Mark and Agatha held each other and laughed until their sides ached, and tears ran down their cheeks. Agatha felt reassured.

But in the following weeks and months, Val's calls continued.

When Agatha answered, she left messages of thanks for meals, gifts—usually lingerie—and outings. When Mark answered, Val plied him with questions. "Do you want me in red stockings or black?" "On top tonight or underneath, cherie?"

They christened Val 'Telephone Sex', and Mark regaled their friends with stories about her calls. He did a very good parody which started, "Do you want me on the kingsize tonight or in the back of the Cortina?" Agatha always laughed along, but without much enthusiasm.

Mark was almost certain that it was a friend of Sam's—naturally Val wasn't her name—whose husband had left her for another, younger woman. She was acting alone, he believed. Agatha disagreed. Surely the woman had Sam's blessing. But she kept this to herself. Only a few months to the day they planned to marry, and then Agatha could rest, certain she had beaten her old inner adversary, the green-eyed serpent.

It was November, the month Mark and Agatha had met.

The telephone rang.

"This is Val."

"Yes," said Agatha, "I know who you are. He's not in."

This was what Agatha always said now.

"I want to leave him a message."

Instead of her usual tone of phoney sexuality, Val was curt and business-like.

"Cosmetics hall, Harrod's, one o'clock. And fingers crossed it's as good as the last meeting."

The line went dead, and Agatha felt a tug at the back of her solar plexus.

"Was that Telephone Sex?" asked Mark, strolling into the kitchen.

"No, wrong number."

In bed, that night, when Mark reached over, Agatha said she didn't want to. Later, while he slept, she stared at the ceiling and the band of light cast across it by the street lamp outside.

The tug was now a stab in her middle. It was jealousy.

In the morning, Agatha promised herself she wouldn't, but she couldn't stop herself coming out with it.

"You've seen your wife, haven't you, and you haven't told me!"

She saw his face redden slightly, and his Adam's apple bobbing as he looked up from his Sunday newspaper.

After a pause he finally said, "Yes, I did, but her solicitor was present. We're tying up loose ends and trying to be civilised about it."

There followed a long account of an innocent meeting in a pub, one lunchtime.

"You're seeing her next week, aren't you?"

"No."

"Don't lie to me. You're meeting in Harrod's, in the bloody cosmetics hall, where you bloody met me. Telephone Sex rang to tell me."

He blinked. Agatha knew she was right.

"We're buying the children's Christmas presents," he said. "It was the only idea that came into my head as a place to meet."

Agatha threw plates. She threw a chair. She emptied her make-up bag and stamped on it, scattering powder, smashing phials of perfume, flattening her lipstick and squeezing the red out.

Mark had never seen her like this before. "You've always been so reasonable about Sam," he pleaded. He was disturbed.

"I hate you," shouted Agatha, hurling her shoes after him as Mark retreated down the stairs.

The front door slammed and there was silence.

Tears rolled down Agatha's cheeks. This was a moment very like another, years before, when her marriage had started to fall apart.

She sat in the kitchen and stared through her tears at the red lipstick on the cork tiled floor. It looked as if it had seeped from the flattened cartridge. Why did this happen at the very moment when she'd almost won through?

As darkness fell, Agatha remained seated, not even bothering to get up and turn on the light.

Wesley

THE TAXI DRIVER WHIZZES through Belfast. It is early morning. Talk is of cars and babies and the new car I bought—this was years ago—and how I was never able to get the smell of the baby's sick off the back seat.

"I know where you're coming from," he says.

He has a pleasant face and wears a chunky identity bracelet.

"A couple of years back now ..."

I feel a confidence looming.

"Pre-ceasefire?"

"Yep. Pick up two suits on the street—we're not meant to but they look okay; one goes in the back, other in the front; he says, 'Town centre'.

"Off we go. Then the one in the back, he says, 'Driver, look between the front seats!' I think, new car—she was new then—and the eejit's been sick. So I look down and I can't believe it."

"What?"

"It's a gun. 'Republican Army,' he says, then the one in the front, he flaps the sun-visor down and takes my license from behind. I keep it there; you know, handy for checkpoints.

"He opens it and he says, 'Hello, Wesley.' And I think, oh God! why am I called Wesley? Couldn't I be John or Tom? But it's Wesley and that's like having Prod tattooed right across my forehead."

"'This your home address, Wesley?'"

"But I can't speak, the words won't come out.

"'Just nod,' he says.

"Thank God, at least he's a pro, I think, and he isn't shitting himself because it's his first time out. So I'm not going to get killed by accident.

"I nod and they tell me where to go. It's in west Belfast. I drive there very slowly, and all the time I keep praying, please, no checkpoint, I'll be killed in the crossfire. And God hears me. No checkpoints. So we

71

arrive, I hand over the keys, we go into a house.

"There are two others there and oh, my heart sinks when I see this! They're in balaclavas. Armed too. 'This is Wesley,' says one of the suits. Oh Wesley, that name.

"'Go and stand over there,' says the other suit. 'Look at the wallpaper. These two will look after you.'

"'Of course, anything you say.' I'm over to that wallpaper quicker than Roger Bannister ran the mile.

"The suits leave and the old cogs start turning. The guards are going to shoot me. That's the plan. It'll be on the news, Wesley X, well known Loyalist, executed by ASU, blah, blah. I start to sweat. I want to pee. I think I'm going mad. I'm a cert for Purdysburn—I know it.

"Then I say, whoa, Wesley! Hold on. You've got to stop this.

"So I look at that wallpaper. It's beige with red pictures—woman on a swing, sedan chair and a guy on a horse—and I look at that wallpaper like it's a woman, or I put it up myself.

"Then I hear the door opening. The suits are back.

"'Alright Wesley. Car's outside, key in the ignition. You just count a hundred and go. But don't go to the cops, Wesley. We know where you live, Wesley, and you don't want a home visit, do you, Wesley?

"They leave. The door closes. I count. I get to a hundred. Then I think, my hundred might only be their ten. I do two hundred. I do five hundred. I do a thousand.

"Then I say goodbye to that wallpaper and I get out of the house. And you know what? No fucking car.

"Then the fear kicks back. It's dark by now, it's west Belfast and I'm a Wesley.

"I run and run and just as I hit the top of the Grosvenor Road, I see the Police Land Rovers. I start to wave but they don't see me. But some guys on the street, they see me waving to the cops. Oh no, I think, that's it, I'm in for a kicking.

"So I have no choice. I just run right out in front of the first Land Rover and it screeches to a stop two feet from me.

"The policeman gets out and I explain and that's it. He takes me to the police station. I hadn't smoked for ten years but I had eight fags then, in a row."

"What about your car?"

"It was up in Poleglass."

"How did it get there?"

"It's a mystery. Someone stole it while I was counting, or the Provos

72

never left it outside. I don't know."

"Had it been used?"

"Yes, they had someone in the boot, drove him quite a few miles. That's what the cops told me."

He looked around his car interior, then jiggled the pine freshener dangling from the mirror.

"She's a good runner, good mileage, but I never open that boot, you know, but I get this really strong smell. I've sprayed it, I've washed it, I've even hung up one of these pine tree thingees—but nothing shifts it.

"You talked earlier about a milk smell; well, in that boot, my friend, I've got the smell of fear."

Christmas

I

MARIE STARED AT THE face in the mirror. Her right front tooth over-lapped the left. At school the other girls had called her 'Rabbit Face'.

Marie was not beautiful, she was pretty, and the best feature was her mouth, with the intriguing freckle which was half-on, half-off her upper lip. When she had her lipstick on, as she had now, the top half of the brown disc stuck up over the red line. It was like the sun rising out of the sea.

She opened her mouth, smiled, and tried to imagine her teeth if they were straight. Her mother could have had them fixed—like her older sister's—only she hadn't. Marie's were just wonky, whereas Rosemary's were proper buck teeth. They stuck so far out over her bottom lip, Rosemary had been able to fit her thumb in the space behind.

Then, about the time Marie was five, and Rosemary was ten, their mother, Angelica, took her sister up to a specialist in the Royal Victoria Hospital. He provided a brace for Rosemary to wear at night. It was a thing of stainless steel hoops and black rubber bands which fitted over the teeth and attached behind her sister's head.

"It tastes of yuck," Rosemary had screamed, a few minutes after she had been put to bed with the contraption in place for the first time.

Marie was in the bed with her.

"I'm going to take it off," Rosemary had roared, "I can't sleep."

"Don't," Marie whispered to her older sister, "she'll hit us both if you go on, you know she will."

Angelica was pretty free with her hand; when one sister was hit, the other invariably caught a whack or two.

And now Marie heard the sound of mother's feet, racing up the stairs of their house. Angelica was on the war-path.

"You'll be beautiful one day," Angelica shouted ahead, "that's why we are making sacrifices now!"

The bedroom door flew open. Mother appeared in the doorway, her bouffant hair like piled candy floss, her mouth a little round 'O' out of which she fired her words.

"I don't want to hear another word out of you. Do you understand?" Angelica hissed at her two daughters, who by now were rigid with fear in the bed. "Not one word. Now get to sleep, the two of yous."

Months passed. The brace reined in Rosemary's upper teeth. Her lower jaw came forward. Rosemary's face lengthened and evened up.

Three years on, Rosemary turned fifteen, and Marie saw that what mother had shouted up the stairs had come to pass. Now that her sister's teeth were straight, Rosemary's physical qualities—always there but hidden before—were suddenly visible; the lovely hair and the clear blue eyes, even the tapering fingers with the tapering fingernails. At weekends, Rosemary was allowed to coat these with red varnish, and when the family watched television, her mother liked to sit with Rosemary on the sofa and to stroke her sister's hands. Sometimes, Angelica whispered, "You have the hands of a pianist."

When Rosemary was eighteen, she met Terry at a disco. Terry was a builder by day, a bouncer by night. Terry lived in Andytown. Terry's parents owned their own house. Terry was a catch. After four months of courting, Terry took Rosemary into Belfast, to a jewellers in Queen's Arcade. The engagement ring he bought that afternoon was a sapphire set with two emeralds.

When Rosemary came home wearing the ring, Angelica cried, and even her father's eyes, Marie noticed, moistened at the sight of it.

It was a Saturday afternoon, about five o'clock. The television was on. Marie's father had been watching the football results which were being read aloud by a lugubrious sports commentator.

"Motherwell 1. Hibernian 2. Kilmarnock 3. Rangers ..."

In deference to the occasion, her father turned down the volume. Angelica and Rosemary sat beside him on the sofa. Mother and daughter began laughing and crying together; meanwhile, her father waited patiently, secretly hoping they would go into the kitchen. Every now and again, he would glance at the silent television set, at the names of the football teams with the scores at the end of each line.

Marie was on one of the armchairs, looking across at them, and she saw that everything about Rosemary that afternoon was lovely. The long straw-coloured hair bunched into a perfect pony tail with a black velvet band. The way her sister's skirt cinched at the waist. Her long legs with their shiny knees and shiny calves, encased in her shiny tights.

Because she was favoured, Rosemary's potential had been spotted by her mother. Rosemary had been made beautiful. Now, because she was beautiful, Rosemary had found a husband.

Marie was happy for her sister, but sad for herself. Rosemary's good fortune was not to be her destiny. Her teeth were crooked, but not enough to warrant fixing. She had nice hair but it was black not blonde. There was a strange freckle on her lip. Builders from Andytown were not a prospect. Ditto sapphire and emerald engagement rings. The beautiful enjoyed good fortune. The fate of the non-beautiful was something else. It was not going to be bad luck, but it was not to be good luck either.

Marie was only thirteen, yet she knew this as she looked across at mother, Rosemary and her father. The understanding brought a lump to her throat. There was a danger she might cry. She turned sideways.

There was a fish tank on a shelf beside the television. Marie pretended to be looking at it. Then she found that she actually was looking at it.

What intrigued her was a blue fish with black stripes. The fish had put itself in the way of the bubbles which were streaming up from below. As they rushed up, they touched the scaly belly of the fish. A few tears rose in Marie's eyes. She blinked them away. She wondered if the bubbles were giving the fish pleasure.

II

When she was eighteen, Marie left school. She had three 'GCSEs' and an E in English 'A' level. She went to Leicester. Her mother had a sister there.

Auntie Carmel was married to Ron. Carmel had met Ron at the bottom of Broadway in 1974. Ron was a British soldier in the Staffordshire Regiment and he was manning a checkpoint. Carmel had followed Ron to Leicester, and married him there. Since then, Carmel returned to Belfast rarely, and never brought her husband home.

Carmel and Ron had two sons, both now away at University. Marie was given the older boy's room. There were several pictures of Eric Cantona pinned up on the walls.

Marie found a job in a shoe factory. Her job was to stamp the brass eyes into the uppers of shoes with an hydraulic press.

After she had been in Leicester six months, one of the factory girls got engaged. At the party to celebrate, Marie met Paul, a Greek-Cypriot.

Paul's eyes were darker than hers. His hair was blacker. His teeth were whiter. Marie married Paul. After the birth of their first child—they named him Justin—Marie went off sex. After two years of celibacy, Paul became exasperated. He went back to Nicosia and the marriage ended.

Marie came home. The Housing Executive put her in a new development in the west of the city. The Executive said the houses on the estate were the best houses built that year anywhere in the United Kingdom. Marie did not dispute this.

The fire drew beautifully. There was hot water all day. There was not a patch of damp. The windows did not rattle when the wind blew. The difficulties began when she stepped outside her front door.

The trees which had been planted along the street had all been snapped in half by young delinquents.

In one of the houses opposite, there were all night drinking parties. The revellers would vomit in her front garden, and worse. Marie had to keep tongs and a spade in a bucket of disinfected water beside her front door all the time. She used these to pick up the turds.

Then, there was the matter of the wind. It always seemed to be blowing in this raw new place, as it never seemed to blow anywhere else in Belfast. It blew very hard, all day, every day, and it always bore a cargo of grit, it seemed.

She and Justin could not venture out without it stinging into their faces. She knew better than to rub her eyes, but her son couldn't stop himself. Of course, this only made the problem worse. Then, he would cry. By the time they got home, his eyes would be bloodshot. She would bathe his eyes with *Optrex* and Justin would scream ...

However, in the scale of things which could go wrong, the grit was only a small difficulty, and of course Marie recognised this. For instance, she could have been one of the girls who lurked in the burnt-out petrol station, drank *Special Brew*, and tore around with their men in stolen cars. Marie had to pass this petrol station where the joyriders hung about every day, when she made her way through the wind, to and from the shops. It consisted of a filthy, bare concrete forecourt, a row of charred lock-up garages, and two rusting stumps. These had once been the pumps. Marie loathed the place, her superstitious fears focussing on her son.

In ten or twelve years time, she imagined, he might become one of them. He might start stealing cars and racing them around the streets. It would end unhappily because, eventually, they would take him up an entry and punish him, as they had always done, ceasefire or no ceasefire, and she knew about punishment. It was why she had left …

The night of her eighteenth birthday—it was the late nineteen eighties, the Troubles were still going—she had been in a bar, celebrating, when two men dressed in boiler suits and balaclavas had come in. It took them less than a minute to find the one they were looking for. He was eighteen, with a little moustache, a thin body, and he wore a back-to-front baseball hat with 'No Problem' on the front. He seemed not unsurprised when the men appeared, and he let them lead him away without complaining.

The bar fell quiet. She heard the shots outside. Everyone heard the shots, and that way everybody knew, the youth with the baseball hat had been done.

Then everyone went out to look and Marie went too. He had got one in each knee. He was bleeding. Someone brought out a couple of towels from the bar with *Guinness* printed on them. These were used to staunch the blood. A barman went to telephone for an ambulance and the youth screamed as he lay on the ground, "My mother,"—he sounded like a little boy to Marie—"I want her, my mother …"

Marie saw his red blood seep through the brown *Guinness* beer towels. She went down the entry and out into the street. She was sick in the gutter. She had been drinking creme de menthe and cider all that evening and her sick was green. Two months later, she sat her 'A' levels, then left the north …

And now, every time she passed the burnt-out petrol station, the memory of this evening was always vaguely in her mind. It wasn't that she was actually thinking about it. It was just with her, like a stone in her shoe, pressing against her foot.

In fact, the memory was so compelling, even if there were no thin bodied mustachioed men in trainers standing around a fire drinking *Special Brew*, even if the forecourt was completely deserted, except for a rook pecking at a styrofoam cup, Marie would always push Justin in his buggy across the road, just in order to put as much space between that place and themselves as possible.

Marie did not like this life she had come back to in Belfast, even after the ceasefires which followed her return. Sometimes she even hated it.

III

Marie stared at the face in the mirror. Her right front tooth over-lapped the left. At school the other girl's had called her "Rabbit Face."

The hair which framed her face was hennaed black.

She pursed her lips. There was a little spot of lipstick on the end of the right tooth where it overlapped the left. She rubbed it away with the tip of her tongue.

She went downstairs to the sitting room. The Christmas tree was in the front window. Justin was playing on the floor. Early that morning he had been excited when they had opened the presents. What happened then had puzzled her, but at the same time, she had not been surprised. Justin had abandoned his presents—the walking-talking robot, the garage with a car lift, the box of *Duplo* bricks—and returned to his favourite toy. This was a white plastic car made by *Fisher-Price*. There were four round holes inside the seats into which four round figures fitted. The figures had the faces of clowns and wore clown hats. Oh yes, she thought, precisely the sort of toy a future joyrider would favour. The car was a present from Justin's father.

Marie went to the kitchen and poured out a small tumbler of *Bailey's Irish Cream*. Normally, there was never drink in the house, but she made an exception for Christmas. She looked at the kitchen clock. It was two o'clock. Where was her father?

She carried the glass back into the front room and sat down. She took a drink. She saw her lipstick left a smudge on the rim of the glass. She would have to put more lipstick on. Two thoughts now began to war in her mind. One, she wished she had got some brandy in. She would have liked to have offered father a drink, and brandy was his favourite. Two, she was angry. Why hadn't he collected her by now? It was past two o'clock, and when she had spoken with her mother very early that morning, Angelica had said, "Your father'll be up to you, twelve midday, latest."

When one o'clock came and there was no sign of him, Marie had rung home again, and her mother had said, "He's just going out the door. We've been a bit held up."

Now it was after two and it didn't take an hour to drive the three or so miles from her parent's house to hers. No, it did not.

Marie took another sip of *Bailey's* and looked across at her son. He had piled up some of the needles which had fallen from the Christmas tree, and he was driving his car through them. The needles were soft and the wheels left their imprint on them.

When she was a child, Marie thought her father was amazing. He drank but he was never drunk—never. He never quarrelled with his wife, Angelica, and he was always back from the car plant where he worked at the time he said he was coming back. Always.

With all the other families who lived around them when she was growing up, it was different. All the men drank, and all the couples quarrelled. Husbands and wives would often shout at each other in the street; on rare occasions, they would even fight out there. And when husbands got roaring drunk, their wives would lock them out. The husbands would spend the night wandering up and down the Andersonstown Road or the Falls, until their wives had cooled down and would let them back into their homes again ...

Marie took another sip. No, she thought, her father was never late, other than when mother made him late. And this Christmas afternoon, she knew that her mother was making him late.

Marie took yet another drink. She wasn't certain what made her angrier? Was it mother's overbearing, domineering manner? Or was it the way Angelica had made her father into a man who always let her have her way, never stood up to her, never contradicted her?

The door bell chimed. Then there was a friendly little rap on the wood.

Marie opened the front door. Father was standing on the step. He was wearing his grey suit, a white shirt and a new tie, green with red stripes. He smelt of after-shave. Mother would have given him after-shave for Christmas. So would Rosemary. And probably the same brand—if Marie knew Rosemary and her mother—a brand her father wasn't allergic to.

"Your father's skin is very sensitive." This was one of mother's key phrases. She said it at least once a day. At the same time she would coo and gently pet his sensitive face. This was mother's way of paying court to the man to whom she never listened.

"Come in, come in," Marie said.

She pulled her father through the door and into her hall. She kissed him.

"I'm sorry, I'm late," he apologised.

Her father's front right tooth, like hers, overlapped the left. He whistled when he spoke. He might follow Angelica's orders, but secretly, Marie had always believed, he was on her side. In all the years she had known him, he had never once shouted at her, or corrected her in public. Now he smiled at her, and her anger evaporated.

"I got entangled with Rosemary and the kids and Terry," father explained.

Marie knew this was a fib yet she heard herself saying, " It doesn't matter. I'll get my coat."

But instead of going to the back of the hall to get her coat, she went into the living room. Her father followed behind. It was as if they wanted to stay there, together, and not rush away.

Justin had heard his grandfather coming in. He was sitting looking down at the ground with a shy expression on his face. As the adults came towards him, he slowly rotated on the linoleum floor until he was facing the wall.

"Come on Justin, say hello, it's grandad."

Justin dropped his head forward until his chin rested on his chest.

"You're a shy boy today," her father whistled gently. "You can't be a shy boy on Christmas day."

"He'll be alright once we get to the house," she said, and then she added, "I expect."

IV

She re-did her lipstick and found her coat. Then the three of them went out to the car. Her father had put one of Rosemary's child seats in the back. He was thoughtful like that.

They set off. The streets of west Belfast were empty, just one row of low houses after another, crouched under a low grey sky. The only points of colour were the fairy lights on Christmas trees glimmering behind the net curtains of parlour windows. Marie was glad she had left her own lights on at home, making their own small contribution towards lessening the gloom.

The McAlister family house was detached. It was not far from the motorway and Dunmurry where her father worked. It was a private house, not a Housing Executive house; her father had made his first down payment in 1969; twenty-five years on and it was his.

The front door was on the latch. They went through. Inside the hall all the coats were thrown higgledy-piggledy into the huge *Silver Cross* pram. This had been Marie and Rosemary's pram when they were babies, and now her mother kept the pram for her daughters to wheel around the grandchildren when they visited. Except they always had their buggies, and so they never did.

Marie put her head around the door into the living room. Her father's younger, bachelor brother, Uncle Patrick, was there, along with Terry. They were drinking beer and watching *Back to the Future 2*. Rosemary's twins were on the floor, staring at the screen.

Her father led Justin towards the Christmas tree—as in her house it was in the front window—and Marie slipped out of the room and down to the kitchen. She found her mother kneeling in front of the oven. She was basting a turkey which was lying in the old black roasting pan, the one Angelica said imparted a special quality to whatever was cooked in it. She always used it at Christmas.

"Hello," said mother. "Happy Christmas." She stood and closed the oven door with a bang.

Mother was wearing a white fluffy mohair sweater with sequins sewn into it, and an apron over the top.

"What kept you?" asked her mother.

The picture on the apron showed a fat man drinking beer, while the wife, trussed in short skirt and suspenders, was bent over a sink of dishes.

"What kept me! Nothing kept me. I was waiting for dad. What kept him?"

"Oh, sorry you had to wait! We were only cooking for twelve."

Angelica puffed her chest forward and pointed at the legend below the picture: *The only one who does any work in the house is the poor woman who has to wear this.*

"Your good sister's present," said her mother, and she pointed at Rosemary, who at that moment was slipping the trifle into the refrigerator.

"Happy Christmas," Marie called to her sister, and that was when she heard a voice say, "Hey! Don't forget about me!"

It was Veronica, hidden in the armchair behind the door.

Veronica had looked after Marie and Rosemary when they were children. This made her an Honorary Grandmother. She always came at Christmas.

"Happy Xmas," said Veronica standing.

Veronica wore a worsted suit with what looked like a dog collar. Somehow, Veronica always managed to look like a priest, and to sound like one as well.

As Veronica's thin arms folded around her shoulders, Marie heard her mother saying, "I cannot tell you how tired I am! I doubt I'd have managed without my two redoubtable helpers here."

Marie felt her face reddening. Only two minutes in the house, and already her mother was complaining that she hadn't helped.

"So what'll you have?" mother was asking now, slurring like a drunk, her standard act when she offered anyone drink. "G&T? Bush on the rocks? What's your Christmas tipple?"

"Ah, Angelica," tittered Veronica. A fellow Pioneer, she loved this performance.

"Sherry, Budweiser ... hic!"

The annoyance which Marie felt at the pose, and the bad temper she already felt because she was the last to have been collected, were now two streams inside her, rushing together to make something bigger.

"You know, I was waiting at least two hours for dad to lift me," she said. "I've been up since seven. I don't have a car, and taxis on Christmas day, as you may have noticed, are not exactly cheap or plentiful."

"Oh boy," said Angelica, this time in her appalling John Wayne drawl, "you sound as though you really could do with a drink. And a double, I should say."

"Just a glass of wine, please," said Marie.

V

Her father and Terry carried the table through from the living room and set it up in the kitchen. Marie fetched the table cloth from the hot press upstairs. It was still wrapped in the paper in which it had come back from the laundry. When Marie unfolded the cloth and spread it across the table, the kitchen was filled for a moment with the wonderful smell of starched linen.

Marie set out the place mats, the good ones with the pictures of Ben Nevis, Edinburgh New Town and Balmoral, and Rosemary fetched the canteen with the good, heavy cutlery. Rosemary and Marie had given the canteen to their parents on their twenty-fifth wedding anniversary. Rosemary was richer and had borne the bulk of the cost.

The sisters set the knives and forks and spoons around the place mats. Then they fetched the good china and the Waterford glass from the cabinet in the front room. Rosemary filled the cruets with salt and pepper. Marie mixed mustard up in an egg-cup, then decanted it into the little blue mustard dish which was part of the salt and pepper set.

As she worked, Marie found herself hoping that by immersing herself in the physical, the intense annoyance that smouldered inside like a hot coal, would simply die, go out.

It was not a theory—this had happened to her before in situations like this—but unfortunately, this time, when the table was finished, she found the anger was still burning inside her.

"Can I do anything else?" she called across.

Her mother was pouring boiling water out of the kettle into the saucepan of Brussels sprouts.

"What else can I do?" she repeated, and then Marie drained her glass.

There were wreaths of steam rising around Angelica's face and her high piled hair. For a moment, it looked to Marie as if her mother was on fire.

"Can you clear the ashtrays and empty the beer cans from the front room? It's probably a pigsty by now."

Marie decided to fetch the ashtrays first. They were heavy, made of cut glass, and they were crammed with butts.

She carried them back to the pedal bin in the kitchen. She lifted the lid with the foot pedal, and was about to tip the butts away, when she saw the greasy cellophane that smelt of fish, in which a whole smoked salmon had come wrapped.

"Are we having smoked salmon?" she called over to her mother.

She tipped the ashtrays. The debris tumbled in, some of the grey ash sticking to the cellophane and forming a coating on it, like city snow.

"No," her mother replied blithely.

"Oh."

"I'm afraid we had that earlier. When Rosemary and Terry came. The kids were so hungry, they practically devoured the wrapping."

Marie re-filled her wine glass, and the little voice inside her head said, You don't need another drink! It won't help things.

She ignored the voice and carried the drink through to the front room. She sat down on the sofa beside her brother-in-law.

"Terry."

"Marie," he acknowledged her.

On the television, the hero of *Back to the Future 2* was at a dance in the open air, somewhere in the American mid-west, sometime in the middle of the last century.

"Are you hungry?" she said.

"Starving," said Terry. "The smell of that turkey and bacon is practically driving me up the walls."

"It's been a long day," said Marie, innocently.

"You're telling me. I've been here practically all day."

Terry used 'practically' a lot, but even for him, twice in a row was excessive.

"I've had five wee cans of *Tennents*," he continued, "which I don't really like, and my head's swimming."

"Did you have nothing else at all?"

"We had smoked salmon," he said, and then he quickly added, "Did we leave you any?"

"No."

84

Terry looked over at the television and Marie looked as well. On the screen she saw there was a car flying through the air. Marie recognised it as a De Lorean.

"When did you get here?" she asked.

"When? I don't know. It must have been … What time did I get here Pat?" he called over to her uncle.

Pat was on the floor assembling a *Brio* wooden train set. The twins were beside Pat. They were each sucking on a little wooden *Brio* man.

"I can't remember. I was here with Veronica a bit before you. Was that ten, ten-thirty?" Pat shouted back.

"So you came, you had smoked salmon and what?" Marie asked lightly.

"Scrambled egg. Coffee," continued Terry. "Since then, that's it. The day's vanished like a puff of smoke. Disappeared into thin air."

Her glass was empty. She excused herself and went out into the hall. She found Justin on the stairs. He was clutching a teddy bear and a Coke bottle with a straw in it.

"Granny gave me a Coke," he explained, pointing to the kitchen from where he had just come.

"And where are you going now?"

Her son sucked on the green straw sticking out of the bottle. There was a faint bubbling sound. Marie could hear the older children squealing in the playroom upstairs.

"I'm going to see them," said Justin.

He stared at her. He was dark skinned, with olive black eyes. There was no other child like him in Belfast, at least that she knew of. Sometimes, in the street, strangers would stop and stare at him. On rare occasions, strangers would even come over and say, "Such a child. I've never seen a child with that colouring."

And it was true; no child was like Justin.

Marie put her glass down on the table beside the telephone, and climbed up the stairs. She sat down, pulled her skirt over her knees, and then lifted Justin on to her lap.

"I love you," she said, and buried her face in his neck. He smelt of himself, and shampoo, but mostly he smelt of Coca-Cola.

"I love you," Marie said. "Do you love me?"

He twisted playfully on her lap as he tried to escape from her. "Don't tickle me," he cried, by which he meant the exact opposite, "Don't tickle me."

"I'm going to blow on your tummy."

"No, no, no," he laughed, "and I promise, I promise to be good."
She set him back on the stairs.

"Now be good when you get up to the big children," she said.

Justin continued to climb, clutching his teddy bear and his bottle. Marie went back down to the hall, found her glass and went into the kitchen.

She found her mother there alone. Rosemary and Veronica, she guessed, were upstairs with her father and Justin and the older children in the playroom. Marie poured herself a third glass of wine.

"You didn't tell me you were all having breakfast."

"I'm amazed you and Rosemary didn't see how dusty the glasses were when you brought them down from the front room?" her mother replied briskly.

Angelica had washed them all, and the wet glasses were arranged upside-down on the draining board.

"They weren't fit to be used in the state they were in."

Mother might be getting her retaliation in first, Marie thought, but she wasn't going to let herself be deterred.

"Why wasn't I invited for breakfast?"

"Sometimes," said Angelica, "I wonder if you two girls have eyes in your heads at all. The glasses were filthy."

"You haven't answered my question."

Her mother slipped past and put a dry glass at the head of the table, where her father sat.

"I don't understand you," Marie heard herself continuing. "I am up at home. You are all down here. Why didn't you send dad to come and get me?"

Mother went back to the sink, picked up a second glass and began to dry it.

"You might think, Marie, that the whole world revolves around you," she said, "but I'm sorry, it doesn't."

The next glass squeaked as Angelica wiped it fiercely with the cloth.

"You had everyone up for smoked salmon," said Marie, "while I was left sitting at home."

"Look, you don't like being *alone*," said Angelica forcefully, "it's down to you to do something about it. It's not for any of us."

"What!"

"Pick up the phone, Marie. Get a taxi. Ask a friend to lift you."

"Mother. Christmas Day. No taxis. Friends busy. With families. Marie at home awaits collection. But all McAlister family here."

"You're being ridiculous," said Angelica, and she glared furiously at her daughter.

"I would have liked to have been asked."

"If you can't be *alone*, that's your problem," hissed her mother, "and lower your voice, please, it's Christmas Day."

There was that 'alone' word again. It was Angelica's code for separated, of course, and in time, inevitably, it would become code for divorced.

A couple of weeks before Christmas, she remembered, her mother had asked about her plans for the future, and Marie had said it was her and Paul's intention to formalise their separation with a divorce. Mother had received the news silently, since when the subject had never been mentioned, or even alluded to until now. But that was it, wasn't it? That was the seed from which all this had come. Angelica couldn't countenance her divorcing. Catholics did not do that.

"What is it?" Marie heard herself saying, the level of her voice rising but what the hell. "What is it about me? Why is it that I don't get the same treatment as everyone else in this family? Why for Rosemary, one set of rules, and breakfast and smoked salmon, and for me, another?"

"It's been fair play in this house," said her mother grimly, "from the moment you were born, to the moment you walked out that door, went to Leicester and embarked on your life. Since when ..." and at that Angelica suddenly closed her mouth.

"Since when?" Marie shouted. "Since when? Go on." She was as much delighted as she was angry by her mother's slip. "Yes. Since when, what?"

"I don't want to have an argument with you. It's Christmas Day," her mother cut Marie short.

"Since when—what?"

"Since when," said her mother, "you've made your bed, and a fine frigging mess you've made of it too. Now, you learn to lie in it, my girl. It's hard, I know, to be alone. I'm sorry for you, but there's nothing I can do about it."

Her mother picked up another glass and began to dry it furiously.

Marie took a huge gulp of wine. To hell with abstinence and caution. And her mother was right, damn her. She was somewhat to blame for what happened. And now her husband was seeing another woman who was giving him what Marie had not.

Of course, Paul hadn't told her this directly, but she knew him that well, she could tell just from the way he said "Hello," and "Goodbye" to her when he rang on Saturday nights to speak to Justin, and again when he had rung that very Christmas morning, she could tell he was seeing another woman ...

But, she told herself, that was not what they were discussing, she and mother, and as a matter of fact they never would. Nor would they ever discuss the way she had felt quite revolted by her husband after Justin's birth, and had never been able to shake off that feeling of disgust, and was now sorry about that, very sorry, in fact was disgusted with herself.

Marie's mind was racing. Wine had that effect. Focus! she commanded herself. She took another drink.

"Has it ever occurred to you," shouted Marie, "that when you chose not to have me up for breakfast, it's not just me you're punishing—because I'm not like Rosemary, with a husband and a house and four children, and doubtless a fifth and a sixth on the way—you are also punishing a three-year-old boy!

"Justin didn't have anything to do with what went wrong. Justin is an innocent. He needs to be loved as much as Sinead and Michael upstairs and the twins down there in the front room, but you don't love him like them because what I've done is wrong according to what you believe, and what the church says. You love Justin less than them because I'm going to be divorced."

Her mother's face had been darkening and shrinking as Marie spoke and now, as she finished, Marie braced herself.

"How dare you," she heard her mother shouting back at her, "how dare you say that! How dare you say I feel any less for one child than another. I've spent as much on his Christmas present, as I have on the other children's. I've changed his nappy, just like the other children. I cuddle him, just like the other children. You are a stupid, ridiculous, spoilt little girl."

Marie heard the door open, which she guessed was her father coming in. She turned and she saw that indeed it was him. He had heard their voices in the playroom upstairs. Now he was coming to make the peace.

Marie turned back to Angelica. A Waterford cut glass was in her mother's hand. Her mother turned the glass against the cloth angrily. The glass shrieked and then exploded. A glass fragment scored across her mother's palm. It cut her from one corner right across to the other. A huge spurt of blood sprang out from the huge slit, and plopped down on to the linoleum floor.

"Look! what you've made me do with your stupid rowing," her mother shouted, and Marie knew she had lost the argument. "You've made me break one of my best Waterford glasses."

Her father rushed her mother to the sink. He turned on the cold tap and he thrust Angelica's hand into the streaming water.

"That was one of a set they don't make any more. I won't get a replacement, you know."

"I'm sorry," Marie heard herself saying, "I'm very sorry about your glass."

"Not now," said her father, with what, for him, was uncommon brusqueness. "It's Christmas. Let your mother be."

In the twenty-three years she had known him, this was the closest her father had ever come to rebuking her. The failure to invite her to breakfast might have been negligent, but this humiliation was crushing. Marie felt a pain in her Adam's apple.

"I'm going upstairs," she said.

She went into the bathroom, not the toilet, and locked the door. She sat down on the edge of the bath. It was green, the colour of avocado. The room smelt of *Radox* and the *Cussons Imperial Leather* soap which mother favoured. It was the only soap to which her father was not allergic, or so Angelica claimed

Marie felt something breaking inside her, and she let out a great rasping cry. Her tears followed, hot and salty.

A few minutes later she heard her Uncle Pat calling, "Dinner. Come on everybody. Come and get it."

She opened the door and called down, "Just fixing my face."

She waited until everyone had trooped through to the kitchen, then crept downstairs to her coat in the hall, retrieved her make-up bag from the pocket, and went back upstairs again to the bathroom.

VI

The turkey was on a platter on the breakfast counter and her father was using the electric carver to cut off thin slices of white meat.

Marie stood and watched while her mother scooted around the table, a white tea towel tied ostentatiously around her cut hand. Her mother was setting the crackers out. Angelica had two types of crackers. She had green and very solid looking crackers from *Marks and Spencer*, and she had cheapos made of flimsy red crepe which she had bought in Royal Avenue, from a street vender, one Saturday afternoon.

"Don't you think I'm marvellous to have the two types of cracker?" mother exclaimed as she flew past Marie. Angelica was blithe and cheerful as if nothing had happened, and before Marie could answer, her mother continued, "The red ones will have keys and pens and rubbish which will keep the kids happy, and for us grown-ups, something with a little style. Thank you M and S." She waved the green cracker she was holding before she plonked it down.

The huge picture window at the back of the kitchen was covered with condensation. Marie saw that someone had drawn a Christmas tree in the wet with a finger, and that darkness had fallen outside. She was holding yet another glass of wine, and now she took a drink. The wine was bitter. She could remember that she had taken a glass before they set the table, then a second and then a third, but after that she lost count.

Marie sat where she was told to sit. She ate the plate of food which was put in front of her. She pulled the crackers that were offered to her. She laughed at the jokes that came out of the crackers, when the older children read them out. She drank her wine, and held the glass out for more when it was empty ...

Gradually, as late afternoon wore into evening, her hurt and anger became a pliant, fuzzy feeling. She had been slighted over the breakfast, she had been rebuked by her father, but none of this was going to trouble her any more. At least not for the rest of the day. The wine made sure of that.

When the plates were cleared away, and the children had gone off to play, Veronica told her story. She told it faithfully every Christmas Day. She was a stern and modest woman but on Christmas Day she couldn't stop herself rehearsing what she regarded as one of the finest moments, perhaps the finest moment in her otherwise loveless and miserable life.

One afternoon, sometime during the early seventies, two men had run into her house. They were carrying a bomb.

Veronica led them to her coal shed, made them lie down, and covered them over with coal.

Moments later, the soldiers who were in hot pursuit of the bombers were running all over Veronica's house.

"They're not here, whoever you're looking for," she told the English Captain haughtily, "and now kindly get out and let me get on with my baking." She gestured at the flour and baking utensils which she had strewn, as a ploy, on the kitchen table. The soldiers apologised and left.

Five minutes later, two black-faced members of the IRA slunk out of her coal shed, muttered their thanks, and disappeared down to the Lagan. According to local lore, they supposedly threw the bomb into the river.

Everyone laughed at the story. Marie laughed as well. Veronica's tale of military stupidity and native Irish cunning was Christmas as much as the turkey and the crackers; they couldn't have Christmas without it. It was also, Marie recognised, the climax, the last obligation. Christmas day was over now for her. She was free to go.

Half an hour later, she was in the front of the car, her father was at the wheel, and Justin was asleep in the child's seat in the back.

Everyone came out to the front door to wave her off, and then her father drove away down the street.

The traffic light ahead of them was red. Her father slowed and then halted. There was an army Land Rover parked against the bollard in the middle of the road. That first ceasefire Christmas, there were still soldiers around. As neither Marie nor her father had been speaking— they hadn't spoken properly since her father had reprimanded her— they were both grateful to have something to look at.

The back door of the Land Rover was open, and Marie saw that there was a loop of silver tinsel hanging down inside the door.

She pointed. Her father nodded. He had seen it too.

There was a soldier on the bench inside and now he ran his finger along the tinsel, much as a child might; and then, suddenly realising he had been seen, he looked back at the pair of them in the car.

The soldier smiled and mouthed the season's greetings.

The traffic lights were turning. Marie raised an arm and waved expansively.

Then she saw that the most extraordinary look of surprise, mingled with alarm, had appeared on her father's face. He was horrified. And her mother, when she heard, would no doubt be horrified. As would Veronica. As would everyone else. You didn't wave at them.

But she had, and now the soldier waved back, his hand curling, his grin wide and surprised.

At the Cinema

THE AMBASSADOR STOOD ON a busy London street. Peter hurried along the pavement and then stopped abruptly outside the entrance.

At the thought of what lay ahead, the adrenalin started to trickle into his stomach. But he had made a pact with himself. It couldn't go on any longer. He was going to say something. When he went in, it was going to be like stepping into an exam room. No going back.

Peter pulled off his gloves and went towards one of the doors that lined the front of the cinema. He noticed the black paint with which it was painted was chipped along the bottom and up the side. The brown wood showing through reminded him, momentarily, of rotten teeth. He pushed the door and went forward.

As he stepped into the foyer, he felt a wave of hot air. He felt it on his face, but the place he felt it the most were his eyeballs. He blinked, twice, and looked up.

The heater on the shelf above his head was big and square, with what looked like miniature Venetian blinds arranged along the front. As the mechanism inside rumbled and whirred, and as the air pumped out, these thin strips of metal trembled like leafs in the wind.

Peter lowered his gaze and looked around. His eyes darted first to the main box office, then to the kiosk where books and confectionery were sold, next to the stairs, and finally to the smaller, second box office, where tickets were sold for the smaller cinema downstairs. The man behind the glass here was reading a book.

Pauline, however, was nowhere in sight. In fact, there was no one standing around the foyer of the Ambassador Cinema except for an usherette. She was an oldish woman. She stood at the top of the stairs. Peter noticed that her hair was dyed the colour of carrot, and that her white, high-heeled shoes, were at odds with the demure maroon of her usherette's uniform.

Peter thought about walking over and asking the usherette if she had noticed a youngish girl standing around and waiting. He was early, but perhaps, for once, Pauline had been ultra-early, and then left in exasperation. That would be just his luck.

He tried the sentence in his head. "Excuse me, I wonder if you noticed a girl waiting?" He hoped and imagined that the tone was simultaneously warm and insouciant, and as he was standing there, trying to gauge whether or not he had managed this, the usherette turned away and slowly began to descend the stairs to the basement. Perhaps, he imagined, she had anticipated what he was about to ask, and had decided to flee rather than answer the question.

Peter unbuttoned his coat. He put his gloves away in the left pocket of his jacket, as he always did; his keys and tobacco lived in the right pocket. He was only twenty years old, but already a remarkable number of patterns and procedures were well in place. Order, he believed, helped him to live.

He touched the Yale key in the other pocket. It opened the front door of the house where he lived with his parents. Why was Pauline always late? he wondered. He glanced at his watch and then stared down at the carpet. It was Prussian blue with a brown motif. Hideous, he thought. He had made the effort to get there in time from college, so why couldn't she? But then of course, hadn't he always known she was going to be late? Yes, he had to admit it, he had. No, the true reason he was irked, he realised, was that he wanted the pleasure of buying Pauline her ticket, and he wanted that pleasure straight away. Now, this instant ...

Funny how the brain went on cogitating, he thought, regardless of how he felt.

He looked at his watch again, futile though he knew it was to do so. There was no need to buy their tickets yet, he thought, and he wandered over to the kiosk and picked up a book: *The Most Important Art: Eastern European Film After 1945*.

He opened the book at random. Two photographs faced each other; one showed a bearded man with his head on the chopping block, a curved, Turkish sword hovering over his neck, and the other, a naked woman chained to the cement floor of a Second World War prison cell.

They were both Bulgarian films and no doubt very depressing, he imagined. Peter reached to turn the page. At that moment he heard one of the doors swinging open behind him, and the foyer was filled, for the next couple of seconds, with the clamour of the traffic from the street outside.

He turned. It was a girl with long, black, crinkled hair. Her companion wore fingerless gloves and a bright red fez with a black tassel which swung as he moved.

Peter put the book back on the shelf from where he had taken it. He walked over to one of the doors. He looked out into the street.

No bloody sign of her, he thought, grimly. Yet why should he be surprised? That was the pattern, wasn't it? He had to agree. That was the pattern.

Outside, beyond the glass, a West Indian in a spotless white coat trundled a fruit and vegatable stall along the gutter of this stretch of Oxford street. Peter could clearly hear the rumble of the iron clad wheels above the traffic. A distinctive city sound of a hundred years ago, he imagined. Oh, his thoughts, so ceaseless, so shark-like.

Peter smoked a cigarette, then extinguished the stub in a sand-filled ashtray from which there sprouted a dozen other brown butts.

He walked over to the wall where the details of the current programme were displayed. The film they had arranged to see was going to start, he saw, in a few moments. He went over to the smaller box office.

"Yes," said the man behind the glass in a testy voice. He wore a frilly shirt and a bow-tie.

"I'd like two tickets, but one is for a friend who hasn't arrived. Can I leave it with you to give to her?"

Two tickets shot out of the slit and slithered towards Peter across the brass. He wrote a cheque with difficulty because the ledge for this purpose, typically, was too narrow for the cheque-book. When the transaction was finished, Peter heard the man saying, "Name?"

" Sorry?" he said.

"Your friend's name? Your friend who you've bought the ticket for." The man in the box office waved an envelope and smiled sarcastically. Evidently, Peter realised, her name was going on the front.

"Pauline Fields."

"Miss?"

"Yes."

Peter went down two flights of stairs to the underground foyer. Down here, the ashtrays were not square, like upstairs, but more like artillery shell cartridges. The usherette with the carrot-coloured hair was sitting on a chair. She was threading half-torn tickets onto a piece of string.

"Hello," she said to Peter.

The usherette stood up slightly unsteadily. She put the string of tickets in her pocket, carefully.

"There's not a soul inside," she said. "Not one person. Terrible, isn't it? No one comes to quality pictures nowadays, do they?"

"No," he agreed.

"I've worked in artistic establishments all my life," the usherette continued, "and let me tell you, there's been a definite coarsening."

She folded her arms and nodded her head up and down.

"Have you worked here long?" Peter heard himself asking.

"I came as the cashier, but I wasn't happy. No head for figures. I've got an artistic temperament, you see. So they sent me down here, to the dungeon. Like the work. Grateful for it too. But I need variety. Every woman does. Work and home simply don't provide the vistas every woman needs. But the films are a boon, naturally."

Peter found himself wondering if the programme wasn't soon about to start. He glanced towards the door, cocking his head to the side.

"Don't worry, dear," she said. "It shan't start 'til the projectionist gets the nod from me."

"Do you go to the cinema much?" Peter waved in the direction of the auditorium.

"Oh, yes, I go a great deal. I like the French ones best. The romantic ones. Not really for chaps like you, though."

"No."

"The women are always so well got up. I think a woman's always got to look nice, don't you?"

"I agree," said Peter.

"It was important in my line of work, looking good. I come from a family of dancers but," she sighed, "it looks like the thing's stopped with me." The usherette paused as if considering what to say next, and then exclaimed suddenly, "Oh, my feet are killing me."

She stepped out of one shoe and then the other. Peter glanced down. He saw through her brown stocking that her toes were twisted and gnarled together, and that there were red bunions at the side of each joint of the big toe. So those were dancer's feet, he thought.

"I'm disappointed, naturally," continued the usherette. "Something's been in the family for generations; then, it goes. But you can't fight fate."

She looked directly across at him. "Can I hold on to you?" she asked quietly. "Stop myself falling over."

When he had first come down and she had started speaking at him, he had wanted to get away. But now that feeling was gone, replaced by a pleasant sense of mild mesmerisation. The usherette's words had a vaguely hypnotic affect.

"Of course," he said, and nodded. He held his arm out.

The usherette grasped him round the wrist. The back of her hand was knobbly; her nails were painted dark red. She raised a foot and began to rub the sole against the shin of the other leg.

Where was Pauline? he wondered vaguely. The stocking material on the usherette's foot rasped as she rubbed. He gazed at the neon exit sign which glowed above the stairs leading back to the foyer above.

"My husband will do nothing at home," Peter heard the usherette saying. "Won't lift a finger. Not even to dry a cup. That sort of chap."

That's marriage, Peter thought, but he didn't say so.

"He's an invalid. So's my daughter. Spinal. She's got a spinal problem. Had it since she was eight, poor little blighter. It's got worse down the years and she's really quite badly handicapped. Has a good job. Luckily. Lives alone. Her only companion is an Afghan dog. My husband calls it 'The Hound'. And my daughter's a vegetarian."

The usherette's words, Peter noticed, were coming out faster and faster. With the detached part of himself that monitored all events, he wondered how long she could keep up the pace? Would she get faster and faster, until eventually, her words became indecipherable, like the words on a speeded up tape.

"The diet thing doesn't help, of course," continued the usherette. "Cooking one thing for my husband, and another for her."

She put the first foot down, lifted the other and began to rub again, this time with her free hand.

"Comes to us for a good many of her meals, does my daughter. And the dog—he has to have white meat. That doesn't help either. Nor does having to walk it every morning before I come in here. My daughter could but she's not inclined to. Doesn't like people to see her, see. She's doubled up because of the disability, you understand. Fact of it is, she's a cripple."

It occurred to Peter then, in a distant sort of way, that perhaps the usherette was never going to stop, and he would have to listen forever.

"They're very good about it at work. She's been nine years a telephonist with the Essex police. Gets depressed—of course!—but that's hardly surprising, I always say. All the other girls having chaps, getting married, having children. You see, I understand her problems. But what I wonder is …"

The usherette looked straight at him. Tears welled up in her eyes.

" … She drives. She might be bent double but she can drive. Automatic, not manual. Now, the bus takes over an hour to get me to her house, and what I wonder is, she does nights, you see, at the police exchange, she's at home in the morning, and what I wonder is ..."

He gazed at her, nodded and waited.

"What I wonder is, why don't she come and fetch me first thing in the morning, that's what I wonder, even the odd time? Bring me there; I walk Tchaikovsky—that's the Afghan; then bring me to the tube; and then I come in here. I look after my husband and her and the dog, you see. Is it too much to ask? I don't think so."

He waited. If you waited, he had noticed, more talk always came to fill the silence, and often, in his experience, the most interesting remarks came after a conversation was ostensibly finished.

"I don't mind walking the dog," she gulped. "I understand she doesn't want to be seen—not looking as she does, bent over and all—and I understand she can't walk the dog at night—well, she's working. But I can't stand the bus, and she's got that car, and I've hinted, and hinted but she's just never offered. Sometimes, God forgive me, I think she doesn't like me."

The usherette squeezed his arm. Peter watched as a tear rolled down each rouged cheek. Each tear left a wet trail after itself.

"I'm so sorry," she said. "What an exhibition I've made of myself."

"No," said Peter. He couldn't think what else to say.

They remained standing close together in this way for what seemed to Peter like several minutes; the usherette dabbing with her handkerchief, blowing and wiping her nose every now and again; he with his hand in the pocket of his coat, turning a ten penny piece. In the bigger cinema upstairs, the film started—there was music and the sound of gunfire—and then, at the sound of footfalls behind, Peter turned to see Pauline hurrying down the steps.

"In the nick of time," she said, breathlessly.

Her coat, unbuttoned at the front, wafted behind her. She was wearing a pale blue suit, the skirt stopping just short of the knee. There was a plain pearl brooch on the lapel.

"I missed the train," explained Pauline. She had blue eye shadow on the lids of her eyes.

The usherette, Peter noticed, backed away from him obsequiously. She slipped her feet into her shoes and then tucked her handkerchief under her cuff.

"You'd better go in," she said. She took his ticket and then Pauline's ticket and tore them both in half.

Peter followed his girlfriend through the door and into the empty auditorium. The seats inside were covered with red velvet. They selected the last row but one from the back, and sat down in the middle.

"Who was that old bag outside?" asked Pauline, smoothing her skirt. Peter looked at her little hands, the neat, rounded ends of her fingernails, and the pale moons of her quicks.

What? he thought, and lifted his eyes.

Pauline's face tapered to a neat mouth covered with a mild shade of pink lipstick, the bow of the upper lip hanging slightly over the lower. On her chin there was a spot covered with flesh-coloured foundation.

"Who was that old bag?" repeated Pauline.

It puzzled him the way Pauline sometimes made these snap judgements about other people. It was also—well, it was also annoying, and, in this case, unkind. He would have to discuss it with her, one day, but not now. There was other business to deal with now.

"She wasn't an old bag," said Peter gently.

"Alright, if you say so," said Pauline.

"Why are you always so late?" It was out before Peter could stop himself. Now he'd lost the advantage.

"Sorry," she said, mechanically, "I missed the train."

Then the screen became bright. Pauline made one of her characteristic noises in the back of her throat. Her face shone beside him in the darkness. He took one of her neat little hands in his own. She did not react.

The film—*The World of Apu*—began. The story was set in Indian city and the film was filled with images of railway tracks, old men smoking Indian cigarettes, crowds in the streets, a beautiful bride squatting at a cooking stove, while on the soundtrack trains were heard shunting and bicycle bells were heard ringing. Peter watched but he could not concentrate. His thoughts were preoccupied with what he'd steeled himself to say that evening. Go on, say it, he kept telling himself.

Then, as he sat there, Peter began to repeat the dreaded phrase in his thoughts and to imagine the different responses Pauline might make. He imagined her turning in the darkness and throwing her arms around his neck. He imagined her whispering that he wasn't to say those words but in such a way that he knew that secretly she was delighted. He imagined her just staring ahead as if she hadn't heard him, but nevertheless smiling to herself with delight.

"I love you," he said, and then he continued. "I've managed to get somewhere to live. A flat. The old tenant's going and I get it next month. Will you come and live with me?"

He was shocked at hearing what he'd longed to say in the weeks before, both during their walks and outings, and during the long walk he made each evening after he said goodbye to her, back to the house where his parents waited, to the house with the vague smell of gas in the hall, to the house from which he was shortly about to escape.

Her hand was still in his. She did not move. Peter wondered if she had heard.

"I love you. Will you live with me?" he repeated.

Her hand came out of his. Where their skins had been touching, the sweat chilled. Beside him her bucket seat sprang back. Pauline's skirt rustled as she made her way to the aisle; her shoes sounded as she circled the auditorium behind him; and finally the door banged after she had gone out.

Peter continued to stare ahead. The black and white images danced in front of him. He recognised nothing. Somewhere, he wasn't certain where, he could feel something like pain. At the back of his throat was the rawness he connected with tears. But his eyes were dry.

When the film was finished and the lights came up, Peter sat where he was for a few moments. It's over, he thought again, and he felt something that was a mixture of wretchedness and relief.

Peter made his way back to the foyer. The usherette was in her chair by the door. There were two or three patrons waiting for the next performance.

"Didn't she like it?" he heard the usherette asking. She stood up.

"No, she felt sick and needed to go home," Peter lied.

"I'd go home myself and have a nice cup of cocoa." The usherette stared tenderly into his eyes.

"I know what it feels like," she said, "when no one understands. It's miserable!"

She was consoling him, he understood that, and signalling that she, a stranger, had read the signs, had seen Pauline stomp out earlier, and did not care for the girl. He saw this.

At the same time, he recognised that he did not know what to reply, because at this moment, he did not actually know what he felt. Not properly. Not yet. That would come slowly. Over the following days, drip by drip, feelings of hurt and resentment were going to leak into his system.

And they were going to pain him; he recognised this. But, he also knew that in the scale of life's miseries, the pain which would fill him would not be that terrible. Actually, nothing much. There were other pains—like that of the usherette whose daughter didn't love her—that were infinitely worse. And my God! what about the pains of those in the Satyajit Ray film he had just seen?

It was startling to observe, once again, how the brain never ceased working. Also, its prescience was amazing. Not only did he now see the pattern of the days ahead—how the pain would come, grow, and then wither away; but also, he saw the importance of the experience. Those feelings, when they came, were going to temper him, to mature him; they would help to change him (although they couldn't do all the work on their own, they simply weren't strong enough), so that one day, he would be able to hear properly what the usherette had said earlier, rather than her words sending him off into a pleasant trance.

He walked to Charing Cross railway station and bought a ticket for Greenwich, and home.

The Cowboy Suit

I

IT IS A JULY afternoon, 1962 ...

I am outside my grandparent's house. It is square. The upper half is plastered and painted cream. The lower parts are bare stones with green dust which is mould all over them. All the stones came from the old house in the yard. Grandfather hauled them down himself on the flat-bed lorry which is now the base of the hen shed. Our address is The New House, then the name of the village, then the county, then the country, which is Ireland.

Our downpipes and gutters are bright red, same as the letter boxes in London. I know this because I once lived in London. But I am no longer there. Now I am with my grandparents.

I slip through the latch gate, walk down the avenue and go out our big gates at the bottom. I cross the road and walk towards the village. After a while I come to another set of gates held open with breeze blocks. A big building with a tin roof stands behind. This is our parochial hall. The blue letters over the front read St. Jo eph's Hall because the 'S' blew away in a storm. Everything in our lives is like that. Needing repair. At least this is what my grandmother says.

I am walking towards the steps. Fr. Devlin's car is parked at the bottom. He drives an Austin Countryman. The car has got wooden struts on the outside, like the timbers outside some houses. I stop and look through the window at the St. Christopher's medal stuck to the dashboard which is almost worn smooth from Fr. Devlin touching it so often. He is such a bad driver, his finger is on it every other second.

Straightening up, I catch sight of myself in the mirror by the driver's door, wearing my everyday clothes and my cowboy hat. This may be a mistake but I couldn't help myself. I am eight years old.

I walk up the steps. Louisa Corrigan is at the top, skipping, her rope banging on the concrete floor. Her hair is long and black and heavy and it bounces as she bobs up and down. It's like a solid piece of moss.

Through the doors and into the foyer. It smells of the sweet lemonade which is all Fr. Devlin permits at the dances he holds here on Saturday nights, and the *Dettol* which Mr. Sulgrave, the caretaker, uses to wash the place every Monday morning. Fr. Devlin says the sweat from the dancers falls on the floor and is turned into germs by flies. That is why Mr. Sulgrave has to disinfect St. Jo eph's every week.

There is a desk in the middle of the foyer. It is a black roll-top, with a money box chained to a nail banged into the side. On the wall behind there is a big poster in Fr. Devlin's pointed handwriting. It says:

St. Joseph's Parish Feis. Saturday, 19th July.
Parents please come and lend your support.
Adults 2/- ; children 1/- ; babies free.

Through the glass panels in the big swing doors, I can see the main hall is filled with children.

I step through. It's like going from the changing room out to the swimming pool. All the children are shouting and their cries are echoing off the tin roof. Fr. Devlin is just inside the door. He sees me and his face goes all cross.

"Take off that ridiculous hat."

Rather than take it off, I push it back over my shoulders, and then it hangs down, held by the drawstring around my neck. In films, this is how cowboys wear their hats inside bars and places. I have seen this on the posters outside the cinema in Drivnagh, although I have not actually ever been in to see a film myself. We don't go. My grandmother says films corrupt people and put nonsense in their heads.

"I said right off!" says Fr. Devlin, "Not half-off."

I do as he says.

"Now go and sit down."

I find a seat and put the hat on the chair beside me.

"All right, quiet please," continues Fr. Devlin walking down the aisle towards the front.

Fr. Devlin is small. His face is round and there is a lot of skin under his chin which wobbles when he talks. This may seem funny but in fact he is frightening. When he looks at you with his black eyes it's hard to move. You feel he might turn you into a pillar of salt.

"Six year old girls, on stage, immediately," Fr. Devlin calls out.

The competitors traipse up onto the stage where the Mr. Sulgrave is waiting. Mr. Sulgrave helps out at all our *feises*.

"May I remind you," shouts Fr. Devlin, as Mr. Sulgrave forms the girls into a line, "that we are doing this today, as we will be doing this on Saturday; today, every one of you will say your bit, and woe betide any child who does not have their piece off by heart today."

Mr. Sulgrave is tall and stooped. Being not too far from the front, I can clearly make out the big cut which runs right down Mr. Sulgrave's nose. It is always bleeding and leaking. He was stabbed there in the war by a Japanese soldier and it's never got better. He says the Jap steel had something in it and that's why the nose won't heal.

Mr. Sulgrave has eight medals and one of these is the 'Burma Star'. They live in little purple boxes lined with red velvet, and the funny part is, the boxes look more important than the medals.

"Are we ready!" calls Fr. Devlin, and claps his hands. "Let us begin."

One by one, the six-year-old girls come forward, recite their poem and bow. I do not listen because its always the same poem, one girl after another, and it's boring, so I drift off into my own thoughts. At some point, I reach out for my hat but my hand touches what I know is the wood of the seat. So I look, see the hat's gone, and immediately get this stabbing pain in my chest.

"Have you seen my cowboy hat?" I whisper to Peter Lynch. He's sitting in the seat behind.

"Meekin has it," he whispers back.

"What?"

This is Mr. Sulgrave's cousin, Dennis Meekin, that is to say his sister's son, who I don't like, and who is unfortunately in my class. Because of his first name, Meekin is known as the 'The Menace' at school.

"He put his hand through the seat from behind," says Peter Lynch.

He shows me what he means by sticking his arm through the gap between the back rest and the seat and waving it around.

"Sure it was Meekin?"

"Course."

"Why didn't you tell me when he was doing it?"

"Meekin said he'd do me if I spoke up."

I look at Peter Lynch. He has a reddish face, freckled and I believe he is telling me the truth.

Looking around the hall, longing for the sight of my hat sitting on Meekin's head but I don't see him or it anywhere.

103

Maybe I should tell Fr. Devlin? He is standing at the front in his black soutane with his hands behind his back. Kitty Maguire is on the stage in front of him.

"Kitty, how long have you had to learn these simple eight lines of verse?" Fr. Devlin shouts.

"I don't know,' says Kitty Maguire in a tiny voice.

"You've had four whole weeks, haven't you child?"

"Yes," says Kitty in a still tinier voice.

No, not a good time to speak to the priest. Instead, I get down on the floor. Chair legs and bare knees and children's shoes in every direction, but no sign of my hat anywhere.

Before I was sad. Now I am angry and wanting my cowboy hat back. Meekin's going to have to give it to me, and I don't care what he says. Then I have my idea. I think, I know where my hat might be.

Quietly slipping out of the hall, down the steps and making my way round to the back, I don't bother to knock on the door of the extension because I know Mr. Sulgrave is still with the six-year-old girls on stage. I go straight in.

This is Mr. Sulgrave's room, and I know Meekin often comes here. There is a table where Mr. Sulgrave eats his lunch and the chair he sits on. There are shelves of tools, and the 'S' of St. Jo eph's on a hook, waiting to be restored to its place above the porch out the front.

I check the boiler room at the back. Nothing. Just a heap of coal with silvery bits glinting in the lumps and the furnace with red flames dancing behind the glass plate in the door. I go back to the other room.

Mr. Sulgrave's brown work coat is hanging on the back of the door. There is something bulging underneath and I am not surprised to discover it's my cowboy hat.

I am happy but then I see the red label saying 'Sheriff' has been peeled off the front.

I sit down at Mr. Sulgrave's little table. There is an old ashtray with *Capstan Full Strength* on the edge. There are several butts and an apple core in the tray and something sticking out of the heap of ash.

I already know what it is as I pull it out. It is the 'Sheriff' label, rolled up on itself, sticky side out.

Why has Meekin done this? It's not as if I've reported him to Fr. Devlin, or anything. I don't understand. Why did he peel it off?

I put the label in my pocket and make my way back to the hall. Unfortunately, Fr. Devlin happens to notice me coming in.

"Where have you been?" Fr. Devlin asks.

I have the cowboy hat under my arm, held by the elbow against my side.

"I've been to the toilet."

"I see, and your hat had to go too I suppose."

Fr. Devlin turns and looks at the boys on stage. These are the eight year olds, my group. Now they have his permission, they all laugh a little but not too much. It's never wise to go too far with Fr. Devlin.

"Get up on stage, Yates," Fr. Devlin barks at me.

I walk down the aisle, ears and face reddening, and climb the steps. Has anyone spotted my blushing? As far as I can see nobody has. This has happened before. I might worry and worry about something, but nobody else even notices.

I go to the back of the line. I am to be last, as usual, because of my surname. In fact, with no surnames starting with 'Z' in my school, or in the village or anywhere, I am always the last.

"Off you go, Armit," Fr. Devlin shouts.

Shane Armit steps forward and says, "'Trouble at the Farm!' by Ivy O. Eastwick."

Armit begins to recite the poem. We have all learnt this poem and we will all recite this poem. We are going to say it today for Fr. Devlin, and then another day for the judge. She is a lady who will come from Dublin. She won't be here until Saturday and this is Tuesday.

When it comes to the actual competition, I'll be wishing I were first. I'll want to get the ordeal over with.

On the other hand, today I am glad I am last, because by the time my turn comes, everyone will have forgotten Fr. Devlin's crack about bringing my hat to the lavatory.

While I think about this, the recitation continues. I do not listen much.

Then I wonder, where is Meekin? He should be in the line in front of me, but he isn't.

Peering out into the audience, I can't see Meekin anywhere.

In my mind, I return to the boiler room. The furnace rests on bricks. It is dark beneath. A good place to hide. Perhaps Meekin was underneath when I was in there? And for all I know, he could still be there.

I have to admit, it is a very brave thing to run away from the practice for the *feis*. Fr. Devlin has all our names on a list, and he is ticking them off as we recite our poems. He's bound to find out.

"Meekin," shouts Fr. Devlin.

Silence.

"Where is Meekin?"

I do not say a word. Nobody does. Meekin is brave but I do not forgive him.

II

It is the end of the afternoon. I leave the hall and go down the front steps. Meekin sits waiting on the wall by the gate, with his sister, Frances.

I am close now. Meekin's eyes are grey. His face is freckled. He sticks his tongue out.

I stare back at him. Meekin starts to make the wet noise the cows make in fields when they open their holes. Meekin is so good that, if you closed your eyes, you'd actually think you were hearing the noise of the brown stuff coming out and hitting the ground and making a puddle, and then more stuff landing on top and the puddle getting bigger.

I put on my cowboy hat and walk past him.

III

When I get home, my grandmother is in the kitchen. Showing her the 'Sheriff' label, I ask if she can unroll it?

"How did it come off?" she asks.

"A small boy did it."

"Why did you let him have your hat? That was a stupid thing to do!"

"I didn't. He took it when I wasn't looking."

"Do you know this boy?"

"No, I don't. I only found the hat on the floor after he'd done it."

"You must be more careful."

She gets a match and splits it. She sharpens the end to a fine point with a razor blade. She tries to open the sticky label but its coiled up so tightly, nothing budges.

Well, at least I still have my cowboy badge that says 'Sheriff', I think. The badge has five points and a ball on the end of each point and the way the word 'Sheriff' appears on the badge is better than the way it is written on the label, although I couldn't say why this is.

Grandmother puts the label in the ashtray on the window ledge and says she will get grandfather to try.

"It's Swiss roll for tea," my grandmother says.

That is the funny thing about disappointment, and I have noticed this before. You have something bad happen, and then something good happens and the bad goes away.

106

"With fresh cream," she says. "You go and play and I'll call you when it's ready.

IV

A few minutes later, I leave my grandparent's house by the back steps, closing the door after myself.

I am now dressed in my complete cowboy suit ...

The cowboy waistcoat is black with fringes on the back. The shirt underneath is black with a lasso stitched on each collar. The trousers are my own covered though with the cowboy over-trousers. These have fringes down the edges and they buckle around the back of the thigh and the calf.

In the brown holster is my Colt forty-five. The caps in the gun are dark discs on a roll of blue paper. When I pull the trigger, they bang and make a puff of smoke and a smell that I like. If I can, I like to fire the gun in the house where the smell lingers for a long time. Outside the smell is just blown away by the wind. I would like to fire the gun before I get into bed, and then drift to sleep with the smell around me, but grandmother won't let me. My grandfather is a nervous man, she says, and the cap fire will upset him.

I am wearing my sheriff badge on my left breast, and the hat is on my head. It is grey and the drawstring is white. It is knotted just under my chin. When I run and the hat blows back, the knot holds it in place around my neck.

When I went to the shop in London with my mother before she died, to buy the cowboy suit, I wanted a plain black hat, but the one in the shop was too big. So I had to have this hat. The edges are decorated with something like lace. It is white and bumpy and sticks up. At first I didn't like it. It was like my mother's corset and suspender belt. Then I got to like it. This was as the hat came to fit me, as the hat became me and I became it.

I make my way to the barrel at the corner of the house where we catch our rainwater. It is only half full because it is summer. I draw my gun and point it into the barrel.

On the surface of the dark water I can see my reflection, and behind it I can see the bits of rust which have fallen off the inside of the barrel and which are lying on the bottom. I can also see the sky and the big fat white clouds behind my reflection.

I squeeze the trigger once, then again. If I can't fire the gun inside, this

107

is the best place to fire it outside. The noise of the caps echo, once, twice, and then a third time. This is the triple echo which my grandfather has told me about. I only have his word because when I asked him to fire his shotgun for me on the lawn, he said it was a waste. He said, how much do you think cartridges cost? I said, I don't know. Of course you don't know, he said, so don't bloody ask.

I walk back round to the front. Our avenue stretches down from the house to the road in a straight line. At the bottom is the demesne wall with our black gates in the middle. They are always kept closed to stop our cattle straying onto the road, but I notice that now they are open. Then a car drives in. It is black with silver headlights. My father's Rover. He gets out and closes the gates. I am puzzled and surprised. No one told me he was coming.

The Rover creeps towards me along the avenue. As it goes over the ruts and bumps, the stones and pot-holes, the car rocks up and down.

Inside the Rover, I imagine my father has both hands on the steering wheel. He is muttering to himself. Bad roads always make him cross. They are bad for the axle, the suspension, the tyres.

At last the Rover comes to a halt on the driveway in front of the house. I see my father's bald head and his thin black hair through the windscreen. He takes the key out of the ignition and then he looks up. I wave but he does not wave back. The door clicks open. He steps down onto the driveway. His shoes are polished. I call "Hello." He makes a small wave and drops onto his knees. He puts his head right down and gazes into the dark place under the car. I do not know how he can see the cracks in the axle because I've never seen them, but he says you can.

Surely they are very fine, like the crack in a tooth? I put my tongue to the tooth of mine that once cracked. It is a big silver lump now which has a funny taste.

Mouth open, staring at the clouds, I fail to notice my father getting up and coming across.

"Hello," I hear him say. I blink, half-puzzled, half-surprised. "Standing like that you confirm what I've always thought," he says in his cheerful voice. "You really are a moron."

"Hello." My voice cracks.

What he is saying is not friendly although it is said like a joke, and I don't know what to say back. I also know that I will say *something*. Then the conversation will go backwards and forwards like the ball in a tennis game, until I miss my shot.

"What are you doing?" he asks.

"Well, nothing," I say.

"'Nothing will come of nothing.'"

"I'm not doing anything. I'm just standing here."

"It's a quotation from a play, although I don't suppose art will ever be of any interest to the likes of you."

"I was just out here looking at the hills."

"You've got your mother's genes and her family are famously stupid."

"I'm not stupid."

"Well, why are staring at the hills like a retard then? And incidentally you look ridiculous in that get-up."

I want to say something but he continues:

"Am I to conclude from your costume that you admire how the cowboy won the West by wiping out the Indians on behalf of American capitalism?" From behind comes the noise of the front door scraping back. It has done this ever since the wood got wet and swelled up after the snow melted last winter.

"Good evening," my grandmother calls, and I realise she is not surprised. In fact, it seems she is expecting my father. My father walks to her, and I follow. He is wearing a tweed jacket and corduroy trousers.

Why hasn't she told me that he was coming?

My grandmother and my father shake hands. My father goes into the house.

"I'll call you when your tea's ready," my grandmother says.

The door scrapes shut. Has he come to take me away? I like living here. I don't want to go back to London. And I wonder if he is the real reason we are having Swiss roll for tea?

I go back to the barrel and stare down into the water. I start to imagine leaving, sitting in the back of my father's car as it moves down the avenue. I turn on the seat and look through the rear window and see my grandmother waving her handkerchief. When the car is further down the lane, she wipes her eyes as she begins to cry ...

In the reflection in the water, I can see the fringes on my cowboy hat are trembling. My Adam's apple is hurting. Its always like this before I cry. But it would be an extremely bad thing if this happened. My red eyes would be spotted at tea. I would be ridiculed.

I leave the water barrel and start running around the house. Once, twice, three times. Feeling better now, I fire my gun. Once, twice, three times. As usual, the caps sound meek in the open air but I do not mind. I nearly cried but I have not. Nearly, but not.

And that is when grandmother calls me in to tea.

The kitchen table is red except where the colour is worn away at one end. This is where my grandmother has been kneading her bread for years and years. That is why the red is gone and the white which was underneath shows through.

Eating a piece of her bread, I wonder why it hasn't got any of the red from the table in it.

I look at the crust. It is knobbly and bumpy and only brown. No red at all.

I often think about this at the table when no one talks to me. It passes the time.

My father is at the head of the table. My grandmother is beside me. We face the window ledge with the big radio on it. I can see the trees of our orchard outside. My grandfather is at the head of the table opposite my father. He has put on a white shirt with no collar. He has also put in his teeth, and his face looks all big and filled out. I have to keep saying to myself, This is grandfather, because I am not used to seeing him like this.

"I thought I might do some fishing," says my father.

My grandfather starts to talk about our lake up on the bog, and the single swan, who lives alone on it. When I go up there with my grandmother for our walk in the evening, we always stop and look at the swan and my grandmother always says the swan is a wife waiting for her husband. I always think it is a mother waiting for her child, but I would never dare tell my grandmother this.

My grandfather is now telling a story about a particular pike which he has hooked and lost many times. It is still up in the lake, but now it has two spinners stuck in its mouth. I start imagining the fish as it moves through the black water, the hooks stuck right through it's cheeks, and the spinners dangling down like the ends of a moustache ...

Father is planning to stay for some days, I gather. He has come to rest, to holiday. He has not come to take me away it seems.

The adults go on talking. A stay of five, six, even seven days is discussed. This will take father to Saturday and the *feis*, and beyond.

I imagine myself in my suit, standing at the front of the stage, and the lady from Dublin handing me the Macnamara Perpetual Cup for Recitation. My father is in the audience, standing, applauding.

My ears are going red. I take a bite of my bread and hope no one has seen this.

VI

Father goes in front of me as we set off down the avenue on our walk. He likes to walk. He breathes in and out.

"Smell that air," he says. "The air here is so clean. My lungs are singing. My God! Paul, you're the lucky one, not like me, cooped up in that box we call home in Croyden, in that awful Imperial country called England. When do I ever get to see green trees, like these?"

He points at the two chestnut trees at the end of our avenue.

"Never," he says. "Oh, you're the lucky one Paul."

We move under the chestnut trees. They stand one on either side of the avenue, but the branches above have grown into one another, making the two trees one, making an arch.

It is said to be a magic place, and that if you walk backwards and forwards under here three times with your eyes closed and no shoes or stockings on your feet, and you repeat the name of the one you love three times, they will love you back. This is what local people say, anyway.

On the branches above there are names carved in the bark. Also hearts and arrows. Should I come down one night myself? But maybe the magic is only for love and it can't bring mother back.

My father tut-tuts. He also has seen the carved names.

"Vandals," he says.

I say nothing.

We pass through and go on. At the bottom of the avenue he opens one of the black gates and I go through.

"Hang on, hang on," he calls after me. "The traffic, mind the traffic, you stupid child."

Our gateway stands on a corner where the road bends sharply. Once, a coal lorry killed a cyclist here and there were so many bits of coal glued to him with his blood, he looked like a black man. At least that's what my grandmother told me.

I feel my father's hand taking my arm. We cross the road.

"When you are left you are wrong, when you are right you are right," my father says. "Yes?"

"Yes."

"You must always head towards the oncoming traffic. Do you understand?"

"Yes."

"What did I say?"

"Always walk towards the oncoming traffic."

111

"Why?"

"Because you said so."

"So you can see the oncoming traffic, you stupid boy."

"Sorry."

"You're dreamy. Did you know that? You'll never do well at school. You'll never be able to hold down a job."

I want to tell him this is not true. I want to tell him I have learnt the poem by Ivy O. Eastwick. I can say it backwards, forwards, any way at all. My head is not in the clouds. My feet are very much on the ground. I am awake. But I decide it is better to say nothing.

We pass St. Jo eph's Hall. Someone has left an empty Guinness bottle on one of the piers, perhaps with the intention of annoying Fr. Devlin because he won't allow drink at his dances.

"Why don't people take their bloody rubbish home?" says my father, pointing at it.

There is a bee wriggling in the bottom of the bottle. His wings have got wet in the little bit of beer that is still in there.

Taking hold of the bottle by the base, I flick it a few times until the bee flies out like a little stone and lands in the grass.

"Oh! Preparing for the sainthood," says father "We'll bring that bottle home later."

I put the bottle on the ground. We walk on, me in front, father behind. At last we come to the back entrance to the Woodvale demesne and turn in. The earth is black with stones bedded in it. This is where my grandfather shoots with Colonel Armstrong. I like to collect their cartridges. They are red and blue and they smell like the caps in my gun. I have a large collection of them at home; I keep them in a square syringe box. It was given to me by the vet after he inoculated the cattle.

In the middle of the wood we come to the cottage. It is made of brick with a white wooden porch on the front. This is the house where the Meekins live. I wonder if Dennis is here, and I am glad that I am with my father. I want Meekin to see him with me. The front door opens, but instead of Dennis, it's Mrs. Meekin who comes out. She is carrying a basket of washing. She walks over to the washing line which stretches between two apple trees at the side.

My father says, "Good day," and Mrs. Meekin says, "Good day."

Mrs. Meekin takes a black stocking and hangs it up on the line. The toe of the stocking has been torn and stitched with white thread. It's squashed like the end of a sausage, not neatly sewed the way my grandmother would do it.

My father and Mrs. Meekin talk as she hangs up the washing. I look around. There is a pile of wood at the side of the house, and a wooden contraption shaped like two 'X's for holding wood when you saw it. There is also a lot of sawdust on the ground. It is white, like snow.

Mrs. Meekin finishes and brings us inside to the kitchen.

There is a table and two chairs in front of the fire. The chairs have been taken out of a car. I am told to sit and I do.

Mrs. Meekin puts the kettle on to the fire. Mrs. Meekin talks and my father listens. Besides Dennis, Mrs. Meekin has several other children. One has died in the county hospital. Mr. Meekin is in England. He is working on the roads. He is in a town called Nottingham. I am interested when I hear this, because I know the town is near Sherwood Forest where Robin Hood lived. I wonder if Mr. Meekin has been out to Sherwood? But I don't ask since my father will only say, "Shut up".

I listen now as Mrs. Meekin talks about money. She gets a little from the government, she says, as well as what her husband sends from England. My father nods. The word "assistance" is used. I don't know what this means.

Mrs. Meekin makes the tea. She fills a cup and hands it to my father.

"Does your boy want one?" she asks.

"No," says my father.

I stop listening to the grown-ups and think about my cowboy suit, lying in the orange box under my bed at home. Later, when my father goes fishing, I will put it on and roam around the fields by myself.

VII

The white shirt scratches my skin as grandmother does up the top button. Then she puts the tie around my neck, knots it and steps back.

"You look nice," she says, "very, very nice."

She wets a comb in the basin of warm water standing on the kitchen table, and starts on my hair.

The comb goes into the bowl again and again and again until I feel the wet soaking through to my scalp. The hair is tangled and grandmother has to tug the comb very hard, and when it hurts, I screw up my eyes.

"I'm sorry," she whispers.

At last I feel grandmother taking my shoulders and moving me into the sunlight coming through the kitchen window.

"Every inch a gentleman," she says, as I open my eyes, blinking.

113

VIII

My father drives through the gates of St. Joseph's Hall. Mr. Sulgrave has got the 'S' up in time for the *feis*, I notice. Fr. Devlin's car is in its usual place. There are many other cars as well. We find a parking space behind the extension where Mr. Sulgrave has his room.

Climbing out, I notice the jacket feels very tight across my shoulders. I only wear this suit on Sundays to Mass, or for an occasion like this, and to my mother's funeral.

I put my hands into my jacket pockets but I don't like the way my elbows are now pushed too much up into the air.

As my father climbs out and locks the door, I change my hands into my short trouser pockets.

"Take your hands out of your pockets, and don't slouch," he says.

I follow him round to the front, up the steps and through the door.

Mr. Sulgrave sits inside behind the desk. He is lolling back on the chair but now he tips forward so the front legs go down on the floor with a bang. He is wearing a huge plaster over the sore on his nose today.

"Mr. Yates, good afternoon," says Mr. Sulgrave, "I hear you were calling up to my sister."

My father smiles. "Do I have to pay?"

"I'm afraid you do."

My father fishes his wallet out. It is black with brass corners. The Henry girls come out of the hall wearing identical green dresses with black stripes. There are several boys in suits, and like me they too have all had their hair combed down flat.

My father hands over an English ten shilling note and Mr. Sulgrave returns his change.

"What about my ticket?" my father says.

Mr. Sulgrave laughs.

The tickets are on a roll. They are green with black writing which says, Regal Cinema, Drivnagh.

"Thank you."

I feel a fluttering in my stomach. Until this moment I have been able to put the idea of the *feis* out of my mind, but now I have seen the tickets, I can't any more. In an hour or two, I will be on stage.

We walk toward the hall doors. My grandmother calls this feeling butterflies. But when I've trapped a butterfly in my hands, the touch of its wings is a faint one, whereas this feeling is like water swishing and swirling in my stomach.

We go into the hall. The curtains are closed. There is a table covered with green felt in front of the stage. The big school bell is on the table, as well as some papers and pencils. There is a nice smell of perfume and tobacco.

We sit down. Fr. Devlin climbs on stage. He appeals to parents in the first ten rows to extinguish their cigarettes as the smoke affects the lungs of the children.

There are people sidling into the seats in front of us. There is a man and two women, and a little girl whom one of the women is carrying, and a boy.

It is Dennis Meekin. The woman is Mrs. Meekin and the little girl is Francis, the sister. The other two are relatives. I have seen them around the village.

Meekin sees me, blinks and turns to face the stage.

Fr. Devlin introduces the adjudicator lady from Dublin.

She has a big bust and white powder on her face. She wears glasses with blue coloured rims. Her pink skirt is pleated and there are pearls stitched into her jacket. Her blouse is white and her bodice underneath shows through.

There is a round of applause. The lady from Dublin bows and sits down behind the table.

Mrs. Meekin looks around. My father leans forward. He touches her shoulder. Mrs. Meekin turns back and smiles. She is wearing lipstick and her hair is pinned up and there are big earrings in her ears.

"Hello," my father whispers.

"Hello," Mrs. Meekin whispers back.

Mrs. Meekin's eyes shine brightly.

The bell peals and everyone falls silent.

"Can I have all the six year old girls," Fr. Devlin shouts, "on stage, please."

Girls flood from the audience, climb up by the steps, and disappear through the curtain to the stage behind; this is where Mr. Sulgrave is waiting to line them up out of view.

The bell rings again.

Fr. Devlin shouts, "One, Ursula Armit."

Ursula Armit, sister of Shane, comes through the middle of the curtain, walks forward, and takes her place at the front of the stage. She wears a big white bow in her hair and a white dress with a pattern of red roses.

"'Autumn Lines,'" says Ursula Armit, "by Edith Perceval Tucker."

115

Ursula coughs. The Dublin lady, pencil in hand, looks up. Mrs. Meekin turns and smiles quickly at my father.

"'The leaves are turning brown and green and red ...'" begins Ursula.

I am itching where the edge of my trousers touch my thighs.

First the six year olds ...

Then the seven year olds ...

Then the eight year olds and it will be my turn.

My stomach is churning. I imagine myself winning and my father smiling and applauding. I hope I will not forget my words.

I close my eyes. A second girl comes forward and starts to recite 'Autumn Lines' while in my head, I begin my poem.

IX

"All the eight year old boys on stage please," shouts Fr. Devlin.

Dennis Meekin gets off his chair and walks towards the stage.

"Good luck!" Mrs. Meekin calls after him.

"Go on," father says to me.

I am awaiting for him to say something else.

"Go on."

I join the other boys who are in a knot at the bottom of the steps, we climb up and go through the curtain.

It is dark on the stage behind. There is a hurricane lamp burning on a table and a smell of paraffin. The drill is, we line up and file out through the curtain, one at a time, when it is our turn.

"All right," Mr. Sulgrave calls, "Settle boys, settle."

I go right to the back. The line forms in front of me. The bell rings on the other side of the curtain.

"One," shouts Fr. Devlin.

Shane Armit disappears through the gap in the curtain to the front.

"'Trouble at the Farm,' by Ivy O. Eastwick," Armit shouts.

"'Help! Help! What's to do?

Dobbin the horse has cast a shoe ... '"

I do not listen. I just step forward each time a boy leaves the front of the line and goes through the curtain. I am number forty-three.

"Twenty-nine, Dennis Meekin," shouts Fr. Devlin.

I watch Meekin disappear to the other side of the curtain. The audience is quiet. A long time passes.

I hear a small voice shouting, "Go for it Dennis". It's Meekin's little sister, Francis. Some of the audience laugh.

"Don't worry, take your time," I hear the Dublin lady saying.

Fr. Devlin is at the front of the line, peering out through the curtain at Meekin. Fr. Devlin is biting his knuckle. He does this when he is angry.

Another long time passes. Meekin has still not spoken. He has either forgotten his words, or he has frozen on stage.

"In your own time," says the Dublin lady again. She speaks louder this time, slightly tartly.

The audience is stirring. It has now been a very long time since Meekin went out and still he hasn't said a word.

"Get off, Dennis!" Fr. Devlin hisses through the curtain, "Go away."

I hear Meekin clattering down the steps and running up the aisle. "Number thirty," Fr. Devlin shouts. "Go on Nolan," he says, "you'd better not bloody let me down."

Nolan goes through.

"'Trouble at the Farm,'" he begins, " by Ivy O. Eastwick ... '"

"Do you know your words?" Fr. Devlin whispers at each of us, working his way down the line. We all nod.

"One more exhibition like the one I have just seen from Meekin, and you will feel my wrath, every man jack of you."

At last Fr. Devlin shouts, "Number forty-three."

I go through the curtain and walk to the front.

"'Trouble at the Farm,' by Ivy O. Eastwick:

"'Help! Help! What's to do?

Dobbin the horse has lost a shoe

Help! Help! What's the matter?

Porky the Pig has eaten the platter.

Help! Help! What is it now?

Shep the sheepdog is chasing the cow.

Oh dear! What a to do,

Such muddles and troubles I never knew.'"

After my bow I walk down the steps and up the aisle, the faces of the audience swimming past me. I try to judge by their expressions how I have done, but it's impossible.

Reaching my seat, I see Meekin is on his mother's lap. He has been crying but the tears have dried. I can see the red streaks on his cheeks. His head is on her breast. My father is leaning forward. He is talking. I cannot tell if he is speaking to Mrs. Meekin, or to her son. I slip past my father and sit down. Nobody says anything to me.

"And now the winners in the category, Eight-year-old boys," shouts Fr. Devlin.

The Dublin lady stands at the front with her arms raised.

"I thought the standard of the boys just now was generally excellent," she says, "as it has been, throughout the day so far, with lots of the boys delivering their words with gusto and drama. And that's what I'm looking for, all the time. Force, presence, energy. You've really got to put those words across, and many of you did so terribly well. Now, in reverse order, third prize goes to ..."

I want to win but now I know that I haven't. I know this because I didn't have any gusto. I just said the words. Actually, I thought the boys who shouted the words were terrible, but seemingly, I was wrong. The three winners are the worst shouters of all.

I look at the floor of the hall. Polished parquet with cigarette burns here and there.

The three boys who have won go forward. The winner receives the Macnamara Perpetual Trophy. The other two get medals. I feel a big lump in my throat. I hear Meekin start to sob. I look up. My father reaches forward and strokes the back of his head.

X

Waking up, I see the picture above my bed of Our Lord on his cross. Where the nails go through Jesus' hands and feet the blood is dark and solid like lumps of sealing wax.

I hear the wicket gate creak outside as someone goes through. I get out of bed and go to the window. I see it is my grandmother. She is carrying two buckets filled with meal down to the hens. The birds are in a cluster around the hen shed which is on the back of the old flat-bed lorry. There are white hens and brown hens and a large black cockerel.

I get dressed and go down. When I get to the bottom of the stairs I see the orange box, which is usually stored under my bed, and which was under my bed when I went to sleep the night before, is now on the hall table. My cowboy suit is inside.

I go into the kitchen.

My father is sitting at the end of the table reading the newspaper. On the plate in front of him are two bacon rinds. Without looking away from his *Irish Times*, he takes a drink of tea and puts the cup back on the saucer.

"Did you sleep well?"

He is going away today. But what is my cowboy suit doing in the hall?

"Your grandmother left out tinned mandarins for you," he says.

I move to my seat. The fruits are little shrimp-sized orange pieces, and their juice is deep yellow, like varnish, thick and sweet tasting. I get mandarins on Sundays at lunchtime, or if I am sick. But this is a Tuesday. Why is she giving mandarins to me today?

I sit down. I lift a fruit on to my tongue and then press it against the roof of my mouth. I squeeze the juice out. Then I begin to chew.

Why has grandmother given me mandarins?

My father coughs and stands.

"I have to run a message," he says. "I'll be back to say goodbye."

Why is my cowboy suit on the hall table?

I sit still. My father goes out. I swallow. I hear the front door scrape open and shut. I hear the sound of the Rover starting.

Why is my cowboy suit on the hall table?

I jump down and run into the hall.

The table is empty. The box is gone.

XI

"Goodbye," says my father.

"Goodbye," I reply.

My father shakes my hand. He turns away, gets into the car and drives off.

With my grandmother beside me, I watch as the car drives away down the avenue.

Why did she give me mandarins?

Where is my cowboy suit?

The Rover goes through the gate at the end of the avenue and disappears.

At last it is safe to ask.

"Where is my cowboy suit?"

"What, darling?"

"Where is my cowboy suit?"

"Well, darling, your father ..."

She stops and I know what she is going to say next.

"Your father thought you didn't need it any more, that you'd had good use of it and played with it often enough, and he thought it would be a good thing to give it to someone who didn't have the same advantages as you, and so he brought it down this morning to the Meekins' house and he left it there for Dennis. Mrs. Meekin apparently said something about Dennis wanting a cowboy suit at the *feis*."

119

XII

She goes inside and I go round to the water barrel.

I look down into the dark water. I can see the outline of my face and I try to imagine I am still wearing my cowboy hat and that I can see its reflection.

Feeling an enormous lump in my throat, I begin to cry. Some of the tears roll off my chin and plop onto the surface below, making ripples which disturb the surface of the water.

Later, I go inside.

The 'Sheriff' sticker has dried out and my grandmother has managed to unroll it. She boils up some gum and sticks it on to the front of one of my grandfather's old brown hats.

I find an old broom handle and grandmother says I can have it for a rifle.

The Fifty Pound Note

I

"HEY BOYLE, YOU THICK mick, wake up. We've arrived," McRory the driver shouted at him.

Boyle opened his eyes, looked out through the filthy back window of the Bedford van, and saw that they had arrived, at last, in the Portobello Road, west London.

"Jesus, I fell asleep. I must be tired." The back of Boyle's neck was itching. As part of his Christmas spruce-up programme, he had visited the barbers that lunchtime for a haircut instead of going to the pub with the other men from the site for a drink and, inevitably, little bits of hair had fallen behind his collar. He started scratching himself with a thick finger as McRory began to address him.

"You know, Boyle," said McRory, "you're always tired. Didn't I see you creeping into those big concrete pipes, this morning, for a kip?"

"It was a call of nature."

"Come off it, Boyle!"

"As God is my witness."

McRory reached up and adjusted the rear-view mirror of the van until he had caught Boyle's gaze with his own.

"And when did you last go to confession, Boyle?"

"Come on," said one of the other lads in the back of the van, "I've a wife to get home to, a supper waiting for me, presents to wrap."

"O.K. so," said Boyle, sliding along the wooden slated seat towards the door which had been opened for him. "Night lads. Happy Christmas."

The young lad Liam, the one with the wife to go home to, slammed the door after him and looped the piece of string around the handle inside which kept it shut. Standing on the pavement, Boyle could see Liam through the glass, bent over now as he knotted the string.

"The governor ought to get that door fixed," shouted Boyle, moving around to the front of the van. "It's a hazard."

"That's right, Boyle." McRory had his head out the driver's window. "Now mind yourself and don't drink it all at once Boyle."

"You can be sure I won't."

"Have a good Christmas."

Boyle slapped the top of the van and McRory drove off; he was headed for Kilburn and Willesden, which was where most of the other men lived. Boyle was the only one in the gang who lived in Notting Hill Gate; and because the area was identified with blacks, the men on the building site often joked that Boyle had a black wife whom he kept a secret. Boyle always laughed at this. Actually, Boyle lived alone. He was forty-five.

Boyle headed up Portobello Road. Outside the Lord Nelson public house, two blacks in felt hats with wide brims were negotiating in whispers. A plump white woman with puffy legs, her slip showing below her short skirt, stood waiting patiently a couple of paces from them.

Further on there was a council refuse lorry, and men in dark overalls were clearing up the mess left after the last market before Christmas. A couple of them were scouring the gutters with coarse bristled brooms, while others, armed with short, light, wooden planks, were organising bruised vegetables and squashed fruits into heaps.

Boyle hurried on. The refuse van smelt of stinking fish—why did it always smell of fish when there was none to be seen?—and he hated fish.

A few steps further and Boyle reached his destination, the *Seven 'til Midnight* shop. He noticed there was a hand-written note stuck to the back of the glass door: UNDER NEW MANAGEMENT.

It was a childish scrawl written with a felt tip pen. Shimmering Christmas tinsel hung in loops beside it.

Boyle pushed through the door and went to the first counter where a young, dark-skinned boy was standing by the cash till. He was aged, Boyle judged, eleven or twelve, although with these Asians it was hard to tell, Boyle thought. In his experience, they were often much older than they looked.

"Half-ounce of *Golden Virginia* and a packet of *Rizla* greens," he said.

The boy behind the counter stared at Boyle with a blank expression which suggested he did not understand what the older man was saying.

"Half-ounce of *Golden Virginia* and a packet of *Rizla* greens," he repeated.

As Boyle often bought his tobacco in this shop, he was now able to point at precisely the place on the shelves where the *Golden Virginia* was kept. As he did this, Boyle became aware of a paper bell made from coloured crepe paper hanging above him, while outside he could hear the mechanism in the refuse lorry, wheezing and groaning as it compressed the rubbish that had just been thrown into the back.

"To—bac—co," shouted Boyle, to the still uncomprehending listener.

The boy called across to the proprietor. He spoke in a language Boyle did not understand. In English, the new proprietor went by the unlikely name of Louis.

"What kind you want?" Louis called back to Boyle. Louis was packing groceries into a cardboard box.

"Half-ounce of *Golden Virginia* and a packet of *Rizla* greens."

Louis left the box and went towards the shelves, circling his hand.

"In the corner and the papers are beside it," pointed Boyle.

Louis found them. As Boyle took his goods and put them in the pocket of his donkey jacket, his mind ran forward ...

The next day, as well as being Christmas Eve was a Sunday and, happily, the Brick Lane Market in the East End would be open. His intention was to go, just as he did every Sunday, and with his Christmas bonus—a lovely, crisp fifty pound note that was sitting in the envelope that was in his back trousers pocket—he was going to buy himself a shirt and a second-hand suit (his current Sunday best being long past its sell-by date). This was part two of the Christmas spruce-up programme. He would wear the clothes to lunch at his brother's on Monday, which was Christmas Day.

Of course, Boyle ruminated, the fifty pound note would need breaking, and they certainly wouldn't have the change in the ticket office in Ladbroke Grove station where he would be going to catch the underground to Brick Lane the next morning; and he would certainly have difficulty getting the note broken at the market itself. In fact, it now occurred to him, there was some danger that a stall holder might even take the fifty pound note on the pretext of getting it changed, and then do a bunk with it. He had heard of this sort of thing happening before.

Well, he decided, as he was in the *Seven 'til Midnight* he might as well get it changed there.

"Can you break this for me?" he asked, pulling the note out of the envelope in which he had received it earlier that afternoon.

As Boyle felt the note being plucked from his hand by the boy, Louis hurried past on his way back to the box he had been packing with groceries.

"I'm sorry I was so slow at getting what you needed," Louis apologised over his shoulder to Boyle.

Boyle turned to listen to the shop's new owner.

Louis threw two pound packets of sugar into the box. They landed in the bottom with a thud.

"We only took over this morning," continued Louis—two tins of *Bachelor's Peas* followed the sugar—"and we don't know where everything is."

"Oh, don't worry," said Boyle expansively, "I got what I needed, didn't I? Isn't that all that counts?"

While he spoke to Louis facing one way, Boyle had his arm stretched out the other way towards the boy, and now he felt the change, his change, being put into his hand. Then the drawer of the till pinged as it was closed. Boyle turned back. Besides the coins, Boyle was expecting to see a sheaf of coloured notes in his palm. However, which was baffling, they weren't there.

"Hey! Where's the rest of my change?" demanded Boyle.

All that there was in his hand were two pound coins and some coppers.

The boy shrugged his shoulders and pointed at Boyle's palm.

"Where's the rest of it? I gave you fifty pounds ..."

The boy moved his gaze to Louis and shifted uneasily from side to side.

"I put it in your hand. I asked you to change it. I want fifty pounds less the price of the tobacco and the papers."

Louis and the boy started speaking rapidly in their own language. Louis' wife, a woman in a red sari, and Louis' twin daughters, ten year old girls with big gold earrings, poked their heads out of the doorway at the back of the shop. The boy opened the till, pulled out a five pound note and waved it angrily at Boyle.

"I'm not a thick Paddy, you know," said Boyle, pointing at the bank note. "I know what I had and it *wasn't* that fiver I'm telling you."

He pulled the wage packet out of his pocket again.

"Look," said Boyle. "Wage here and bonus at the bottom—fifty pounds."

The details were in biro on the front of the envelope.

"I worked hard for that. Now you can keep your tobacco."

He put the *Golden Virginia* and the papers back on the counter.

"I just want my money back."

The boy was pulling out bank notes from the till and flicking through them. There were five pound notes and ten pound notes and even twenty pound notes, but Boyle's fifty was nowhere to be seen.

"There's no fifty pound note," said Louis finally. He was standing behind the counter and looking down into the cash register.

"But I gave the young lad the note."

Boyle's tone was more and more exasperated.

"It's a fact as plain as this hand in front of your eyes ..."

Whilst the argument went on like this, Louis' wife slipped into the alley at the side of the shop. She ran down to the Portobello Road where she found a young policeman making his way along the street.

"There's trouble in the shop," she burst out breathlessly.

"What kind?"

"There's a man. He wants money."

"Armed?"

"No, no. He wants change."

The police constable was puzzled.

"I'm frightened for my husband," said Louis' wife. "The customer is shouting at him."

"All right then," said the policeman, "lead the way," and whispering into his walkie-talkie, he followed Louis' wife across the pavement and through the door of the shop.

Inside, the policeman found Boyle going at full belt. "The money was there," Boyle was shouting, "Now you give it to me!"

The policeman asked what the trouble was.

"These people are robbing me," Boyle explained angrily. "I gave them a fifty pound note and they're trying to palm me off with the change from a fiver. Look here. It's written down. Fifty pound bonus."

Boyle showed the policeman his wages packet.

"The bonus was a fifty pound note. The governor's idea. Every lad on the building site got one."

"Now, just a minute," said the policeman. "Simmer down. Let's go through this step by step. What's your name?"

The policeman had just completed a community training scheme.

"Boyle, James."

"Right Mr. Boyle. You allege you handed over a fifty pound note."

"Not allege, I did."

"Can I see the till please?"

The boy moved aside and the policeman stepped behind the counter. He examined the bank notes in the till with great deliberation. No fifty pound note. He lifted out the drawer. Underneath the policeman found a pile of luncheon vouchers and a receipt book. Again, no fifty pound note.

"I tell you, I gave that young fellow the note," said Boyle furiously, for he could see the policeman's search had been fruitless. "It doesn't mean a damn thing that it's not in there. Search him. Go on. He's got it in his pocket or stuffed it down his shoe."

Louis caught the policeman's eye and shook his head.

"It's not here, Mr. Boyle," said the policeman, "you can see that for yourself."

"Ring the governor, Mr. McCarty," persisted Boyle. "His home number's in the telephone book. He'll tell you. Every lad on the building site got the bonus. A fifty pound note." Boyle was shouting now and unaware of the other customers staring at him from around the shop.

"Have you just returned from work, Mr. Boyle?"

"Yes."

"How?"

"Van."

"Perhaps you dropped the money in the van?"

"The proof is there in black and white." Boyle waved his wage packet at the policeman again.

"It's not here, Mr. Boyle. I think the best thing you can do is to make an official report, at the station tomorrow, that the money is missing."

"My God, these people are crooks. It's daylight robbery! It's protecting me you should be. Search that lad."

As Boyle made a lunge for the boy's collar, the policeman got hold of the older man's arm. The boy went white and jumped back.

"Mr. Boyle, I'm only going to warn you once."

"By Jesus, if you're not going to help me, I'm going to help myself."

Boyle tried to snatch a fistful of notes from the till. The policeman caught his arm again and twisted it behind his back.

"Let go!" shouted Boyle. The policeman was hurting his arm.

"I'm going to put you outside, Mr. Boyle, and if you're still there in two minutes time, I'm going to call a squad car. You'll be bounced inside the station so fast your feet won't touch the ground."

Louis opened the door and the policeman propelled Boyle through it.

"What about my money. I'm being robbed."

"You clear off within two minutes, or else you'll find yourself in the cells for Christmas."

"My fifty pounds. My fifty pounds," Boyle shouted.

The policeman shut the door and the young boy leapt forward to bolt it. Louis turned and called out to the other customers, "Trouble over, ladies and gentlemen."

Meanwhile, out in the street, Boyle shouted, "My money! My money!"

Through the glass which had 'Merry Christmas' written in fake snow, Boyle saw the policeman was looking back at him and threateningly touching his watch.

A few moments later, a Panda car drew up behind Boyle. It was a routine follow-up to the message received at Ladbroke Grove police station a few minutes earlier. A second policeman climbed out, his radio crackling. Boyle walked off down the Portobello Road as fast as his legs would carry him. He felt shaky and there were tears in his eyes. There'd be no new shirt and no new suit now.

"Those fucking darkies," he murmured, "I'll get those fucking darkies."

Boyle wiped his face on his sleeve and went into the Lord Nelson public house. It was a gaunt, inhospitable place with a dirty floor and worn velvet covered seats which were split and losing their horse-hair stuffing. The lavatories at the side were not properly boxed off and could be heard continuously flushing and gurgling. In the corner, an old man was staring at an E.T. doll which was flashing on the table in front of him. He was the only customer.

"Hello, James," said the barman to Boyle.

"Bushmills—make it a double!"

"What happened? You look like you saw a ghost."

"It's worse."

Michael the barman wheeled around and lifted the glass to the optic.

"Can you spare a fag?" asked Boyle.

"Sure."

Michael the barman threw Boyle a packet of *Major* and a box of matches.

"Smoke away."

Boyle took the glass, drained it and asked for a second.

"It must be bad. Were you laid off?"

"No. Them fucking darkies up the *Seven 'til Midnight* shop. Gave them a fifty pound note to change and it disappears. Policeman comes and takes their side. It was daylight robbery. But I tell you, I'll have them. I'll fucking make mince-meat out of them."

"What? Come again. I don't understand."

"It was a young lad. I give him the money. I turn to talk to the governor. The money disappears. The young lad put it somewhere."

"Ah!" exclaimed Michael. Now Boyle had acted out the scene for him, Michael understood.

"They'd sell their grandmothers," said Boyle.

"Send the bollocks home."

"Give them a hiding first."

"Better still ..."

For some minutes they talked on like this until Boyle became aware of someone touching his elbow. He looked round. It was one of Louis' daughters, curly black hair and dark eyes. She touched Boyle again and stared back up at him.

"What is it?" he asked.

She pointed at the door.

"Is your father that imbecile from the shop?"

She had not a clue what Boyle meant but she nodded all the same. He stubbed his cigarette out and marched towards the door.

Outside the pub there was a flagged area set back from the pavement; customers sat and drank there in the summer, using large wine barrels as tables. But it was winter now, so the area was empty except for Louis standing in the darkness, the boy snivelling beside him.

"What do you want?" demanded Boyle.

Louis said something to the young boy in their own language and then pushed him forward. The boy was wailing and rubbing his hands on his face. Louis' daughter, who had followed Boyle from the pub, took her father's arm and watched a passing car.

"I'm sorry," said the young boy stiltedly and something crumpled went into Boyle's hand.

Then the young boy turned and ran back past Louis and away down the street, his wails trailing after him. Seconds later, his little figure rounded the corner under the yellow street light, and he disappeared.

Boyle opened out the crumpled piece of paper. 'I promise to pay the bearer ... ' It was his fifty alright.

For the last half-an-hour, Boyle had felt like a man wrongly accused of a crime he hadn't committed. Now the money was back, he felt vindicated and relieved all at once. A surge of delight went through him. He *had* been right. He *had* had the note. He *had* handed it over. He *was* innocent.

"Have a drink," he heard himself saying.

Louis shuffled nervously, then pointed at his clothes.

"My overall," he said. It was white, nylon, with biro marks above the breast pocket where Louis always kept a pen.

"I wouldn't worry about that."

Boyle indicated his own donkey jacket.

"I know the landlord. He'll pass no remarks."

In the Lord Nelson, a few minutes later, over pint glasses of bitter, Louis explained, haltingly and with embarrassment, how the young boy had slipped the note, which was new and crisp, into the tiny but note-friendly slit between the bottom of the till and the top of the counter on which the till sat. After the policeman had left, Louis had noticed the boy poking in there with a playing card. Louis had found the money and then beaten the boy. It had been Louis' wife's idea to find Boyle and apologise.

"Get rid of him," said Boyle, when Louis finished his account, "You can't have a thief in a shop."

"But how can I?" said Louis, "he's my brother's son. He's come here from India."

II

Boyle was woken the next morning by the sound of his alarm clock ringing. He got up and went straight to his trousers, turned his back pocket inside out, and discovered that from the fifty pound note, all that he had left was about seven pounds. Oh well, he thought, he hadn't enough to buy anything, and as he had a terrible hangover, he might as well go back to bed. So he went back to bed, and slept until twelve ...

On Christmas morning, Boyle went first to Mass and then to his brother's house in Ealing. He was clean, his hair washed, his nails cut, his shoes polished, and his landlady, Mrs. Pearse, had ironed his clothes for him. However, though they might have been crease-free, it was impossible to disguise the fact that his old suit—good God, he'd been wearing it for ten years—was so threadbare it was shiny, while the collar on the white dress shirt, which was nearly as old, was floppy and fraying.

And in response to his appearance, the brother and the family were true to form. They called Boyle a tinker and a pauper and a mendicant. The banter seemed fairly good humoured but Boyle was left wondering if there wasn't something hostile behind it. If it wasn't meant to hurt.

Sipping a sherry in the afternoon—this was during the lull before the meal—Boyle began to feel sorry for himself. How dare they call him names. He would have been togged out if he hadn't spent the money in the Lord Nelson with Louis. But he had and there it was and anyway, what did his brother and the family know about the real Boyle? It was what was inside a man that counted, not his outside appearance.

Then Boyle remembered the boy and his judgement, "Get rid of him. You can't have a thief in a shop." Why had he said that! He found himself wishing now that he hadn't. Christmas was the time of forgiveness, charity and brotherly love. His own should be showing him a bit more of that, he thought, and he, in his turn, should have shown some too. He felt a great wave of remorse sweep over him. He emptied the glass of sherry and called out to the sister-in-law for another ...

Two days later Boyle went into the *Seven til Midnight* shop not knowing exactly what he intended to say, but determined to say something.

However, before Boyle could speak, Louis came over to him and said, "I got rid of him."

Boyle decided to play dumb though his heart was beating very fast.

"You can't have a thief in here," continued Louis. "You were right. So I sent him up to my sister in Bradford. That'll teach him."

It was too late to say anything. Boyle saw that clearly now. The damage was done.

Then, to console himself, he found himself wondering if perhaps the boy thief wouldn't in fact be better off in Bradford? After all, he thought, it did gave the boy the chance to wipe the slate clean and start again, didn't it ... ?

"Change for a fifty?" he heard Louis saying wickedly beside him. They were friends now, rock solid. That, at least, was one good thing to have come out of the whole mess ...

And over the next few weeks, 'Change for a fifty?' became a catch phrase, first in the shop and then amongst the children in the neighbourhood; and before very long they were chanting it after Boyle as he moved around the streets, although they had not the faintest idea what lay behind it.

And soon Boyle himself had quite forgotten too.

A Short Story

I

MY CAREER IN FICTION is unspectacular. At least it always has been. Maybe this will change that. And what an odd thing that would be.

When I started, my models were Borges and Robert Louis Stevenson. These writers investigated unknown worlds, took notes, and published the results. They were generous, tender-hearted souls; they gave to life; and I longed, when I began, to take my place beside them.

But now, I am about to write about myself as a writer, despite having vowed never to do this. But promises are made to be broken, I mean those pious promises that we make to ourselves. But enough preamble, here goes ...

It starts with a girl. She was a photographer who sometimes worked for *Architectural Heritage*, a magazine for which I also worked because I wasn't getting stories published in those days, and reverent articles about stately homes and their owners were a rather neat way to pay the rent.

Her name was Hazel although she liked to be called Haze. She had once been a model and then, as she put it, she moved from the front of the camera to behind the camera.

We were brought together, Haze and I, by the State Apartments at Hampton Court. After the fire they were refurbished (at considerable expense), and then I was commissioned to write a piece about the new look State Apartments, and Haze was asked to take the snaps.

Never having met Hazel before, I got on the telephone to make arrangements.

"I'll meet you in the Maze," she said.

"Why can't we meet somewhere normal, like the entrance?" I said.

"You wear a carnation; I carry a rolled-up *Evening Standard*."

"You'll recognise me," she said.

"How? Do you have a wooden leg?"

"I am extraordinarily beautiful."

I went to the Maze and located Hazel with absolutely no difficulty whatsoever. The camera case with its ridged steel exterior, of course, was a giveaway, but without that aid I would have found her anyway. Amongst the ordinary mortals who were milling around, nobody could have failed to notice her.

She had wonderful, long, wavy auburn hair and a fullish unwaifish body, which is my code for saying she had large breasts. I saw her before she saw me, standing in the middle of a corridor of hedge, her face tilted towards the sky. She was contemplating the clouds, which that day were huge, plump confections hanging in a blue and, for London, surprisingly clean sky.

She had the soul of a poet I decided instantly; she had to have; who else but a poet would stand in the middle of the Maze at Hampton Court, children screeching with excitement, mothers and fathers pushing past, staring resolutely at the heavens.

"Hello," I said, and she turned it towards me—her poet's face. It was heart shaped and her eyes were large and expressive.

"Hello," she said back.

She had this slightly trembling voice which made her sound as if she was nervous, and yet, as I knew from her gaze, she wasn't nervous at all.

She came towards me, smiled, shook my hand. Her palm was warm, not cold or clammy—an unfailing indication of good character in my book.

We went inside Hampton Court and, to my great surprise, I functioned perfectly well during the interview with the Keeper of the State Apartments; I remembered to turn on the tape-recorder, I didn't get the two sides of the cassette confused, and I asked the questions which I had prepared in advance.

But, at the same time, I was also following Hazel out of the corner of my eye, watching her wherever she went. Even when she was out of sight, I was watching her. It was a schizophrenic experience, working away while following her.

The article that I wrote for *Architectural Heritage* about the State Apartments at Hampton Court was liked; ditto Haze's photographs. This emerged when I went to see the editor—a rather nice but dull woman (as I then thought her) called Cynthia—in order to discuss what I was going to write next for the magazine.

"Oh, I'm so glad you liked it," I responded, and then I began to tell her how magnificently Haze and I had got on, how much we had in common, how we had plans to go and see the Turners in the Tate Gallery together, and so on. We had something, I enthused. We had good chemistry. We worked well together.

Of course, inevitably, I overstated my case.

"I think you're telling me something else," said Cynthia, who was not lacking in insight, nor directness, for the next moment she said, "You want to fuck her, don't you?"

You have to picture the scene. We were in the offices of *Architectural Heritage*. It was on the eleventh floor of a nasty high-rise development in Coin Street near Waterloo. Below the window lay the Thames, grey and sooty-looking. There was a boat moving through the water.

Out of the corner of my eye I could see Cynthia regarding me. She was a blonde haired woman—the hair was dyed—in her fifties, who disguised the lines on her face every morning with the careful application of brown foundation. (I ran into her once, in a butcher's shop, one Saturday morning, when she was without her make-up; I failed to recognise her.)

Was I to tell the truth, or was I not? I wondered, not a little anxiously, as the boat chugged on below, the froth of its wake the same grey as city snow.

On the one hand, Cynthia might applaud my honesty, but on the other, she might just as easily lean across and say, "Thank you very much for being so candid, Morgan, but I think you will understand that I won't be putting you and Hazel together on any assignments in future."

Then I thought about Alexander the Great and the Gordian knot, as I often do in moments of moral queasiness, and I thought, oh, to hell with it.

I said, "Yes, I want to."

Cynthia put a finger under the fluffy bow of her blouse and scratched her neck.

"I can understand that," she said.

On the Thames the boat had passed and now half a dozen seagulls had settled in the water and were bobbing up and down in the waves the boat had left behind.

I feared a lecture looming; the older and experienced woman was about to warn the callow youth against the ensnarements of physical beauty. But Cynthia surprised me.

"I can understand that," she said again, "I would want to, I think, if I were you. Hazel is very beautiful."

133

Yes, she was beautiful but it wasn't beauty—or so I believed, that was the driving force here; it was the spirit inside her which I had glimpsed in Hampton Court—that was what I believed I was reaching for.

A period of intense courtship followed now between Hazel and myself. For our first outing we did lunch at a Lebanese reataurant in Marylebone ("Oh, I love the food, it oozes Middle-Eastern heat," she said); we took in a Rock Hudson/Doris Day movie at the National Film Theatre ("Isn't Doris subversive?" she said afterwards); we did a boring play at the Bush Theatre about the life and death of the photographer Margaret Bourke White ("What an inspiration," she said); we spent a day in Hyde Park reading—I read a Russian novel, she read the memoir of one of Louis XIV's mistresses ("It's so good to nourish the brain,") and so on.

Finally, Haze came to my flat one summer's evening, bringing a bottle of *Vinho Verde* and a large bunch of green grapes. We were in the kitchen. I was running the grapes under the tap. The water frothed and fizzed. I imagined the coldness of the fruit of the grapes. I heard myself saying, "I'd like you to stay tonight."

Surprised as I was by what had slipped out, it was as nothing compared to her reply.

"Yes, all right," she said.

There was a magnificent insouciance about it. Yes, sex let's do it, was what it said to me.

I didn't kiss her. I just turned off the tap and undid the drawstring of her cotton trousers. She slipped off her espadrilles. Her clothes dropped to the floor.

I led her to the bedroom. We had sex. I don't remember much about it except that her breasts were, surprisingly, much smaller than I had thought, and she was rather passive. Haze just lay there while I did it. In retrospect, and as described in cold print on the page, it seems a rather joyless occasion; however, at the time—no, it didn't seem like that at all. No, at the time, I saw what I now understand was a sort of disinterest on her part, as a stunning form of maturity.

We were grown-ups and we had decided to do this thing together. And it was going to be painless, angst-free, straight forward. Party on.

Sounds cold? Unengaged? But it didn't feel like that. It was what I liked then to think was adult, unfussy, unmessy.

After the event was over, we lay side by side on top of my bed together, and I had a good look at the body I had coveted for months. Her thighs were extraordinarily long and her pubic hair, I saw, was very black and very bushy.

"I want tea," she said, got up, went to the kitchen naked, made it and came back.

It was a summer's night. I lived then in a top floor flat in Little Venice. The bed was in an alcove in the huge living-room and the windows looked down to the communal garden. Haze carried her teacup to the window and sat down on a stool. I got up and went and stood behind her.

There were three young American boys in the garden below, playing with a frisbee, and in fact it is this moment, this post-coitus moment, that glows most brightly in the memory. Yes, more than the sex, this is what I remember from that first coupling; Hazel at the window and the lusty American voices rising from the darkness, and the flat, green, fluorescent plate that was the frisbee, floating through the air.

That was the start and what followed was like before—ethnic restaurants, films, plays, Sunday walks, the odd weekend away—the only difference was that now we slept together. Strangely, but not untypically, I have no real recollection of these times. Not of what we did at any rate. What I do remember, is that as we saw more and more of each other, I fell more and more deeply in love. And the key to that deepening and (laughable as this sounds) maturing of my feelings was her absence of feeling, her coolness, her 'O.K. I don't mind. What ever you say, Morgan', attitude. Air rushes into a vacuum, and similarly I found myself pouring everything into her.

Then, one night, we were in my flat (she never liked me going to her place in Kings Cross; she didn't want me, as she put it, to find out too much about her.) I had a gramme of cocaine and some beers and a bottle of wine. It was a very dry wine; very cold; very sharp. I remember that. Its taste and the sour taste of the cocaine crumbs which we picked up from the mirror and rubbed on our gums, these are the details I recall.

I was lying on the bed. Hazel was beside me, wriggling her toes. When people talk about cocaine they say it makes you speedy and that you talk too much. But sometimes it doesn't. Sometimes it does the opposite. Sometimes it makes you rather pensive and careful with your words.

I was holding my glass and observing the condensation as it formed on the outside. I could taste the bitter cocaine taste in my mouth and my head was filled with that lovely, fake, cocaine clarity. Haze was wearing a skirt and I had lifted it back from her knee and I was stroking her leg. The mirror was on the table, with the little white envelope of cocaine, the razor blade and the rolled-up bank note. A good sight. The CD on the CD player was *Let it Bleed*.

Suddenly, and totally unexpectedly, Haze said "I feel happy."

It was what I had been waiting to hear for months.

"Hazel," I said, "Hazel, darling."

She turned her face towards me wearing what I recognised was her alarmed expression. I had come across this look at other moments of intimacy or near intimacy, and it was her infallible means of preventing emotional disclosure. But I was fired by wine and coke. What did a look mean to me? Oh no, baby; I knew and I saw, suddenly and very clearly, what I had to do, and I was filled by the fatal inspiration (personally, I blame the coke for this), that despite any misgivings that I might have, tonight I was going to triumph.

"Hazel," I said, slipping my hand between her thighs, (slightly tasteless, I admit, but my feelings were utterly sincere), "Hazel, I want to marry you."

I came out strong. I came out straight. I took a drink, swallowed, rubbed my tongue over my gums. Hazel was the woman whom I thought I wanted to marry, and I had just told her; and now I settled back and waited for her to speak ...

And what happened? Nothing! Not, "No, I won't marry you." Not, "Morgan, do you mind if I think about it. Not, "How dare you". No, nothing, absolutely nothing was what happened.

"Well, Hazel ..." Eventually I had to speak, didn't I? "Do you not have anything you want to say? A response? Yes! No! Maybe!"

But Hazel simply took another drink and said "If I have another line of coke, I'll lay one out for you too, shall I?"

Later we undressed and got into bed and began to make love. I drunkenly whispered "I love you," to which her response was to put her warm and very lovely tongue into my mouth ... What followed was hell. This thing had happened—or at least for me it had happened; I had asked her to marry me. But it also hadn't happened, because she hadn't said anything. Suddenly, in the succeeding weeks and months, I began to see what a wonderful weapon silence is, what a massively brilliant device for control. If you don't respond to what is actually the truth of a situation, you achieve far more than you achieve with a rebuttal or a denial; what you achieve with silence (which the wankers in the Tory government of that day knew only too well), is that you disinvent; you make, by not responding, you make what has happened disappear.

In my case, what was disinvented, made to disappear as if by magic, was not only what I had asked, but the enormous weight of commitment which I obviously had to have felt in the first place in order to have asked her to marry me.

But nothing had happened because nothing had been said and, therefore, we were able to go on seeing one another. We were able to go on having sex. We were able to drink wine and take coke together. And my dreadful impertinence asking her to marry me was never alluded to. Not by her.

I, on the other hand, couldn't keep Haze and what had happened out of my thoughts, and I endlessly found myself talking to close friends about her and what my friends called for no good reason, 'le situation'.

At the beginning, the advice which I received from friends—including Cynthia (who became a confidant during this period)—was that I was not to worry. "Oh, she'll come round to you," Cynthia used to say, "her biological clock is ticking away."

It made sense. I agreed.

But then weeks became months, and the quality of the advice changed. "Have a good time," Cynthia used to say, "but don't bank on her."

I always felt Cynthia wanted to say something harsher about Haze when we had our heart-to-hearts, but forbore from doing so. If she vilified Hazel too much I would stop listening to her and she would lose what influence she had. So I went on complaining about the necessity for relationships to progress (my late-eighties anthem), the importance of commitment, fidelity, blah blah, and Cynthia went on listening and advising me to enjoy myself with Hazel but to put my heart elsewhere.

It was good advice. 22 carat. I paid no attention. I was 'in love'. This went on for two years. Then, through Cynthia, Haze and I were asked to do a job together.

II

The piece was to be about a castle on the Antrim coast. It was owned by a family called the Picots who had arrived in Ireland with the Normans and somehow contrived to hold on to their property (possibly because they changed their religion half-a-dozen times during the intervening seven hundred years.) The owner was a brigadier, ex-British Army, and our brief was to produce three thousand glowing words on the history and architecture of his pile, illustrated with a dozen or two magnificent photographs. The Brigadier was an unknown quantity but Cynthia was fairly certain about one thing. The Picots were not poor Anglo-Irish folk living out the twilight of their days in a hostile land. The Picots had money which came, bizarrely, from a successful sardine and pilchard canning operation which they owned in Spain. "I don't want anything melancholy or elegiac," were Cynthia's last words to me on the telephone, "I want something upbeat."

Haze and I flew together to Aldergrove and drove north through the Glens. Grey rain was falling on the landscape which was half-green, half-brown. Eventually we found Picot Castle standing on its lonely promontory with a view of the grey sea. It was surrounded by a very high, very thick, stone wall.

"We're in Ireland all right," said Haze, unnecessarily I thought, as we drove into the keep and under the portcullis. On the far side we emerged to find ourselves facing a big, square, Norman bawn with windows and turrets. This was Picot Castle. It was a pillbox, medieval yes, but nonetheless a pillbox.

We parked at the front door and got out. The Royal Coat of Arms hung above the lintel; there were little gun slits at the side which had been glazed sometime in the eighteenth century; and furthermore, which greatly surprised me, there was an intercom. I pressed the buzzer.

"Yes, hello." The voice was that of a woman, a toff alright but her tone was warm and friendly. "You've come to see my father."

"This is true," I said.

"I will tell him. Then I will come and open the door. Welcome to our house."

A few moments later the door scraped back and voice was standing before me in person.

And she was everything I didn't like—or at least I didn't like then. She was short, brown haired, a little plump; she was wearing a dress and make-up. I couldn't stop myself looking back at the car where Hazel, slim and long legged, her face fresh, clean and unmade up, was retrieving our bags and her cameras.

"My father is coming down," I heard the voice behind. I turned back. She introduced herself as Anne (never a name I had liked) and explained that she was the owner's daughter. Then we shook hands, and I noticed that her skin was cold.

It took in all five, maybe ten seconds and in that time I had already made my mind up and decided that Anne belonged in the 'Not of interest' box.

Shortly afterwards, the owner appeared. He was in his mid-sixties and dressed exactly as I might have predicted; he wore a Prince-of-Wales flat cloth cap and a green Barbour jacket, a tweed jacket and a tie underneath.

"Have you seen that?" he asked, after we shook hands. He pointed above the door.

"Yes." I nodded. I had noticed the Royal Coat of Arms. "When my family had their lands restored by Charles II 'cos they supported him," the Brigadier explained, "of course the king didn't have any bloody money to give them (the Picots spent a fortune supporting a regiment) and so the king said that in lieu of cash, they could put that thing up. But it didn't pay any bloody bills!"

Hazel had drawn her camera out of its case. She was looking up and simultaneously winding on the film.

"Don't you think that would be somewhat obvious," said the Brigadier to Haze, "Royal Coat of Arms as shorthand for Irish Ascendancy?"

"The light's good," said Hazel, side-stepping the Brigadier who was blocking her path.

The camera shutter clicked.

It was time for some diplomacy. A little massaging of the ego. Rule number one of managing the stately home owner. Having slapped him or her, flatter immediately.

"How do you like to be called, sir?" I said. "Are you Brigadier Picot?"

"Round here they call me sir, and they usually do so before rather than after they do something," he said.

He looked straight at Hazel, waited a beat to ensure that his remark had hit home, and then continued, "But you can call me Michael."

We entered the house. The door closed behind us. The key was turned in the lock. We traipsed across the gaunt Irish hall with its bare black painted floorboards, empty fireplace and vast turf box.

We climbed a bare wooden staircase to the first floor. We left our bags down and went into the library. It was a small, compact room, lined with bookcases, and with mullioned windows at one end which overlooked the bawn below.

"Sit down."

Our host indicated an armchair and sofa.

"I'm not allowed to sit on low chairs because some years ago I did my back in."

"How?"

"So I've got a good excuse for keeping my own chair, if you know what I mean."

Selective deafness is a very old trick with stately home owners, but I persisted.

"How did you do your back in?"

"Wielding a pick-axe. I farmed. I don't think it's very wise starting to farm, which I did, at the age of forty-seven."

"Where?"

"Around here."

"I see."

"I was in the Guards." he continued. "My father was. My brothers too. We all four were, we four boys. I suppose you want my background?"

"No, I don't think he does." It was Anne, wheeling in a trolley. There was a large plate with small white sandwiches sprinkled with cress, several pieces of fine bone china, and a teapot in a striped woollen tea-cosy.

The dance which followed was one I had been through many times before. Tea was served. I got out my tape recorder and asked if I could turn it on. "Yes," said Michael. I began to ask questions about the two eighteenth-century architects who had been brought—one from London, one from Dublin—to work on Picot Castle. My host answered. He was formal to begin with; these big house owners always are; but gradually, seeing I wasn't a fool and that my questions were fairly intelligent, he began to relax, open up; he even tried one or two rather pallid jokes.

Haze, meanwhile, sat sipping her tea and nibbling egg mayonnaise sandwiches. She was waiting for the conversation to reach the point where she could say "Excuse me, do you mind if I take some photographs?" Long experience working in the field together, and long experience of each other in bed I suppose, had made us very, very good at gauging together when was the right time to ask. We never got it wrong. (Well, almost. We'd got it wrong on the doorstep but I think by now that was forgotten.) I was brilliant at the shmoozing part and she was very acute and sensitive to the tiny little movements I would make with my head meaning, Yes, Go, or No, Stop, Don't ask yet. We were almost telepathic, and that's the irony of course; we never spoke so much or so eloquently or so truthfully, as when we were in a room together speaking in our secret language of nods and winks about the subject of the interview, its progress, and so on.

Anyhow, at some point I became aware of Haze looking sideways at me and in response I looked sideways back at her and made a very slight movement. No one else would have seen it but I know that she saw it because she flashed back her 'I'm-impatient-to-get-on' look.

Again, I made a just barely perceptible movement of my head.

No, not yet, it said. My gesture was very categorical. Not yet!

Her response was to openly shake her head, in exasperation. Michael, meanwhile, was staring at me with his slightly hooded blue eyes and I saw that he hadn't seen but I saw that Anne had. She had seen Haze and I semaphoring.

Anne reached the plate of sandwiches towards Hazel and mouthed "Do you want a cup of tea," and then put her hand over her mouth and looked at the tape recorder and then at me.

"I haven't spoilt it, have I?"

People's exaggerated deference to the sensitivity of tape recorders, which they treat like ancient dowagers, is something I have always found amusing and touching in some way that is difficult to put into words.

I smiled and shook my head. Anne smiled back. I saw that Anne had a rather strangely shaped face; she also had a high forehead, very clean, very clear grey eyes, and a generous mouth. It was the same woman I had seen downstairs, but it was not the same woman. Her face was appealing, or strangely stirring.

At the very moment I was having this insight, and while Michael Picot was still talking, I become aware that Hazel had stood up and was walking over to her camera case. This was sitting on the oak table in front of the window. Hazel then opened her camera box noisily, pulled out a camera and turned back towards me.

I made a big and expansive and absolutely unmissable gesture. I shook my head, hugely. But Haze glowered back at me and I knew she was just going to go right ahead and do what she wanted, and no one was going to stop her.

A millisecond later my stomach began to tremble with the release of adrenalin. It's amazing how quickly the body works.

I continued to watch Hazel out of the corner of my eye as she came back to her seat and dumped herself down. Michael, oblivious to what was happening, was still rambling on about the difficulties the English architect, Jonathan Ashford, had with his Italian plasterers and the peat content of the local water; it had discoloured the Italian plaster.

Now everything went in slow motion. "The peaty water made the plaster go a sort of pale brown," Michael was saying. Haze raised her camera, and next moment I heard the shutter clicking.

Michael turned round and glared at Haze.

"What did you do that for?" he demanded firmly, and then he continued, gently but still firmly, "You didn't ask." His manner at this moment surprised me. There was no anger or temper, no attempt to pull rank. His tack was much cleverer because it alluded to something human—the fact that we all like to be asked, because it gives us the freedom to be able to say yes or no.

Hazel, who should have known better, much much better, because she

141

had been doing this sort of work for years, had violated an important part of the contract, the unspoken but nonetheless very clearly understood rules and terms of agreement, which exist when two people come into a rich stranger's private house with the license to probe and pry and take photographs.

But why had she broken the rules? Telepathy, of course. Fatally, I had allowed to seep from my thoughts to hers, the sense I had that Anne was pretty and her mouth was nice. It made Hazel very angry because never, until now that is, had I shown any interest in anybody else but herself. But I did, I had—and that made her irate, jealous, incandescent.

However, the way Haze showed her anger was not by shouting at me; she did it by taking the photograph. (It is not for nothing that when you go to work with your camera, you do something which is called shooting. The camera is a weapon, oh yes, with which we hurt, humiliate and murder, usually while pretending we are doing something noble, warm-hearted and generous.)

Now at the very same time that I was realising all of this, I was also aware—because the auto-pilot is still working—that Michael's remark, "You didn't ask," was still there, hanging in the air.

Something was going to have to be said, and as it wasn't going to be Hazel who would, it was going to have to be me.

I cleared my throat.

"What we're trying to do," I said, "is a bit different from what photographers and writers normally do on assignments of this kind. Usually the work is formal and posed, but what we're trying to do is the very opposite of that. What we're trying to do is something informal, unposed."

"So you want me as I am, *au naturel*. Well, I'll get this bloody tie off then," and he smiled.

III

That evening, the four of us ate together in the dining room (the Brigadier's wife was dead, Anne was his only child) and for reasons that I can't recall, the subject under discussion was the environment. The old soldier, like many of his class, had strong leanings towards conservation and the preservation of the landscape, et cetera. But Hazel, who thought of herself as greener than green, was quite unable to accept that the old fellow was anything less than a perfidious rural pollutor. With what I didn't think was particular astuteness, she wheeled the conversation round to shooting and fox hunting, and when Michael Picot foolishly fell into the not very cunningly laid trap by admitting that he had indulged, when younger, in both these pastimes, Hazel pounced.

"How can you call yourself a caring man when you've set your dogs on foxes and had them torn to pieces! When you've murdered ducks by pricking them with dozens of lead pellets! ..." She went on like this for some while.

Unfortunately, Haze had not noticed the old man's plate. We were eating steak and carrots, while his dinner in fact was a nut cutlet. The cunning bastard was a vegetarian and he allowed Haze to dig her own grave before he quietly said, "I don't hunt any more because I don't eat meat or fish."

Hazel went red when she heard his words, and then, as people so often do when they've been made to look foolish, she got affronted. She huffed and puffed and called Michael Picot "contemptible", "callow" and "complacent". He parried by politely enquiring if she really meant what she was saying. In his old-fashioned and gallant way, he was giving her the opportunity to withdraw. Unfortunately, she didn't want to make the peace.

To cut a very long story short, we then got on to the subject of tactics. Hazel adumbrated that it was a jolly good idea for conservationists to tie themselves to Norwegian whaling boats, or to throw themselves before the bulldozers of Canadian lumberjacks.

"You won't get anywhere unless you bully them," she said, "you've got to bully, bully, bully."

Now I, who was sympathetic to a great deal of what Hazel was saying, felt myself suddenly feeling very irritated at the way she used this word.

But before I could start, I heard Anne speaking from the other side of the table.

"Surely you don't actually mean that it's good to bully, do you? You can't be serious?"

"I am."

"Bullying is something that's horrible, isn't it? Bullies bully other, weaker children at school and make them cry. Are you seriously saying that's what we should be doing?"

"Yes, we must bully, it's the only thing they understand."

"Who?"

"The multinationals. They have such power, they have to be bullied and humiliated."

And as I sat there listening to Hazel's declaration of the right of the

143

green to hurt, and Anne's quiet and reasonable rebuttal of this position, I saw my entire life with Hazel unfurling before my mind's inner eye, from the moment we met for the first time in the Maze at Hampton Court, to this present moment in the dining-room of Picot castle.

Thus, I saw our first meeting, our first date if you like, in the Lebanese restaurant. I was early and I saw myself waiting. I saw the tables and the chairs, the pink table-cloths and the dark-skinned waiters. I also recalled the smell of tahini and parsley, and the aniseed drink on the table. And then I recalled looking out through the window of the restaurant while I sat there, and seeing Hazel walking out of the Seymour Baths on the far side of the road, and then walking across to the restaurant.

"I love this place, it's so romantic," she said, when she came in, (for the venue was her choice) "and I love the way it oozes Mediterranean heat." I agreed and I was charmed.

However, as I recalled the moment now, sitting in a freezing Irish dining-room, I was forced to admit that in all probability, the true reason for chosing the venue was convenience. It was opposite the gym where she went to her aerobics class. Proximity to her previous engagement; that's why we were there, and all the stuff about it being Middle Eastern and exotic and so forth, that was all guff, 22 carat crap.

While the ecological debate continued, I shuffled on to the next memory, our visit to the National Film Theatre, and I saw that her observation that Doris Day was a rebel who challenged Hollywood, this was nothing more than a re-hash of the thinking of the times. It wasn't her opinion at all; it was the opinion of the film critic at *Time Out*.

I went on to our third outing, and it was the same—more fakery; and on and on I went, spooling through the years and the hours, and every single event, it now seemed to me, had something untrue at the centre from which, until this moment, I had averted my gaze.

All this happened in a matter of seconds (whereas it seemed like hours), and when I turned back to the table, I was quite surprised to discover that the conversation was more or less as it had been only a few moments earlier, only the subject now was sealing.

With what enormous rapidity do you see and understand and comprehend something very enormous and, having seen, with what speed do you then change. Your epiphanous insight hits you, you turn 180 degrees and, in a fraction of a second, you find yourself facing in entirely the opposite direction to the direction which you were facing a moment earlier.

I looked across at Anne. Her face was lovely in the candlelight. And at that moment I knew, and I knew that she knew too.

Of course what happened then was ugly and mucky. Hazel and I spent the night together in a four-poster bed. We made love. I fell asleep to the sound of the sea sighing in the distance, with Hazel lying on my shoulder. We made love again in the morning. Then we went back to London. It was as if nothing had happened. But something huge had happened. A week later, I rang the Picot's, ostensibly to check some facts. As I had hoped, Anne answered. We talked and talked. She came to London ...

Our insights—like that I had had at the Picot's dining table—are marvellously quick and efficient. We understand and we see so clearly. Alas, we do not then act on what we know. We prevaricate, we dither. We don't know, we think maybe we're wrong, we doubt our certainties ... But in the end they can't be avoided, or this one couldn't be avoided and, to cut a very long story short, Anne and I, we married. Yes, I married Anne. But it's not the ceremony that is the point, not in this story. The point is that somehow, out of all of this, out of knowing that I loved someone, and that they loved me back, I found, I hardly dare to say it, my voice, and I began properly, seriously, unselfconsciously, to write down one word after another. In other words, I began.

Four Pesos

I

SHE WAS ALWAYS LATE, so this once Mary determined to be early. She was at the café by half-past ten although their meeting was arranged for eleven.

It was the slack period between breakfast and lunch and *Pierre's* was almost empty at that time of the morning. The only customers were an ancient couple eating muffins. They were chewing slowly, patiently, with blank expressions on their old, creased faces. And the reason they ate so very slowly, she found herself thinking, as she took off her coat and hung it up, was because they had so much time on their hands.

But a moment after, Mary regretted having such a sour thought. What did she know about this husband and wife who were each, she guessed, in their eighties? Of course she was anxious, she told herself, about what was looming, and the effect was to make her temporarily mean spirited.

Mary sat down at a table in the corner, made a porthole in the condensation on the window, and looked out at the grey city snow piled on the sidewalk outside. For the next few minutes her mind was empty.

Peter arrived just two minutes before eleven, as always prompt and punctual. As he sat down she saw that he had seen the envelope which she had brought and which was lying in front of her on the table. It was a long white envelope with a bulge in the corner.

"There isn't much to say," he said.

"No, there isn't much to say," she agreed.

She felt a pain inside, somewhere behind her stomach, pressing outwards. This was not how the conversation was meant to go. This was not how she had envisaged it. This was the moment of termination, long anticipated, but now that it had arrived, she was resisting.

"Have we come to the end of the road?" she heard herself asking.

146

"I'm sorry," he said, picking up his gloves, "I never thought this would happen."

Which was why he had come, she realised, to say these words. Then he stood up and walked out of the door of *Pierre's* into the Montreal street and back to his life as a civil engineer on Prince Edward Island. Just like that. He hadn't even taken off his coat.

The envelope, she thought, I've forgotten to give it to him, and with the sharp end of her spoon she pressed on that part of the paper that was stretched over her wedding ring inside like a drum skin, and she went on pressing until at last the paper broke.

Mary finished her coffee and asked for another. It came and she drank it without thinking about anything, and then, when it was finished, she put on her coat and walked slowly outside. There was a cold wind blowing up the street between the high buildings on either side. Mary stopped, took her hat out of her pocket and pulled it onto her head and down over her ears.

"Hey!"

Mary turned and saw the young man who had served her was calling from the café doorway.

"You forgot this."

He was holding her envelope towards her. Mary took it with her mittened hand and put it in her pocket.

At the end of the afternoon, Mary booked seven days of February sun in Cuba. Two days later she flew first to Havana, then on to the provincial town of Cienfuegos. Here she caught a gleaming tourist bus which would take her to the hotel.

There was a public address system in the bus and among the tunes played she recognised *Eine Kliene Nachtmusik*. Outside the coach window, Mary could see an undulating landscape of red-brown earth and green sugar cane. Her first impression was that Cuba didn't look very interesting. Then, from the top of a hill, she suddenly saw the blue sea in the distance and her heart lifted. But a few minutes later, it sank again, when she saw the hotel where she was going to be staying.

The *Cienfuegos Excelsior* was a gaunt, white, modern building standing in the middle of nowhere. It really did look as if it had been dropped there from the air.

Mary registered at the desk and changed some money. She was only allowed to change ten dollars, and in return she was given eight pesos.

"In Cuba, tourists pay for almost everything in hard currency," the clerk told her, "so you'll hardly spend these pesos in a week."

A bellboy with bow legs showed Mary up to her room on the fourth floor. She gave him a dollar tip and he left the room whistling. She opened the balcony doors, went outside and leant on the parapet wall. Beyond the swimming pool, which was just below, and the grounds of the hotel beyond, she could see a channel, half-a-mile wide, which connected Cienfuegos bay to the Caribbean, and on the other side of the channel she could see a village which came right down to the water's edge. It was then she noticed the wall at the front of the village on which was written, for the benefit of those in the hotel presumably, *Bienvenidos Cuba Socialista*.

II

It was dark when she left her bedroom that first evening. In the lift Mary pressed the wrong button and, when the doors opened, she found herself not in the lobby, as she expected, but in the basement below.

Mary was going to stay in the lift and let it take her back up, but then she noticed that in the middle of the basement there stood a shop with large glass windows. She wandered across and went in.

The shop was filled with racks of clothes, fans, televisions, and other electrical items, bottles of liquor, and cosmetics—all prices marked in US dollars. There were customers milling around and, judging by the way they spoke and acted, she assumed they were all eastern European workers—Czechs, Russians, Hungarians—and they were in the shop to spend the hard currency with which they had been paid. Mary bought a packet of *Marlboro Lights*, paid a dollar (she knew they wouldn't take her pesos), and was returned 20 cents change.

After supper in the cavernous dining-room, Mary went back to her room. Her handbag was lying on her bed. Before she knew what she was doing, in other words before she could stop herself doing what she knew she must not do, she had taken the photograph out of the side pocket, and looked at it.

It was a photograph of her husband, Peter, taken when she first knew him, when he was a student and had a moustache and long hair. She felt a little kick inside and heard laughter from below. She went out onto the balcony, and saw people were sitting around the swimming pool underneath.

Mary put on lipstick and went down straight away. The pool was large, with tables and chairs arranged around the edge and a bar at the far end. She sat down. A waiter brought her a beer and took away a dollar.

"*Bon soir*," she heard and realising she was being addressed, she looked up and saw a man. She guessed he was about the same age as herself, early thirties.

The man came forward and introduced himself as Eduardo. He explained that he was in charge of customer relations in the hotel. He asked if he could sit down and was already reaching for the chair when she said, "Yes."

"How are you enjoying our beautiful country?" he asked.

"I've only just arrived."

"Would you like another beer?"

She nodded and he called out, "Psst, psst," to the old waiter. It was an extraordinarily offensive sound which she had heard the Cuban men along the bar making already at the waiters; nonetheless, she was surprised to hear this man make this sound; he had been so polite up to this point.

The old waiter brought two *Claros*, as the local beer was called. There was a jukebox and somebody put on a record. It was a song in Spanish. Two girls started dancing, jumped into the pool with their clothes on, were pulled out by two men, and went on dancing, their wet dresses hugging now against their bodies. Eduardo smiled and Mary smiled back at him.

III

The next morning Mary was woken by the sound of rapping on her bedroom door. She sat up in bed, a little dazed, trying to remember the Spanish from her phrasebook for, 'Come back later'.

Then the door opened and a trolley appeared, followed by a black woman in her thirties. The woman was wearing a nylon housecoat, and the top of her trolley was piled with sheets and towels. Mary realised it was the chamber maid. The maid said something in Spanish and backed out, closing the door.

Mary went down to the dining-room. She took a table at the far end from where she could look out over the channel to the village on the other side. Eduardo had told her the village was called Jagua, and boasted a sixteenth-century Spanish fort. After some minutes, a cup of coffee arrived; it was oily and sweet tasting, and it had been made, Mary realised as she drank it, with condensed milk.

When she went back upstairs, Mary found her bedroom door was open and heard music coming from the bedside radio inside.

"*Hola*," the maid greeted Mary as she came into her room. It was the

149

maid who had woken Mary up earlier. The maid had a pillow gripped under her chin and was working a clean pillowcase around the end.

Mary went into the bathroom, sharpened her kohl pencil and began to run it around the rims of her eyes.

"Ah, *que lindo*."

In the mirror Mary saw the maid had come into the bathroom behind her. She was holding the dress Mary had left on her bed—she had planned to wear it later—the domino dress that had been a present from her husband on their first wedding anniversary. It was white and green and decorated with dominoes. Mary liked it more than any other single thing that she wore. It made her feel lucky.

"*Es muy bonito*," said the maid holding the dress up against Mary's body.

"*Si, si*," the maid continued, looking her up and down.

Then the maid caught Mary's eye, and put a hand over her mouth to stop herself laughing at her own audacity. Mary felt herself smiling. She walked out onto the balcony and looked across at the cranes and the rising blocks of flats in the distance beyond Jagua. This was a new town, Eduardo had told her, and was still in the process of being built. It was going to house workers from the new nuclear power station.

IV

Eduardo had also mentioned, as they had talked by the pool the night before, that there was a bus to the town of Cienfuegos.

Wearing the domino dress, Mary now went down to the lobby to enquire about this, and to her surprise she found Eduardo sitting at a table beside the hotel desk. There was a poster on the wall beside him advertising the Cuban National Ballet.

"Very beautiful," said Eduardo, pointing at the ballerina in the middle of the poster. The dancer was rising on her toes and her shoes were tied with silk stays around her ankles. Then Eduardo smiled, showing his immaculately white teeth.

It now crossed Mary's mind that when he had introduced himself the night before, Eduardo had lied to her. He wasn't in charge of customer relations as he'd told her. He just sold tickets for the ballet and other 'touristic attractions', as the Cubans called them.

"Today I am a servant," said Eduardo suddenly, as if reading her mind. Then he shouted, "Psst," across the lobby, and a young man who was walking past came over and agreed to mind the table for a while.

Eduardo brought Mary behind the hotel desk. He showed her a map of the area on the wall. Then he wrote down the times of the buses.

"Have you money?" he asked.

"Only about eight pesos," said Mary.

"That's fine. You won't spend that in Cienfuegos."

Mary went outside and made her way to the bus-stop. It was on the brow of a hill about a quarter of a mile from the hotel. There were several Cubans waiting there. She showed her pesos to a man and he pointed to the ten centavos piece she was going to need to pay the driver. Finally, the bus came, and she crowded on with everyone else. There were no seats but someone got up and gave his place to her.

Mary smiled and sat down. The bus lurched off, the standing passengers swaying together and jostling her. Mary was uncomfortable and crushed but, for the first time in ages, she realised she was not completely miserable. She looked at the black tulle bow tied in the hair of the child in the seat in front, and then at the beautifully smooth shaven armpit of the woman standing beside her and who was holding onto the handrail overhead. The woman's skin, Mary saw, was dusted with talcum powder.

Yes, it was a good idea to have come to Cuba, she thought. It wasn't going to vanquish the pain—no, how could it?—but it was going to take her out of herself, and at that thought, her spirits rose another notch or two.

In Cienfuegos, the sun beat down into the still streets of low, Spanish-looking houses. Mary found an ice-cream parlour and went inside. It was a cool room with iron tables and chairs, a zinc counter, and a couple of waitresses in white blouses and black skirts.

Mary sat down at a table and waited. Nothing. She lit a cigarette. Nothing. She tried to catch the eye of the waitresses who were standing talking. Nothing. She tried to say, "Psst," as she had heard Eduardo and others doing, but lacking the courage to do so forcefully, Mary's version came out as a limp, snake-like "Ssss", instead, which of course was totally ineffectual.

At last Mary got up to leave and, as she did, one of the waitresses approached her.

"*Aqui esta cerrado*," said the waitress, "*pero alli esta abierto.*"

She ran a hand down the middle of the ice-cream parlour and Mary understood.

Where she had been sitting was closed, for some mysterious reason known only to Cubans, while the other half of the ice-cream parlour was open.

Mary transferred to a new table on the other side of the invisible line. The waitress gave her a menu listing many different flavours. Mary pointed at what she thought was coconut.

"*No hay.*"

The waitress waggled a finger flecked with old nail varnish and then pointed. It was either chocolate or vanilla. Mary chose vanilla.

She looked out into the street as she waited for the ice-cream to come. The impression Mary was forming was that in Cuba there was nothing to buy, unless she counted the Dollar shop in the basement of the hotel, where she hadn't seen any Cubans anyway. The shops in the city of Cienfuegos all had queues outside and hardly anything on sale inside. The cars she had seen were all old U.S. cars, many of which looked as if they were in imminent danger of falling to pieces. All the houses were also very decrepit looking, with tiled roofs and cracked walls from which the paint was invariably flaking away. It was the opposite of Montreal in every way, but Mary decided that she liked it. Yes, as she had thought on the bus—she was getting out of herself, and that was good.

V

The following morning, Mary was woken early by a knock on her door.

"*Campanera?*" The maid, the one from the day before, now appeared at the end of Mary's bed. The maid was wearing a head scarf and had a piece of graph paper which she showed Mary. On the graph paper there was a childish drawing of a dress with a pocket on the left breast. The maid began to speak slowly in Spanish while pointing at the picture. But it wasn't until she she wrote $11.00 and then 44 pesos, that Mary realised what was happening. She patted the bed and the maid sat down on the very edge. Mary pointed at the dress and then in the direction of the basement and the Dollar shop, and the maid nodded ecstatically.

"What colour?"

The maid looked puzzled for a moment and then started to look around the room.

"*Rojo ... marron ... verde, no importa.*"

"Any colour, O.K. then, big or small?" Mary asked, moving her hands.

The maid pointed at Mary. Mary pointed at herself.

"Like me," she said.

The maid nodded.

"Eleven dollars," said Mary pointing.

152

"*Aqui*," the maid pointed at the other figure, "*es igual a cuarenta y cuarto pesos*." Her rate was four times the official one.

Mary took the pen and wrote out her name. The maid did likewise. The maid's name was Pata. The women smiled and shook hands.

After breakfast, Mary went to the Dollar shop in the basement. As she was searching through the clothes on a rack, she suddenly realised this task was absorbing her to such an extent, she had actually forgotten her ache for a couple of seconds. Her self-consciousness brought the pain back, of course, but surely, she thought, this remission, albeit short-lived, represented a massive step forward.

Mary bought a medium-sized denim dress like the one in the drawing with a pocket on the left breast, and paid in dollars. Then, for no particular reason, she walked up to the lobby to catch the lift back to her floor. Eduardo was waiting by the call button.

"Mary," he said, "are you still liking our beautiful country?"

"Yes."

The lift door opened. They stepped in.

"Which floor?" Eduardo asked.

"Fourth"

"Me too. Today I check on the maids up there."

The lift stopped. They stepped out and started to walk along the walkway in the direction of her room. All the bedroom doors on this level were a vivid, hideous orange. Pata was at the other end of the balcony, wheeling her trolley towards them. As Pata drew closer, Mary thought she saw the chamber-maid moving her head as if to say 'No', although the movement was very faint and certainly imperceptible to Eduardo. But Mary saw it and acted instantly. She put the bag with the dress behind her back, in rather the same way as she might have hidden something when she was at convent school.

Mary and Eduardo drew level with Pata.

"Goodbye," said Eduardo, stopping, "I have to talk to this maid." He put his hand out and squeezed Pata's shoulder.

"Goodbye," Mary said.

As she unlocked her door, Mary heard Pata shrieking. She turned and saw that Pata was swinging at Eduardo with the flat of her hand. Eduardo caught Pata's wrist and started to laugh. Neither seemed to be aware that Mary had seen.

Half an hour later, Mary found Pata in a bedroom at the other end of the walkway. The maid seized the dress and immediately thrust it under a pile of towels where it could not be seen. Then Pata pulled her purse out

153

of her overall pocket and opened it. There were ten crumpled pesos inside. She handed them to Mary and wrote 34 with her finger on the wall.

"Thirty-four pesos," said Mary.

"*Trienta y cuatro, manana, si.*"

"What about Eduardo?" Mary said.

Pata made an 'O' with finger and thumb and then jabbed the index finger of her other hand in and out of the hole. Then she sighed a couple of times as if she was having sex.

"*Es un jefe. Me desea.*"

VI

Pata woke her the next morning with the money she owed Mary and another drawing. This time it was of a jacket. Mary agreed she would buy it, again at a price of eleven dollars.

After breakfast, Mary went down to the Dollar shop. While she was looking through the jackets hanging on a rack, an argument broke out in Spanish between a young man smoking a cigar who appeared to be drunk, and the girl at the cash desk. Almost immediately, two policemen arrived with night sticks and revolvers slapping against their thighs. They slapped the young man, made his nose bleed, and then dragged him towards the door.

As Mary stared in amazement, she heard someone saying, "Cubans aren't allowed in the Dollar shops."

She turned and saw she was being addressed by a man in a white peaked hat who had clearly noticed her appalled expression. "In Hungary," he continued, "we wouldn't put up with it, shops like this for foreigners only."

He was about fifty, with very bright, blue eyes.

"I thought it was just our police who did that sort of thing," said Mary.

"Pity the poor Cuban caught with dollars," the Hungarian mused, "or caught with anything from here."

He held one wrist over the other, indicating handcuffs.

Mary quickly found something like the jacket in Pata's drawing, and when she came to pay her hands were shaking. They were still shaking when she handed the garment over to Pata ten minutes later.

"*Pesos, manana,*" said Pata as she hid the jacket under the towels as she had done with the dress the day before. "*Manana.*" She pushed her trolley away along the walkway.

"*Manana ...*" she called again over her shoulder.

VII

On Thursday morning, Pata came into Mary's bedroom and dropped a bundle of crumpled notes onto her bedside table.

"*Ciao y gracias*," she said. Pata quickly shook Mary's hand and sped from the room.

Mary counted the notes. They were four pesos short. She felt annoyed. It was a cheap trick, and the type of deception that was only practised on foreigners.

She went to the beach and lay in the sun. At lunch-time she went to the Cuban cafeteria by the roadside where, she had discovered, she could spend her pesos.

In the afternoon it was so hot down by the sea, Mary had to sit under one of the reed umbrellas. She had a book—a novel by Danielle Steele— but when she tried to read, she found that although she could decipher the individual words, she could not see how one linked to the next linked to the third. The text was literally meaningless to her. So after a few minutes fruitless struggle, she closed her book and began staring out to sea.

For a while, she had imagined Cuba was going to save her, or at least divert her from her own anguish. But Pata's little scam had put paid to that. As she watched the waves running up the sand, Mary felt as if the small bulwark against despair—laboriously thrown up over the previous few days—was now crumbling away. Next, she sensed herself growing melancholy; and finally, although she tried to resist this, she could not stop herself remembering the events as they had occurred ...

It started the evening Peter came home to their flat in Montreal and told her about the job.

"I don't think you should come with me," he said, when he had finished.

"Why?"

"The job's temporary. I'm coming back. Why uproot both of us?"

Mary didn't agree but she acquiesced. He went away. She felt lonely. He felt lonely as well, he said, stuck out in a camp on Prince Edward Island. This made her feel better.

Then, one day, his letter came. He'd been thinking. He'd gone away so he could do some thinking, he confessed, and now he'd come to a decision. He didn't think they were right for each other any more. That was exactly the phrase, and Mary could see it, just as he had written it in the letter in his small, sloping handwriting, 'I don't think we're right for one another'. There wasn't another woman, he said, and she believed him ...

Recollecting this now, Mary found herself starting to cry, and in order that no one would see her, she got up and went into the sea, squatted down and cried there for several minutes with the water lapping around her.

VIII

On Friday morning when she woke up, Mary felt her skin was sore and slightly tight. She had stayed a little too long in the sun, she thought, the day before, when she had cried in the sea.

In the restaurant she drank her usual cup of the sweet, oily coffee made with condensed milk, and afterwards walked down to the jetty below the hotel. She climbed aboard a water taxi which would take her across the sound. The boatman took her ten centavos and threw it into an old cigar box.

On the other side of the channel, the houses of Jagua came right down to the water. From the hotel, the front had seemed attractive, but when she got close she saw the ancient buildings were crumbling and dirty.

She disembarked onto a pier and wandered up the hill into the village. Her route took her past houses even more dilapidated than those at the sea front, and as she walked Mary glanced slyly into dark rooms where men sat on old car seats watching flickering black-and-white television sets, and children lay asleep on pieces of sacking on the floor, flies buzzing around them. There was a strong smell of refuse and sewage.

She looked around for a café in which to take refuge, but there wasn't one. However, she did notice a church at the top of the village, and at the sight of this small but solid looking building, her heart rose.

Hurrying towards it, Mary imagined the interior as quiet and cool and filled with the intoxicating smell of wax and incense. She reached the church door, opened it, and went in. She saw mould on a wall—smelt it as well—then saw a bare, bare altar, and half-a-dozen miserable pews. She turned straight round and marched back down to the jetty.

An hour later, walking along the balcony towards her bedroom, she was surprised to see Pata, without her trolley, coming towards her.

"Where's my four pesos?"

"*Si, si, manana, manana*," said Pata quickly. She had something behind her back and, as she passed, Pata kept her front to Mary so that she couldn't see what it was.

"Give," said Mary. "Now."

156

Pata turned and started to run and Mary saw what she'd been hiding behind her back; Pata was hiding her purse.

"Pata! What a cheap trick."

"*Manana*," the maid shouted, and disappeared down the service stairs.

<h2 style="text-align:center">IX</h2>

On Saturday morning, Mary was dressed and waiting in her room at seven o'clock.

After waiting until nearly nine, Mary went onto the balcony and saw Pata and her trolley outside a bedroom half-a-dozen doors away. Pata saw Mary too and fled into the bedroom.

Mary ran along the walkway after her.

When she reached Pata's trolley, Mary found the door beyond it was open, and Pata was inside by the bed.

"Four pesos," Mary shouted.

Pata shrugged, walked forward and tipped the door shut, right in Mary's face.

Mary took the lift to the lobby. Her intention was to speak to the manager, but when she stepped out into the lobby, she saw Eduardo was at his table. Without thinking, she ran across and told him everything. His face grew very dark and he looked angry. It worried Mary, who had thought no further than telling someone what had happened, but it was too late to undo her words. "Where is she?" Eduardo asked, and Mary heard herself saying, "Upstairs."

They travelled up in the lift together, and when they got to the balcony they saw Pata wheeling her trolley away from them.

"Is that her?" Eduardo asked.

"Yes," said Mary.

"Hey, *chica*," he called.

Pata stopped. He went forward, Mary following. Eduardo started shouting at Pata in Spanish. Pata looked at the ground and chewed her lip, and even with her face at that angle Mary could see Pata was frightened.

"It doesn't matter," Mary began to blurt. "I don't care about the money. Can't we just forget it?"

"Miss Mary," said Eduardo angrily, "what this one has done is very illegal; it's wrong; it's bad. She's going to be punished. Now you go to your room. I'll speak to you later."

His tone alarmed her. Mary thought it best to retreat. She went to her room, and closed the door carefully after herself. She could hear Eduardo shouting outside. After several minutes the shouting stopped. Mary opened her door and looked out.

There was no one on the walkway but Pata's trolley was still there, piled high with sheets and pillowcases. Mary crept along to the bedroom door which was nearest to the trolley. She put her ear to the wood, and it was then that she heard the sound of Eduardo making violent love to Pata on the bed inside.

X

On her last night, Mary did not sleep at all, and the next morning she was up well before seven. She dressed and went down to the dining room. Instead of taking her usual seat in front of the window, which looked across the water to Jagua, she sat with her back to the glass, facing towards the waitresses who stood in a cluster around the entrance to the kitchen. And instead of her usual single cup she drank five cups of the sweet, oily coffee. When she finished, Mary put five dollars under her saucer and left smiling.

Mary returned to the fourth floor. Stepping out of the lift she bumped into a maid she had never seen before. Mary smiled at the strange woman. She was pleased to see the staff were already at work at this early hour— it wasn't even eight yet—for this meant she would see Pata sooner rather than later. And she wanted to see Pata urgently, desperately; she wanted to make some sort of amends for what she had said, the trouble she had caused.

Mary started moving along the walkway briskly. There was a trolley half-in, half-out of a doorway. It was not her bedroom—that was much further down—but it was Pata's trolley, wasn't it? It had the same door on the side with the dent in it.

Mary ran forward. Her heart was beating, her hands were hot. She was excited and anxious. Something would come to her, she didn't know what, but something; a gesture, a phrase, something; and from whatever that was, Pata would not fail to understand how truly and deeply sorry Mary was.

Mary reached the door. She put her head around the lintel and then she saw, to her great surprise, that it wasn't Pata, but another woman, rounder, older, and white.

"Pata?" Mary asked. "Pa—ta?"

158

The maid lent her broom against the wall, licked her index finger and pointed into the distance, at Jagua, on the far side of the water.

"*Se acabo para ella.*"

Twice more the maid repeated the phrase and the gesture, and then Mary understood. Pata was gone; she had lost her job.

Back in her room, Mary folded her clothes without care and stuffed them into her case. At eleven o'clock the bow-legged bell hop came. He was not whistling. He carried her bag to the lift while she followed. They rode down to the lobby together in silence.

Coming out of the lift, Mary saw that Eduardo wasn't at his desk. This was disappointing, for now she couldn't smile at him, sarcastically, as she had planned.

She got onto the courtesy coach and made her way to the back. She sat and put her handbag down on the seat next to her so that none of the other tourists, who were travelling to the airport, could come and sit near her. The idea of any kind of conversation with anyone was unbearable. At the start, this vacation had promised to be wonderful, but it had turned out to be the worst vacation of her life, ever. All she wanted now was to go home to the north, to the cold, go to her apartment, and sleep, and until then, all she wanted was silence.

A few minutes later, the driver came aboard. It was the same man who had driven her at the start of the week. He drove the bus slowly out of the hotel car park and turned onto the main road.

Mary looked back, and as she saw the great, gaunt white form of the *Cienfeugos Excelsior Hotel* receding into the distance, thoughts of Pata came to her involuntarily. Mary had done something very stupid, something very small and petty, and she had possibly ruined someone's life.

For a few seconds, Mary registered her guilt as a hot feeling somewhere in her chest—it was a sensation like heartburn—but then that feeling was eclipsed by a great rush of different and much more powerful feelings ...

In a few hours she would be home, Mary thought, and she imagined herself coming out of the lift in the condominium where she lived, turning the key in the lock of the front door of her apartment, and stepping into her hall. It would smell of wood and coffee, she thought, as it always did, and in her mind's eye she could see the two letters on the side table addressed to Peter. They had come on the morning she had left for Cuba, and she had not had time to re-direct them. She would have to write out Peter's new address on them, and the very idea of doing this later now made her tremble ...

And as the bus rumbled on, Mary began to picture the evening which would follow ...

She would unpack; she would load the washing machine and turn it on; she would boil a can of soup; and at some point the ache which now throbbed would turn into a full blown, red-hot pain, like a burning coal in the middle of her being; and after that her mind would be filled with half-formed thoughts, with conversations and memories of Peter. These would overwhelm and exhaust her, but when she eventually went to bed, she would not be able to sleep for a long time, and would just lie in the darkness, wet-cheeked and mournful ...

When she had put her handbag on the seat beside her, Mary had sincerely believed that more than anything she wanted to be alone and home; now, minutes later, it seemed that she was dreading that.

Yes, that was true, she conceded to herself; but it was also enormously consoling and reassuring to know that she would be overrun and by what? She saw that too. All she had left of the marriage was the grief, but it was something, and that something was better than nothing.

Mary lifted her eyes and turned now to look at the village of Jagua beyond the foamy blue sound. A moment later she felt a hot tear trickling down her cheek and running into her mouth. She savoured its salty taste before swallowing. Pata was forgotten; Mary's thoughts were now entirely of herself.

There was an electronic click at the front of the coach as the public address system was turned on, and an instant later the first notes of *Eine Kleine Nachtmusik*—played not with real instruments, but with a synthesizer which imitated real instruments—began to drift from the speaker in the ceiling above Mary's head.

Connemara

I

IT WAS A LAND of low houses, small fields, and trees arched by wind. Rain hovered in the air like heat from a city street. The handkerchief in his pocket was damp: the steering wheel was cold and sticky in his hands: the moisture had even got under his fingernails, for Christ's sake!

Jack turned on the de-mister and hot air poured from the slits in the dashboard. The back of the glass began to clear and Jack felt his eyes growing tender from the heat.

He blinked and stared ahead. The narrow road coiled away through the brown, boggy landscape. They passed a hunchback with a coal scuttle who waved, and Benjamin, sitting beside Jack, waved back nonchalantly.

"They seem to wave to everyone here," said Benjamin, who was his best friend. "Have you noticed?"

On they went. He was vaguely aware of their boxes of geological equipment rattling in the back. He considered getting out to re-pack them but he decided it wasn't worth the soaking he would get. And besides, he scarcely heard the racket from behind; all his thoughts were on the road that wound ahead and what lay at the end of it. And these thoughts worried him now, nagging him like a sore tooth.

They stopped for lunch at an old quarry by a lake, and ate bread and tomatoes and processed cheese. Afterwards, they had monkey-nuts out of a red sock ...

It was still pouring with rain. Jack turned on the wipers, watched as the wet was swiped away and the grey lake water sprang back into view. Then Jack cracked a shell with his thumb-nail and put the kernel into his mouth. He felt a small but unpleasant tightening in his stomach. Why hadn't he written a letter? he wondered, and at least taken the curse of uncertainty out of the situation.

"It might not be very much fun this evening," he said quietly. He tossed the shell into the ashtray, where there were already many shells piled.

"Oh, I'm not worried," Benjamin replied. "Even if he's only half as good as your mad uncle in Armagh, I'll be happy."

"But he might not be there," said Jack.

"Of course he'll be there," said Benjamin, waving at the wet world beyond the window, "where else would he be?" and that closed the conversation.

II

They came to a 'V' in the road. One signpost pointed north and the other towards the village where his father now lived. Jack felt another flutter of apprehension as he followed the sign and drove on.

It had stopped raining around tea-time. Puddles lay along the margins. Jack could hear the tyres crashing through them. His thoughts were filled with innumerable images which together formed a speeded-up version of childhood. They were repeating themselves over and over again ...

The sequence began with the family holiday which they had taken together amongst the melancholy lakes around Roscommon—his mother, his father and himself. They travelled by camper van. It rained incessantly. He remembered his father, smoking *Woodbines*, grim and silent; his mother, weeping as she shredded one tissue after another until the pieces formed a heap on her skirt like a pile of snow; and himself, in the back of the camper van, with his *Spiderman Colouring Book*, and his waxy crayons impregnated with pencil shavings.

They had returned to London early from that holiday and, soon after, his father had carried away his possessions in cardboard boxes. "It's a trial separation," his mother had explained to him the first evening they were alone.

After that, his father would come to the flat on Saturdays, uncomfortable in a suit and tie and smelling of aftershave. He would exchange a few stilted words with his wife and then take Jack on awkward outings to Madame Tussauds and the Tower of London. Then, around the time of Jack's eleventh birthday, the meat packing company for whom his father had worked for several years, decided to re-locate to South Wales; they offered redundancy payments to those who didn't want to move. Jack overheard his father telling his mother about it in low tones as his parents stood one evening on the doorstep.

"It's risky," his father said, "but I've decided to go home and try my luck there." Then he added, "There's nothing left for me here."

Jack and his father had just returned from Greenwich—they had visited the Cutty Sark—and as he heard his father talking to his mother, he was staring at a postcard of the famous sailing ship which his father had bought for him that afternoon. For a moment he envisaged sending it to this father with the message: 'Don't leave me'. Then he realised he didn't have the address where his father lodged. He wasn't even certain that his mother had it. But, more importantly, he sensed that his father was unlikely to be swayed by his plea. So instead he stuck the postcard in his scrapbook that night and wrote underneath it in his childish writing, 'Dad gave Jack this'.

Their last outing together—before his father returned to Ireland—was a trip up the Thames on a pleasure boat, followed by strawberry sundaes in a coffee bar near Westminster Bridge. To round off the afternoon, they posed together in a passport photograph booth near the Houses of Parliament. While they were waiting on the pavement for the processed prints to drop into the wire cage at the side, his father's eyes filled with tears. Jack saw and looked away. His father pulled out his handkerchief and blew his nose loudly. The following day, when Jack woke up, he imagined his father was on the boat sailing back to Ireland, and all that day the thought stayed with him. He felt it as a pain somewhere in his chest.

During the years that followed, his father wrote to his mother from time to time, while at Christmas and on Jack's birthday, his father always sent a card and money for his son. Details of 'O' level results and 'A' level plans were sent across the Irish Sea in the opposite direction. Holidays with his father were mooted, but never came off for reasons Jack was unable to ascertain. Then, come Jack's seventeenth birthday, there was no card; nor was there any communication the Christmas following.

When he was eighteen, Jack won a scholarship to Oxford and his mother suggested, not particularly forcefully he noted, that he should write to his father with the good news. Jack promised his mother he would, but then, because now two birthdays and two Christmases had been and gone without a word, he had not really felt like putting pen to paper. Why communicate with someone who showed no interest? When he told his mother that he had decided not to write, she had received the news without comment, since when, nothing more was either heard from his father, or said about him in the home. The situation was, as his mother termed it, one of 'Radio Silence.'

The day Jack went up to Oxford, his mother came with him to Paddington to see him off and cried. He remained dry-eyed but felt a kind of heartburn in his throat. As the train pulled away, she waved after him from the platform, and he found himself wishing she wouldn't make quite such a show of herself. For a day or two she was depressed—he gathered this from speaking to her on the telephone—but then that disappeared. She dyed her hair and invested in several pairs of stockings. She started socialising and quickly met a man called Stephen at an Antrim Association dinner dance. By the time Jack's first summer holidays came round, she and Stephen were living together.

It was the end of one type of relationship with his mother and the beginning of another. This had many consequences, of which the principle was that it started Jack thinking about his father. Jack became curious to know what he was like; however, he lacked the will to follow through, to write, or to telephone. Then, in the autumn of his second year, the Geology Department sent him to Ireland; he took this as a sign, and that was when he decided to pay the unexpected call which he was now due to make.

"You know what I used to think about when I was in trouble," said Jack suddenly, "and I had to go and see the headmaster? He was a particularly violent Brother and pretty free and easy with the strap."

"What did you think about?" said Benjamin.

"The story—'The Tortoise and the Hare'."

Jack peered along the road that stretched ahead; it was straight and flat, darkening fields to each side where the earth was banked in ridges.

"Although the hare doubles and re-doubles its speed," he continued, "it never actually catches up with the tortoise, does it? That's what I'd wish; my speed would double and re-double but I'd never arrive at his door."

"Ah, so," said Bejamin in his Sigmund Freud accent, "you wish you go towards your father forever but never actually reach him?"

"Yes, doctor."

"All I ever thought about," said Benjamin, "was whether the head'd rumble the exercise book I'd tucked down the back of my pants." He ran his hands through his hair. Twenty years old and Benjamin was already grey. "You know what your trouble is Jack?" he continued.

"What?"

"You never went to public school. That would have toughened you up."

The road turned inland and widened. The tarmac looked mauve in the gathering dusk. He drove the van around a corner and saw a lake like a dark sheet of polythene stretching on his right. A man wheeling his bicycle was coming along the road in the opposite direction.

Jack braked and wound down the window.

"Hello," he called politely. "I'm very sorry to trouble you."

"He's not a work of art, for fuck's sake. Get on with it," Benjamin muttered beside him.

"We're looking for Cyril MacDonagh," Jack blurted out.

"First house on the left."

They went on. In the growing dusk, the boulders along the verge were like crouching animals. The road wound down and the lake loomed closer. There were houses scattered along the shore.

"There she blows," said Benjamin pointing.

It was a white modern bungalow on top of a hill, with a steep tarmacadamed ramp leading up to the door. A sign hanging by the roadside bore the words 'B & B. *Bord Failte* approved.'

They drove up the incline, the engine roaring, and stopped at the top.

The net curtains were pulled tight behind the windows and there was no light to be seen. It was pointless to have come, thought Jack, and at that moment he felt his friend touching his arm.

"There's got to be someone about," said Benjamin, "it's a guest-house for Christ's sake."

They got out and walked up to the front door. Jack pressed the bell. They waited for footfalls from inside but none came. Benjamin stepped back.

"There's smoke coming out of the chimney," he said.

"And I can hear a T.V." added Jack, who could indeed hear a faint murmur which he indentified as a newscaster.

"Well, they say it's the land of the thousand welcomes," said Benjamin throwing open the front door, "let's take 'em at their word."

Inside the door stood a coat rack with a mirror. The hall smelt of new concrete.

"Hello?" called Benjamin. "Anyone at home?"

The door at the end of the hall opened and Jack saw a young woman lit by the glow from a television in the room beyond.

"Yes," she said. "If you're looking for accommodation, I'm afraid we're closed."

"No, we're not," said Jack.

His heart was beating. How did he explain himself? Did he use his father's christian name or did he ask for Mr. MacDonagh?

165

The woman looked back into the room behind.

"There's someone at the door, Michael," she said loudly, which was more for their benefit than for Michael's, whoever he was.

She shut the door and walked towards them. She was wearing a pair of men's leather moccasins and a denim skirt.

"It's cold," she said.

She took a shawl from the coat rack and threw it around her shoulders. Her skin was white; her hair was dark black; she was quite beautiful.

"Is Mr. MacDonagh at home?" asked Jack.

"No, I'm afraid not." She spoke slowly. "He's gone to Galway. I don't know when he'll be back."

He heard Benjamin sighing behind.

"Could he be back this evening?"

The woman folded her arms.

"He could be," she said. "But I couldn't say for certain."

"That's a pity. We've come all the way from Oxford. Is there anywhere we could stay in the village?"

"All the B & Bs are shut," she replied. "It's out of season. You could try the hotel; it's on the Galway road, about four miles out."

She knotted her shawl and looked up. "Would you like to say your name and I could say you called."

"You could say," said Jack, "that Jack MacDonagh, his son, was here."

They went back to the van and climbed in. She was still standing in the doorway with the shawl over her shoulders. Jack looked at her again, saw the slippers, the bare legs, the shawl; she wasn't the housekeeper as he had at first assumed; she was living with his father.

"Drink," said Benjamin.

They drove into the village and found the pub. It was a long low brown building with Hansel and Gretel shutters. The interior was decorated with ploughs and old whiskey bottles. A partition ran across the middle. On the other side they found a room with bales of hay dangling from the ceiling and a snooker table.

"Good! We can play," said Benjamin cheerfully.

He ordered drinks while Jack leant against the bar. Leaving his father's house, Jack felt dazed; now he was thinking again, particularly about the girl. What a thing to do! Not to ask them in.

On the other hand, why should she welcome the son from the old marriage who was almost the same age as herself?

166

They took their drinks and settled on sticky seats. Apart from two girls in white high heels, the snooker room was empty.

"Well, it could have been worse," said Benjamin.

"Yes," echoed Jack.

They drank slowly without speaking. Then the girls came over to the snooker table and began to play. Jack watched them carefully; grateful to have something to look at. He did not want to be left with the thoughts rattling around in his head ...

Time passed and then he felt Benjamin nudging him gently and saying, "Who's that?"

Jack's eyes travelled from the snooker table to the partition. Here, in the gap, he saw a balding man with a pointed nose. A moment later, the man started to move towards him, his mackintosh swirling around his knees.

"It's my father," said Jack.

He started to stand.

"Hello Jackie," he heard his father saying. "Don't get up."

Jack found himself looking down at his father. He had not expected to find that he was taller.

"What would you like to drink?" asked Jack, the question coming automatically.

He looked at his father shyly. The skin around his nose was red with the eczema which always flared up when his father was nervous.

"No, it's all right," his father said, gesturing at the bar. "It's all taken care of."

"Let's sit down," said Jack.

"Are you comfortable there?" asked Jack.

"Yes, thanks," his father said, and then he added, "You've grown."

"I have, well, yes, I suppose I would have," replied Jack.

The barman appeared with a tray; pint glasses for Jack and Benjamin; a tumbler for Jack's father.

They all toasted one another, swallowed their first moutfuls in silence, then returned their glasses to the table.

"What's yours?" Jack asked his father. It wasn't Guinness, like theirs, but something red and fizzy.

"Red lemonade."

"Don't you drink?"

"It's the ulcer." His father held his stomach with his two hands.

"Oh Christ," said Benjamin. "Do you have to have barium meals and all that carry on?"

167

"I have to drink milk and eat bread and stay off the alcohol."

His father and Benjamin began to swap hospital stories, after which Benjamin told his father about what they were doing, the geology course at Oxford and the Irish field trip. At several points Benjamin praised Jack exaggeratedly. When his father beamed back, Jack felt embarrassed, just like he had on open days at primary school when his parents had enthused about his childish paintings. It therefore came to him as a relief when he heard the conversation turning to other matters—the comforts of academic life and a decision by the dons at Oxford University not to grant the Prime Minister, Mrs. Thatcher, an honorary degree, much to her annoyance.

As the talk rambled on—the next subject was whether the Labour Party would ever get elected—Jack took the opportunity to look closely at his father. He saw that his blue eyes were surprisingly mild and not at all angry and resentful as Jack remembered them as being at the end of the time his father was in London; he saw too that he was wearing a tie which looked brand new, as well as a clean, white shirt that was slightly too tight around his neck; and finally, that although his father's hands were calloused and roughened from years of manual work—his father was now a central heating engineer—his fingers were surprisingly elegant, his fingernails neatly clipped.

As he gazed, Jack tried to imagine what had happened in the pristine modern bungalow that was his father's house in the moments following the departure of himself and Benjamin ... Had the girlfriend fetched his father from a workshop? he wondered, which Jack presumed was at the back of the house. Or perhaps his father had been hiding somewhere in the house the whole time, listening and even watching. It was possible.

Had his father then washed himself rapidly in soap and water, maybe even shaving as well, while she ironed his shirt, filling the whole house with the smell of starch? How long had it taken his father to finish getting ready, and what feelings had quickened his father's heart as he clicked his way out of the house in freshly polished shoes and climbed into his car? When he had arrived at the pub door, mock-German to match the shutters, had his father hesitated? Had he felt butterflies of trepidation? Had he wanted to turn round and go away again? And finally, how had his father been so certain that he would find his son there?

As he wondered about this last problem, Jack heard his father coughing, exactly as he remembered his father doing when he was a child and his father had something difficult to say, and a moment later the question followed.

"How's your mam?" Jack heard his father asking him.

He thought of his mother and Stephen in the flat in Tooting Bec. It was Saturday, early evening; so they would be in the front room, drinking *Martini* and lemonade before going on to the Wimbledon Irish Club. The aquarium in front of the fire place would be bubbling, filling the room with a fishy smell.

"She's very well," said Jack quietly and he realised he had no idea what feelings remained, on the part of either parent.

The next moment a man passed his father.

"Cyril," the man called, and his father turned and cried after the man, "Peter! Hey, Peter, I've a little business needs attending."

Then Cyril turned back and squeezed Jack's arm and said, "Excuse me."

III

A moment later, Cyril was in the next room—Jack could see him through the partition, some of which had been folded back at some point; Cyril laughed and joked with several drinkers, then followed Peter through the main door and vanished from view. Yes, Jack reflected grimly, his father's world, after so many years apart, was quite unknown to him.

Now he began to wonder if there had been any point in coming?

The question panicked him. In order not to think about it, he looked first at his drink and then at the snooker table. Two youths were playing a slick game, intended to impress the girls who had played earlier.

Jack began to watch, toting up the scores in his head before the tallies were altered on the score-board. Anything to keep dark thoughts at bay.

After some minutes he became aware that his father was standing between himself and the table.

"I have to go, lads," he heard his father apologising, "I have to go home to my dinner." His father's face, he saw, was turning red. "I'd have made arrangements if I'd known you were coming," he continued.

"It's alright," his son replied. In fact, in one way it was a relief not to be invited along to the bungalow. The girlfriend would have been heavy going, for a start. This thought gave Jack considerable comfort.

"And don't touch that wallet of yours," his father continued. "You'll be looked after this evening."

"Well, goodbye." Jack stood up, knocking against the table.

"That your van outside?" his father called from the other side of the partition.

"Yes, it is," Jack said. "Why? Is it in the way?"

"Not at all. Work away. It's a fine looking van."

Then his father turned, hurried through the crowds of drinkers, and disappeared into the night outside.

IV

Jack sat down slowly. He felt cheated and relieved all at once. He had sought out his father and had re-established contact. He, who had always been the child, had been the adult for the first time in his life.

On the other hand, what *actually* had happened? He had called at his father's house but his father's girlfriend had not asked him in. Later, his father had found himself and Benjamin in the pub. They had had twenty minutes conversation—and not very significant conversation at that, most of it conducted by Benjamin—and then his father had made his apologies and gone home to his dinner.

When he had thought about this encounter in the past, Jack had imagined arguments; he had imagined reconciliation; but he had never imagined something so modest, so—he hardly dared to use the word—so uneventful, even banal.

"O.K., lads?"

It was the barman with another round of drinks. He set them on the table and walked away, throwing his tray in the air and catching it as he went. Jack swallowed his pint and said, "Let's go."

They walked through the noisy bar, and stepped outside.

It was a cold, crisp October evening. They walked across the road, their shoes crunching on the tarmac, and reached the van; Benjamin was on the passenger's side, Jack by the driver's door.

"What shall we do?" he asked.

Benjamin pulled a small polythene bag from his pocket, and waved it at Jack across the roof. It was a coin bag, with *Allied Irish Banks* printed on the side; and it contained, as Jack knew, a small, greaseproof paper envelope of damp but good cocaine that was cut with Italian baby laxative, and a dark oblong of hashish the size of a toffee. Benjamin had bought the drugs in Dublin from a man he had met in the toilets of a public house. He was good at that sort of thing.

"To the hotel," Benjamin commanded. "we'll play canasta."

Jack opened his door. He was about to climb in when he saw something on the driver's seat, and he didn't remember anything having been there before. He slipped in and lifted the package on to his lap.

It was a plastic bag from *Quinnsworth*—and from out of it he drew a *Southern Comfort* bottle. He turned on the internal light and held the bottle up to it. The screw cap was broken and, as far as he could see, the bottle was filled with a clear liquid.

Jack unscrewed the top and put the stem to his nose. The liquor inside had exactly the same sour apple smell as the stuff his mother kept on top of the wardrobe in her bedroom, and which she claimed she only took for medicinal reasons.

"It's *poitín*," explained Jack.

Benjamin reached for the bottle and took a swig. The drink made him shiver twice.

"Wow!" he shouted enthusiastically.

Jack nosed the van out of the car park gate and down the road. He passed a row of terraced houses, and in every front room there was a television glowing behind the net curtains. After about a quarter of a mile, they passed out of the village and into the countryside. The road stretched ahead of them with a stone wall on either side.

Jack took a gulp from the bottle and returned it to Benjamin. Up to that point, the evening had been an anti-climax; but now the gift of the *poitín* changed everything. It was illegal and Jack supposed that his father had made some effort to obtain it, from Peter presumably. One didn't just go and buy it like a box of chocolates.

On his left a sign appeared reading 'Hotel'. His heart lifting, Jack turned the van on to the track and headed towards the lights twinkling in the distance.

The Kitten

I

THE TABLE WAS SQUARE with an electric light hanging above. The shade was made of raffia. A faint breeze moved the shade and the shadow cast on the wall by the raffia moved in turn. It was like sitting inside a huge spider's web, he thought.

Something moved outside under the veranda. Richard looked across. He saw the cat climbing up the outside of the mosquito screen, as she usually did in the evening, and then hanging there with the fur of her under-belly poking through the mesh.

"Look at the cat," he said.

Martha looked across.

"Do you suppose it's hungry?" she asked.

They had just finished eating their supper in the kitchen. On the table there were olives which shone dully in a bowl; a huge halved tomato; a broken loaf of bread; Greek salami on the coarse brown paper it had come wrapped in; pickled peppers, gnarled like roots, a gift from the Yannis next door, the caretakers of the chalets; a *White Huzzar* vodka bottle with a greasy label which was filled with olive oil; and half a bottle of *Domestica*, water droplets running down the sides.

"Hey!"

Richard got up and went towards the doorway.

"Get down."

He clapped his hands. The cat jumped back. He slid open the screen and bent down. Its eyes were long diamonds like those on a playing card.

"Good puss."

Its small, pink tongue came out and rasped over his fingers as it licked. He scratched the animal behind the ears. The cat began to purr.

He closed the screen and said, "I'm giving up smoking."

"I don't think you're ready yet."

"Why?" he asked.

"I don't think you've found a reason."

But he had. That day he'd swum out several hundred yards, and then, when he'd started to swim back and found the going hard because of the current, he had been overcome by a sense of panic. He'd started swimming harder, which caused his heart to race and his lungs to hurt. When he had finally reached the shore and felt the shingle running over his toes, he had thought, it's time to stop.

He went out on to the veranda and turned on the lights. There was sand in the ashtray on the table, butts sticking up from it in a parody of young shoots. He sat down on one of the cane chairs. The cushion was slightly damp. He took a cigarette out of the packet on the table and put it into his mouth. Then he put it back in the packet again. Martha was moving about in the kitchen. There was a faint sound of tinkling glass as something fell.

"It's alright," she called.

Moments later she waved, a dark shape behind the mosquito mesh.

"Goodnight," he replied.

She padded away. Richard saw the square screen of the Yannis' T.V. glaring behind the net curtain of the caretaker's house next door. He opened the *International Herald Tribune* on the table. The headline read 'Is Nakasone a Racist?' He closed the paper. He was sitting out under the veranda while his wife was going to bed. He shook his head and said, "Tut-tut," to himself out loud.

He went back into the house, sliding the door shut after himself. What the situation needed was dramatic action.

He went to the bathroom. She was looking at her face in the mirror. With her tongue she bulged out a freckled cheek. There was a small blemish on it, a spot. She was dabbing it with perfume. He remembered her asking him not to kiss her there.

"Do you fancy a bit of … Shall I come to bed?"

She caught his eye in the mirror.

"Oh hon!" she wailed. "I'm tired. Can't you see? Aren't you ever satisfied?"

"I thought it would be nice."

"No, it wouldn't."

She screwed the top back on the perfume.

"I thought it would be nice," he repeated.

In the mirror she caught his eye again and looked up towards the ceiling—an infallible signal of irritation. Then she took hold of the bottom of her green cotton blouse and pulled it off. Her breasts were brown and smooth. She pushed her skirt and knickers to the ground, stepped out of them and hung them on the back of the door. He reached forward and touched the bottom of her back. She slid past him and disappeared through the doorway into the dark bedroom. He heard the bedside lamp clicking on and the shutters banging shut.

"You've left the top off the toothpaste," he called.

In the bedroom he could hear Martha sighing as she wriggled into bed. The light in the room went off.

II

The following morning, when he awoke, the top sheet was moist and moulded to his body.

He rolled over. Martha's twin bed was empty. The top sheet was thrown back over the wooden bed end.

He got up and looked through the window. He could vaguely remember hearing Martha opening the shutter when she had got up earlier. Outside, he could see an empty cloudless sky and the edge of the enormous fir tree which grew in front of the chalet. Every evening, the caretaker's mother sat beneath it and played patience on a tray laid on her lap, while the wind sighed through the boughs overhead. Through the wall came the sound of the shower.

Sometime, during the night before, after he had climbed into bed and before he had fallen asleep, he had come to a conclusion.

Go on, he said to himself. He got out of bed and went to the bathroom.

Martha was standing on a towel in front of the mirror. She was naked and wet. He watched her run the mascara stick along her eyelashes. Martha always put her make-up on straightaway after showering. She did it, she said, because she didn't like drying herself, and she knew from experience that in the time it took to apply the foundation, eyebrow liner, mascara, rouge and the cerise-coloured lipstick she favoured, and then pop in her small gold earrings, she would be dry. It was one of those peculiarities that made Martha Martha.

"You make me feel ugly in bed," he said.

He noticed his stomach hanging over the elastic of his boxer shorts and pulled it in. There was something else that he wanted to broach and that had come to him in those dark moments before sleep, but now he couldn't remember what it was.

174

The pollinating mascara stick went back into its sheath.

"I'll never mention you're fat again," said Martha. In the mirror he saw her eye was on his middle, red from the sun but white in the well of the belly button.

III

After breakfast they bumped into town in the little Fiat they had hired. From a rack outside a shop, Martha selected Richard a sun cream with a high protection factor. He gave her his purse, went off to the bank with his passport and joined the queue inside. Middle-aged holidaymakers in their summer clothes stood stoically in front of him, varicose-veined, paunchy, grey-skinned. He admired their indifference to ageing. The woman who cashed his traveller's cheques was vast, with sweat on her upper lip and a lovely smile.

He returned to the car to find Martha sitting in the front seat, and holding his wallet. She had bought a snorkel, a mask and a Lilo. They lay on the back seat, rubbery smelling in the sun.

"Spending my money?" he said.

"Our money," she replied.

They drove down to the harbour, then along the quays covered with market stalls. He glimpsed the red flesh of lopped watermelons, and green peppers being tumbled from a brass scuttle into a sack.

At the end they turned on to a causeway, a narrow road which connected the town to the isthmus opposite and saved a laborious journey round the bay. Halfway across stood a memorial to the original builders, a four sided Egyptian needle with a globe at each corner. In the barber he'd visited two or three times for a shave, dozens of models of this memorial had shared the shelves with tubes of *Palmolive*.

On the far side, the road began to climb. There was a dusty smell of tarmac and a faint sweet smell from the yellow broom which covered the mountainsides. The Fiat laboured on the steeper inclines. Whenever he changed down, he would glance at Martha beside him, moving her jaw from side to side.

He touched the cigarette packet lying on the dashboard. The cellophane had warmed in the sun. He stared at the tarmac, glistening and blue, the white line along the middle, and the parapet to the side, the only protection against a fatal descent. Go on Martha, he thought, say something about smoking. He pulled out a cigarette, put it into his mouth, and picked up the box of matches

"I thought you were giving up," she said.

"If I die at forty from cigarettes," he replied, "it won't matter if I've packed in eighty years of living, will it?"

It wasn't an original thought. He'd overheard it at a party. She had too. He was relieved she didn't remember.

"I could be killed by a bus tomorrow," he said.

Suddenly, he remembered what he'd wanted to say when he'd gone into the bathroom that morning.

"When you smoked, I never shied away from you," he said.

"Why have you never said this before?" she asked.

The filter was swelling with his saliva. He put the unlit cigarette and the matches in his shirt pocket.

"I need time to reflect on these things," he said.

"Humph."

They found the turning for the beach and inched down a track of packed mud and white scree. Chalky dust drifted through the window. He could sense it coating his brow. At the bottom they found a place to park in the shade of white chalk cliffs. He got out and started to walk towards the sea. He carried the basket with their towels and a bottle of water. It was a shingle beach, the stones large and grey. He could feel them pressing through the soles of his sandals. He fixed his eye on the shore. The foam which had formed where the sea broke on the shore, reminded him of floating cream.

At last he reached the sea's edge and found a place to lie down. He spread his towel. He could hear the small stones along the shore rustling and murmuring as they were pulled back by the drag of the surf. He took off his shirt and knelt by the basket. The sun was hot on the skin of his back. He took out the bottle of drinking water, their towels and their two paperbacks. The bottom of the basket was filled with crinkly onion skins but there was no sign of the sun cream. Damn, he thought. He pulled his shirt back on to cover his red torso.

He got to his feet and started walking back towards the car. Martha was coming towards him, lugging the Lilo behind, the heavy inflated shape banging on the stones. Funny to have blown it up by the car, he thought. Probably she'd done it so he wouldn't be able to offer to do it for her.

"Where's the sun cream?" he called. His voice echoed off the cliffs.

She dropped the Lilo and started walking back to the car. He returned to his towel and lay down. It was blue and coarse and smelt faintly of salt and perspiration.

He heard Martha coming. She dropped the snorkelling gear and sat down with a sigh. He could hear her huffing into the plastic nipple of the Lilo as she topped it up.

"Well?"

A last puff and the sound of air escaping before it was closed with the plastic stopper.

"I couldn't find it. I must have left it in the shop."

"Well, that's marvellous. Here I am on the beach in the boiling sun and I've got nothing to stop myself from going red."

"I'm sorry."

He squinted at Martha staring out to sea, her honey gold legs stretched in front of her.

"You don't know what it's like not to tan," he said.

"No, I don't."

He changed into his trunks and walked to the edge of the sea. The waves were coming in very hard. He saw that the water was cloudy, as if chalk had been dissolved in it. He wet his swimming goggles, took two steps and plunged forward. The Mediterranean felt cold for an instant, and then it felt warm and milky. He began to swim, moving his arms and legs slowly. Whenever he put his face under water, he couldn't see more than a few inches ahead because of the chalk particles.

He decided to swim the entire length of the beach. At the far end he was exhausted and he had to lie down for several minutes. His chest was heaving, his heart was pounding. When they grew quiet and he began to feel cold, he started to make his way back. He walked close by the edge of the sea where the tiny shingle stones were made firm by the wet. They provided the most comfortable surface on which to walk.

"I must go in with the snorkel," Martha greeted him when he returned.

"You won't see a thing," he said.

She plunged into the sea. He watched the snorkel moving upright through the water. A few moments later she stood up and pushed the mask back from her face.

"It's amazing," she called, "you can't see a thing."

"That's what I said. Everything's stirred up."

She came back up the beach and threw herself down on the Lilo.

"I was only trying to make conversation," she said.

He dried himself and went back to the car where he sat in the driver's seat. In the distance he could see Martha moving between the water's edge and their towels, while behind he could hear the wistful echo of the surf bouncing from the cliffs.

When the sun was high in the sky he returned to her. She was naked, lying on her front. Lipstick still coloured her lips.

"It's lunchtime," he said.

"Yes, I was just going to have a swim, and then I was going to come and suggest lunch," she said pedantically.

"Yes, why don't you have a swim, then come to the car and we'll go and have some lunch."

IV

In the village there was just the one taverna. It had a red awning and they sat underneath. Two Swedish tourists were writing postcards at another table. The waiter came to take their orders. His was swordfish, hers was pork. Neither spoke as they waited for the meal. He looked at the fishing boats in the harbour.

"That looks good," she said, when his swordfish arrived. It was white meat sprinkled with a green herb like parsley. "That looks very good."

He ate slowly. The flesh was strong tasting. Finally, with only two mouthfuls left on his plate, he said, "I'm not going to give you any swordfish unless you ask."

He forked into his mouth the last mouthful but one.

"I don't want any. If I'd wanted any, I'd have ordered it myself," she said.

"In that case you've missed a great experience."

With his fork he ran the last piece of fish around the oil on his plate and put it into his mouth.

The plates were cleared away. Martha ordered a dish of grapes and two coffees. A dog came out of the taverna. He was brown and white with dull eyes, and clearly he had some beagle in him.

A man appeared, a friend of the waiter, and began to stroke the dog. The dog wagged his tail. A small lizard ran across the floor. The dog turned. The lizard froze. The man urged. The dog lunged. Martha turned away but Richard kept looking. He saw the dog with his head thrown back, the lizard like an elastic band hanging between his white teeth. The man applauded the animal. The waiter appeared with their grapes. He smiled and put them down on the table. On the floor, Richard noticed, was the torn form of the lizard and a mess like saliva.

The coffee arrived and they began to eat the grapes. Pips accumulated like pieces of gravel on her plate, but Richard swallowed his whole. Suddenly, there was a sound of running and scratching on stone. In the

178

square in front of the restaurant, Richard saw a scrawny kitten beginning to run. The dog shot forward and caught the kitten on the steps at the far end. Then another dog ran up and joined in. The waiter rushed out of the taverna and began to shout at the dogs. The kitten flew into the air. A stone hurled by the waiter missed the dogs and landed in nearby shrubbery. The waiter threw a second missile. Then it was all over. The mongrel from the taverna was coming down the steps towards them, and the other dog was disappearing in the opposite direction. Richard could see the kitten was lying at the top of the steps, a grey rag on grey stone.

He stood up and swallowed his coffee. Then he slowly walked to the end of the square. The kitten had been split along the belly and its intestines had spilled out on to the stone. They were moving vaguely and he realised the creature was still breathing. You'll have to put it out of its misery, he thought.

He looked at the little neck with its grey ruffled fur. The tiny eyes were half closed and there was a sticky mixture along the lids. The little pink tongue was sticking out. He put his foot on the neck. He pressed. Through the sole of his shoe he could feel the neck, like bird bone. He pressed harder, but he knew he wasn't pressing hard enough. With his other foot he raised himself off the ground. He bounced once. He bounced twice. As he was about to bounce the third time there came the shriek of bone. He turned and ran down the steps. He was sweating. He rubbed his hand over his forehead.

Martha had left their table and was standing on the quayside looking into the harbour. He came up behind Martha and stopped. The sun hung just above the hills on the other side of the bay. Soon it would sink behind them, out of sight. The hot still air would chill. Night would fall.

He took a step closer and touched her back. She did not move but went on staring down. She was watching a swordfish snaking through the water. It was small, pipe shaped, ribbed like a mackerel, its snout sticking ahead and its shadow moving on the stones below. They stood there for some minutes and then he realised Martha had started to cry.

He took the cigarette out of his pocket, the one which had been in there since the car that morning. It was bent and some tobacco had come away from the end. He put it into his mouth and lit it with a match.

W.9.

I

IN THE DARK HOURS of the night Amos always thought of Jonathan. Sometimes he thought of him as a baby, bawling in his cot. But on this night, Amos thought of his son Jonathan at the end of his life, at their last meeting ...

It was unplanned. Amos had opened the front door and there he was.

And as his son had stepped across the threshold, Amos had seen that his son's face was red and puffy, and that his son's eyes had the same vacant expression they had had when he was born. Amos wondered if Jonathan had been drinking, but later, when they talked, he realised he had been wrong; he realised that Jonathan's swollen, bloated expression was caused by unhappiness. Depression, Amos realised then, could change the face just as much as alcohol.

Amos shivered. What time can it be, he wondered. Had the birds started yet? Amos strained his ears, but beyond the windows of the bedroom, thrown open to the sweltering summer's night, he heard nothing except for the faintest murmur of wind in the trees, and a solitary taxi rumbling along the Edgware Road. Damnation! he thought. If the birds had started singing, he could have listened to them; and then, he would have been able to put Jonathan, and the whole unpleasant business, out his mind. He felt old and out of temper, and he had a pain at the bottom of his back. He pulled some of the duvet away from his wife, Katya, who was in the bed beside him, and tucked it around himself.

"Look at the man on the horse," Katya muttered now in her sleep.

"What man on a horse?" Amos asked his wife.

His question woke Katya up.

"I was dreaming," she said. "I was in France with Jonathan. There was a man in a uniform with gold epaulettes. We were happy together.

But there was no man on a horse as far as I can remember." Then she added, "After I've had a dream like this and I wake up, I always think it was Jonathan's spirit visiting me."

He felt Katya take his hand under the sheets. Her hand was warm and there were beads of moisture on her palm, yet Amos' hand was cold.

"Do you ever dream about Jonathan?" she asked.

"You know I don't," he said.

"Never?"

"Never!"

Amos was lying. He dreamt about Jonathan often. But as far as he was concerned, the whole subject of Jonathan was a Pandora's box and, for Katya's sake, he wanted to keep it firmly shut. Right from the beginning, he had decided that he was going to talk about Jonathan as little as possible, just in case reminiscence led to soul-searching and this, in turn, led to self-doubt and guilty, self-lacerating speculations. Similarly, he had also decided, from the beginning, that he was going to stamp ruthlessly on any conversations of a recriminatory kind; he was not going to tolerate attempts to lay the blame at one door or another. As for his own fears and self-doubts, these too were to be absolutely taboo. 'If you tell Katya how guilty you feel,' he had often said to himself, 'then her guilt will come out too. All sorts of terrible ideas will spring up in her mind. These thoughts will be like weeds in a garden, and it will be the end of her.'

"I'll make some tea," said Katya and got out of bed.

Amos turned on the electric light so she could find her way to the door. She was naked on account of the heat. As she took her dressing gown and put it on, he watched her carefully. She was old now, and her flesh like his, was raddled. Yet beneath her skin, she was still his young bride. As she tied the cord of her dressing gown, Katya turned and saw him looking.

"You still make me blush," she said.

Moments later, as she moved around the kitchen, Katya's bare feet kept sticking to the floor; every time she took a step she made a funny sound. To pass the time Amos sat up and looked out of the window. The night sky, lit up by the lights of London, was muddy black instead of pitch, but at least the stars in the heavens were silver. Then he lowered his gaze. In the triangle-shaped communal garden at the back of the house, he saw the brooding forms of trees and, beyond them, the two terraced rows that formed the other sides of the triangle. They were dark, except for a couple that had lavatory lights that stayed on all night.

Beyond these houses lay the Edgware Road, and although he could not see it, he could imagine the street, with its hi-fi shops fronted with protective grilles, its kebab houses smelling of mint tea and grilled meat, and its greasy pavements.

Katya came in with two cups of tea and a plate of buttered matzos. These were one of the few reminders of their otherwise vanished faith. While the city slept, Amos and Katya sat side by side in bed, and noisily consumed their little meal.

"So, what were you dreaming when you woke up?" asked Katya.

As soon as she asked the question, Amos remembered.

"I was in Warwick Avenue tube station," Amos said, "except the station wasn't here in W.9., in London—it was in Paris! I was late and I was in a hurry. I went and looked at the underground map, but it was in French and its strangeness frightened me. I decided to go and ask the ticket collector for help, but of course he was French too. By this stage I was getting really anxious. Precious seconds were slipping by. I decided to go back to the map and have another go at deciphering it. A futile move, for of course I couldn't. Everything is lost, I thought. I shall give up and go home. However, just as I was leaving, a girl came up to me, blonde ..."

" ... Oh you bad man!" Katya murmured.

"'I will lead you to your train,' said the blonde girl. I followed her along a series of twisting passages. Eventually, we got to a platform, but my train was nowhere in sight. 'Where's my train?' I demanded. 'It's in the tunnel,' the blonde girl replied. 'It's being kept in there for safety.'"

"We jumped down from the platform and started to follow the tracks towards the tunnel. As we walked along, I was careful not to step on the electrified rail. Then we stepped into the tunnel, it got dark, and that was when I woke up ..."

Katya was now snoring quietly. Outside he heard the first bus coming along Clifton Road. It hurtled along without stopping; there were no passengers waiting at the bus-stop. Too early. He noticed daylight glimmering faintly outside and he heard that the birds had started to sing. Again, he was struck by the idea that no matter how hard he tried, no matter how attentively he listened, he never caught the first notes of the dawn chorus. It always crept up on him. Now chains swished against metal. This was the Warwick Avenue tube station being unlocked. Shortly after came the sounds of the first travellers making their way to work. Their footfalls were peculiarly resonant in the morning air, their voices a soft susurrus, like conversations whispered in the corner of a church, or synagogue.

182

And mingled this morning, with the noises which he could hear, was an overpowering sense of Jonathan. Today was the day before Jonathon's birthday, so he presumed this was why his son was so particularly on his mind. Did the spirits of the dead come back on these occasions? he wondered. Amos did not like to have these vaguely occult thoughts. He prided himself on being a rational and practical man.

II

Mid-morning, Amos decided to go and see Elsie in the Ritz café before it got too hot.

He put on his white panama hat and left the flat. On the landing and the common stairs of the house it was cool, but out in the street it was boiling. He began to walk. A man, naked to the waist, with blue-black tattoos up his arms and his pale white skin reddened by the sun, was sponging down a green Jaguar. Two girls in summer dresses sat on a wall. They were listening to a transistor held between their two heads. Hunched together, shoulders touching, they reminded him of Siamese twins he had seen in freak shows as a boy in Poland. A marmalade-coloured cat lay on a front door step, luxuriating in the sun. The cat was the only living thing in the street which seemed at peace with the heat.

Everything he now saw made Amos long for water, huge expanses of it, cold and inviting and preferably surrounded by dark pine trees. For a moment he considered going up to the canal. Looking at it might cool him down, he thought. But it was such a hike. No, he decided, he would do what he set out to do. He turned into Clifton Road.

The street was broad and tree-lined with a wide pavement. The houses were white, peeling a little, with fluted columns beside their big front doors, large shuttered windows behind them, and ornate wrought-iron balconies crowded with huge earthenware pots, lines of washing, and unidentifiable pieces of machinery. On one balcony there was even a crude weather-vane on the end of a bamboo cane. It was Amos' favourite street in London, for there was something about the architecture and its configuration which reminded him of the leafy avenues of Lódz where he had spent so much time so long ago; and now, unsought memories from then came flooding back ... He was at a party in a big house, drinking champagne. It was his first time and he found the drink unexpectedly prickly in the throat. In his pocket he had a thick bundle of zloty notes just won at the card table. He held them tightly, frightened of losing them. Glancing nervously up the stairs, he saw a girl sliding down the bannister. Big eyes, red lips and a red dress billowing behind her. As she swept towards him, he imagined himself, victor of the card-table, kissing her bare shoulders. He took his hand out of his pocket. The champagne was taking effect. Everything was suddenly attainable, whatever he wanted ...

Another memory, this one from boyhood. It was December, the day of his mother's funeral. He was standing in the street waiting for a tram. His scrubbed raw face was smarting in the cold. He could see his breath in the air and all around wreaths of steam poured from drains. His grandmother and his great-aunt were beside him. The tram appeared, screeching along the metal rails, sparks flying from under its iron wheels, and as it curved towards him, a feeling of wretched loneliness closed in on him like a fog.

After this, he remembered something that happened much later. He was in a park with Katya, sitting in a café by a lake. On the water, men in shirt-sleeves were rowing boats and laughing, while he and Katya sat in silence, eating ice-creams. It was their first date and they were shy. The ice-cream was runny and his metal spoon tasted of cod-liver oil. Suddenly, the autumn afternoon got dark, and then someone turned on the coloured carnival lights hanging in the trees around them. "Beautiful," she whispered ...

"Hey darling!"

Amos looked up. A workman on a roof was shouting down at a girl in the street. She had dyed, maroon-coloured hair which was piled on top of her head.

"What's your number? Go on, give us your number!"

The girl walked on saying nothing. Amos smiled to himself. They are all so young, he thought. What did they know?

He stepped into the Ritz café. It was dark inside. Automatically, he made his way to the staff table. It was at the back, underneath the grimy statue of a flamenco dancer with flying skirts.

"Hello!" called Elsie, the owner, "I'll be with you in a minute."

He sat down, took off his hat, and started thinking about Jonathan again ...

One day, years before, he had left the Ritz and gone to the local bookshop. To his great surprise, he had run into Jonathan in there. This was long after his son had left home and married. Jonathan did not look well; he was perspiring and his hands were trembling.

"What's the matter?" asked Amos, when they were back in the street.

"Nothing." But after much badgering from Amos, Jonathan eventually told his father that he and Sarah, his wife, were going through what he called a 'rocky patch'.

"A rock what? What's that? Damn my English."

"It means that we're unhappy," Jonathan explained.

"Have you been unfaithful?" Amos asked.

"No."

"Are you angry with her?" Amos asked.

"No, I'm not angry."

Amos looked into his son's eyes and saw that the expression there was that of a man who did not understand what was happening to him. Amos had brought Jonathan up to believe that the world was benign, and now he regretted that.

"Did you put your books on my account?" Amos asked him abruptly.

"No, of course not," his son said.

"Well, please, let's put them on my account," said Amos, "I would like to make them a present to you."

He took Jonathan's books back into the shop. He was surprised to see that one of them was the *I Ching*, and the other a book on astrology.

A moment later they said goodbye, and Amos let his son slip away. In itself, this was a small omission; but there were so many like it, and added together, he felt, they amounted to a huge indictment.

Elsie brought over two cups of coffee and sat down opposite. Taking a careful sip, Amos noticed the coffee tasted burnt. In the Ritz the coffee was mixed with chicory for economy. It was a taste he quite liked.

"Are you ever lonely?" he asked.

"You're very serious this morning," said Elsie.

"Are you ever lonely?"

"Yes, sometimes I wake up in the middle of the night and I put my feet out to feel for Charlie but he's not there," replied Elsie. "I hate Sundays most. There's only myself to argue with in the flat. The silence gets on my nerves. I go for walks although these old pins aren't what they used to be! But what am I talking about? Look at what you've made me go and say. You don't want to listen to an old woman wittering on."

"Yes, I do."

"You miss Jonathan."

"Yes, I do."

They touched each other's hands.

"Two coffees!" a customer shouted.

"Harold," Elsie bellowed down the stairs to the cook in the kitchen, "two coffees …"

The café suddenly fell quiet. It was a conspiracy of silence, thought Amos. They were being left alone to talk.

"I often feel my old Charlie's watching me," said Elsie. "I just get this feeling and I know he's around. Sometimes, I think I see him in the street, but it's always a stranger. But he hasn't gone, I know. Your Jonathan too. He hasn't gone either. He's just gone somewhere else."

"Yes," said Amos, "I know."

Elsie's views were all very well and it was touching that she believed they would console him, but what Amos wanted to talk about was his guilt and the feeling that he had failed Jonathan. But could he, he wondered? And did he dare? His courage was wavering.

A customer appeared at the counter, jingling change in the palm of his hand.

"You'll be alright," said Elsie.

Then she squeezed his hand and stood up.

He picked up his coffee cup and took another careful sip.

III

When he got home, Amos found Katya had been crying. The rims of her eyes were red and there were little swellings on her lips where she had bitten them.

"What's wrong?" said Amos.

"*She's* coming round."

"Who ... ?"

"Sarah ... she telephoned while you were out. She's coming to see us. Why can't she leave us alone? Why does she torture us? She's done enough harm as it is."

"You can't say that, Katya."

"Of course I can! She drove him to it!"

"We don't know that."

"We do know it as certainly as we know that kitchen table is here!"

Katya buried her face in her apron and started to wail.

"Katya, Katya," he said, putting his arms around his wife. "Our son was unhappy and he took his own life. No one is to blame."

"Yes, she's to blame," sobbed Katya.

"No, she's not," he said, "and nor am I to blame, or you, or anyone else."

As he spoke, Amos felt himself growing irritated. He was fed up with repeating himself. He wanted to tell her what he really felt. "Forget

186

Sarah!" he wanted to say. "Think about us. Think about how we let him down!" But he did not. Years of habit could not be broken in an instant.

For half an hour he told Katya that no one was to blame. She resisted him at first, then slowly succumbed; it was a bit like hypnosis. Finally, Katya dried her eyes and they had a bowl of cold soup together.

IV

After lunch, Katya took a siesta and he went down to the communal garden to sit on a bench in the shade. He felt weighed down. In the first place he had not been able to tell Elsie what he felt and then, on top of that, he'd had to spend half an hour telling Katya what he did not actually believe himself. Would it ever end? Was he condemned to carry his remorse and guilt to the grave? Would he never know the sweetness of sharing the burden with someone? His life had to change. He could not go on waking up every morning and thinking automatically of Jonathan, yet denying that he did. Nor could he spend his days going over everything in secret. He felt his heart was going to burst and he wanted to shout out: "Is there no one I can tell? Is there no one who will listen?"

The last time Amos had seen Jonathan was a week before it happened. Jonathan had called on Amos unexpectedly ...

As he slowly walked down the hall of the flat, Jonathan kept his hands in his pockets and his shoulders hunched as if he were nursing an internal wound.

"Have you been drinking?" asked Amos gently.

There was nothing censorious about Amos' tone. On the contrary, he was blithe and happy.

Jonathan turned and looked him in the eye.

"No, I haven't been drinking," he said, very seriously. "I'm in love."

They sat in the back living-room overlooking the triangle garden. Jonathan asked for a pencil and paper. Amos gave him a sheet of paper and coloured pencils. His son started to draw. Outside, in the street, Amos could hear workmen banging with hammers ... ton, ton, ton.

Katya brought in a tea-tray and, as tea was poured, Jonathan cleared his throat.

"Mother and father," he said, "I have come here to tell you something important. My marriage is not a success as you know. I have not been happy. And now, after everything, I have met a woman whom I love."

As he spoke, Jonathan's Adam's apple bobbed like a cork at a sea, and Amos remembered how it would do this when he cried as a boy.

187

" ... Sarah is not happy either. I am going to leave her—I think it is best for both of us—and I am going to live with Eliza."

The name, when he heard it, shocked Amos far more than the idea of the failed marriage and the new union. It had always been Jonathan and Sarah. Now it would be Jonathan and Eliza. It seemed an unlikely combination of names.

Amos and Katya were silent for a while, then Katya said:

"Does she love you?"

"Yes. I think so."

"Well," said Amos, "you must do as you think best."

"Yes, you must do what makes you happy, and whatever your choice, you have our blessings."

As he and Katya spoke, Amos was overcome with a sense of how old they were, and how platitudinous they had become. They were like Old Testament figures passing pronouncements.

After finishing his tea, Jonathan crumpled up the piece of paper on which he had been drawing.

"I have to go," he said.

Katya and Amos went with him to the front door.

"Our thoughts and prayers are with you," said Katya, and kissed him.

"Yes, our thoughts are with you," said Amos as they embraced.

After shutting the front door, Amos retrieved the crumpled paper ball. When he opened it out on the table, he saw that it was covered with rows of circles, each of which had four petals inside, arranged symmetrically, like propeller blades. At the bottom of the page Jonathan had written over and over again, in spiky writing, 'Work on what has been spoiled'.

Amos and Katya heard nothing for a week. Then a policeman called to their door with the news. The constable had dandruff on his shoulders and a crackling radio. Jonathan had drunk weed killer, then hung himself in his garden shed.

The Coroner's Court was in Ashford, Kent. When Amos, Katya and Sarah arrived, they found the strange woman, Eliza, was already there. Jonathan had written to her and posted the letter shortly before he killed himself. The letter was read out in court.

It began as a love-letter. Eliza, Jonathan wrote, was the first woman he had ever loved. She was also the first woman, he believed, who had ever really loved him ...

When she heard this, Sarah broke down and had to be taken outside. Katya went with her, but Amos stayed. He felt oddly numb inside and as if everything was a dream or a blur. And he wanted to know everything.

In the letter Jonathan went on to say that he was burdened with debts. His company had gone to the wall. So many depended on him. He had let them all down. He was worthless. He had no right to live and no wish to live. Nor could he stand the humiliation of public bankruptcy.

Jonathan ended the letter by writing that he was going to post it. After that he would return home, and by the time it arrived, he would be dead.

As he sat listening in the Coroner's Court, several pictures of great vividness formed in Amos' mind. He saw the half-timbered house where Jonathan lived out in Kent, with its white gate, flint-studded walls and lattice windows with their diamond-shaped, lead-beads. Then he saw Jonathan's study—Amos assumed this was where Jonathan wrote the letter—small and cluttered like a ship's cabin and crammed with the maritime objects—quadrants, compasses, maps—which Jonathan collected. Then he pictured the lane along which Jonathan walked to the post-box. The sun was shining and there were daisies and buttercups growing along the verge. Finally, Amos imagined the garden shed with its creaking door, smelling of old twine and creosote, and full of the chatter of the chaffinches that nested in there. These thoughts left him dizzy. But the feeling passed, and a few minutes later he felt better.

The Coroner's verdict was that Jonathan had taken his own life, being of a disturbed state of mind.

Sarah, Katya and Amos took the train back to London together. They had not spoken to Eliza. When Sarah left the compartment to use the lavatory, Amos asked Katya—who had not left Sarah since she had led her from the court—if Sarah was all right?

"She wishes she'd had a child by Jonathan," said Katya curtly, "but it's too late for that sort of whining now ..."

Amos looked out of the window and remembered something Jonathan had once said to him. They had been in the sitting-room in Jonathan's house, Sarah's collection of Victorian dolls and Edwardian teddy bears on shelves around them.

"Do you know what they are?" Jonathan suddenly asked his father, and he pointed at the collection.

Amos looked up. The dolls all had pale sinister faces, while the teddy bears looked inane with their buttons for eyes and brightly coloured bows around the necks.

Amos shook his head. He did not follow the drift of his son's question.

"Those are Sarah's substitute babies," said Jonathan. "She hasn't the courage to have one of her own."

Beyond the grubby window of the train stretched green, lush meadows.

In one field there was a shire horse, his head turned at an odd angle as he grazed, and two little girls who waved at the train as it rumbled by. It was then that it hit Amos. His son *was* dead. He started to cry. Inside, he felt the same as when he was waiting for the tram to take him to his mother's funeral. But, along with the grief, there was a new feeling which had been beyond him in childhood, and this was remorse. Jonathan's last hours and weeks, he imagined, must have been so dark. How had he failed to notice, to act?

Sitting now in the garden below his flat, Amos winced at the thought. 'I should have interfered,' he said to himself, 'as it is the duty of every human being to stretch out his or her hand if they see another falling, and my failure to do this will be to my eternal shame ... '

As he heard the words booming in his head, Amos imagined himself standing before a tribunal—he called it *The Tribunal for the Hearing of Crimes of Omission*. He was on the floor of the court, while in front of him there was a judge, sitting on a dais. This was one of Amos' most frequent daydreams.

Suddenly, the usually silent and inscrutable judge spoke.

"What do you want from life?" he asked.

Amos did not have to think twice about it, for every day he wished the same thing.

"What I wish for more than anything," he replied, "is to be able to unburden myself to Katya. I want to say—Katya, we are guilty. We have failed. Let us shout it from the roof tops. Let us confess it to the world. We let our son fall. We did not think."

Amos looked around himself. The trees and bushes of the garden were baking in the sun. He looked at his watch. He had been sitting thinking for more than an hour. An hour!

Children shrieked in a plastic paddling-pool, and the music drifted from a transistor. Standing before the Tribunal, he had been oblivious to all. It was time to go.

He got up and walked slowly across the scorched grass towards the gate. Underfoot, the earth seemed abnormally hard, and the sunbathers that he passed on the way were like dead corpses laid in the sun.

V

Sarah—she came straight from work—arrived at their flat at six o'clock. As she came through the front door, Amos saw she was quite different from how he remembered her. Instead of the habitual scrubbed face and black jeans, she had dyed her hair a yellowy blonde and had it curled. She was wearing lipstick and a short summer dress. She had become a girl again.

"How are you?" he asked, as he bent to kiss her on the cheek, for he was very much taller than Sarah.

"Tiddly," she replied, "I've been celebrating!"

As his lips brushed her cheek, he smelt alcohol on her breath.

He led Sarah to the living-room. She greeted Katya then flopped down on the sofa and put her knees together in a way that reminded him of a schoolgirl.

"Any chance of a Campari?" asked Sarah. "I need something long and cold. It's so hot ..."

Amos was standing by the drinks cabinet. He took the lid off the ice-bucket. The cubes inside had stuck together to form a huge block. He began hacking with the tongs and, as he did, he remembered the girl in Lódz ...

As she jumped off the bottom of the bannister, he had winked at her; they had fallen into conversation. Later, that night, they had slept together.

"You went to bed with a virgin," she had said to him the next morning, "but you're waking up with a woman."

"Did you get drunk last night so you could go through with it?" Amos had asked.

"Yes."

Since which exchange Amos had always been a little nervous of a young woman drinking. He decided therefore to give Sarah a slightly smaller measure. As he poured in the liquor it made the ice crack, an eerie sound.

Ten minutes later, Amos had swallowed his drink and exhausted his small talk. In the silences, he swirled the melting ice in the bottom of his glass in little nervous circles. Katya and Sarah, he noticed, were doing the same. The air was heavy.

"Listen folks," said Sarah suddenly. "I think this is going to come as a shock to you ... but—I'm not going to be Mrs. Rubilinsky any more. I'm going to be Mrs. Ward-Smith. I've fallen for this man you see ... I wanted to tell you ... I hope you won't take it amiss ..."

Out of the corner of his eye, Amos saw Katya wince and her green eyes fill with tears. Sarah was a living connection with Jonathan and it was painful, Amos presumed, for her to think of it being severed, even if Katya also blamed her.

"My dear Sarah," he said, reaching out to touch her hand, "I am so happy for you. I am grateful you have had the courage to tell us this. It must have been very difficult for you. And we understand, life goes on, it cannot stop—don't we, Katya?"

"Yes, we do. Our heartfelt congratulations. It's wonderful news."

Both women shed a few tears.

"We should be laughing and celebrating," said Amos, "not wailing."

"Yes," said Sarah, laughing and wiping her tears away with her sleeve.

With great animation she took a half-melted ice-cube out of her glass and started to rub her temples and the back of her neck with it. Where the droplets of water splashed on her dress, the fabric darkened.

"Gosh, it's hot!"

It was hot. All the windows of the sitting-room were thrown wide open, but there was no trace of a breeze. From the distance, voices and the rumble of traffic floated in. The inhabitants of the entire metropolis, hot and grubby, were hurrying home to their showers and bathrooms.

"What about the lucky man?" Amos asked, politely.

Sarah told them that he was called Douglas, he was tall and kind, he had bluish eyes and blondish hair, he had made his money in the City, and he owned a house in Lincolnshire.

Her description made Amos fractious. He yearned to be told one small, true thing rather than this welter of clichés.

A few minutes later, he walked Sarah to the front door. She was sober now, and he realised that what he had earlier taken for drunkenness was actually nervousness.

"If you would both like to come to the wedding," said Sarah, as she stood on the threshold, "you would be my guests of honour."

As she spoke, Sarah squeezed his arm and looked into his eyes. Amos sensed her guilt, and how important it was to her that he should agree. But the question had taken him by surprise, and he did not know what Katya would say.

"If we can come, I am sure we will," he said.

Sarah was disappointed, but she said nothing and he shut the front door after her.

Back in the living-room, he found Katya where he had left her.

"So, she is marrying again," he said.

"Yes."

"You are sad?"

Katya said nothing.

"How do you feel?" he asked.

"I feel like a stone. I feel nothing. I am numb."

Amos walked to the window and looked down. In the garden below, three boys were playing cricket. They had chalked their wicket onto a tree, the trunk of an elm. There were deck-chairs, toys and towels, scattered on the ground around them.

"Hey!" a woman shouted down to them. She was at the upstairs window of a house on the other side of the garden.

"Supper," she continued.

The boys ran home—shoes crunching on the gravel path—and now the garden was empty.

Looking now at the shadows which lengthened across the grass, Amos suddenly felt quite frozen and petrified, like something that had been buried in the ground for a thousand years. Life was changing all around him, yet he seemed to be fixed by grief and unacknowledged guilt at the moment in time when Jonathan had died. He was old, he thought, but was he so old that he couldn't change? Surely not.

VI

The evening was dreary and Amos went to bed quite early. The sheets, when he climbed in, felt scratchy. He thought, I'll never sleep! But surprisingly, he fell asleep almost immediately and his dreams that followed were extraordinarily vivid.

He was in the Clifton Road, the road that so reminded him of Lódz. He went into the small, Pakistani-owned supermarket, the one on the corner, near the Edgeware Road. It was crowded. He filled a basket from the shelves and joined the queue to pay. The line moved slowly. As he got close to the cash till, a dark Iranian woman stepped up to him.

"Excuse me," she said, "would you mind if I went in front of you?"

"Not at all," said Amos.

"Thank you so much," she gushed. "I'm in such a rush. I've got the Messiah at home, you see."

"*The* Messiah?"

"Yes. He dropped by, unexpectedly. I'm going to give him fish."

When the dark woman came to pay, she found she had no money.

"Oh no," she wailed. "Can I have it on credit?"

"Certainly not," replied the shop assistant behind the till.

"But the Messiah is waiting at home. I must feed him."

"I'm sorry. I don't care who you've got at home. No credit."

"But it's *the* Messiah."

"Messiah or no Messiah—*no* credit!"

"Listen," interrupted Amos, "I'll pay. The Messiah would never come to me, but at least I can buy Him his dinner!"

A few minutes later, Amos left the shop. To his great surprise he found his grandmother and his great-aunt waiting outside for him. Both women were wearing long black dresses and little white bonnets on their shaven heads. Together, the three of them walked back down Clifton Road towards his flat. The trees overhead were in bud and the pavement was sticky with sap. Suddenly, Amos's grandmother scowled and shook her head, then rushed to the kerb and began to scrape the bottom of her boot on the edge. She had stepped in dog-mire, black and evil smelling.

"Oh, grandmother," Amos exclaimed, "you've stepped"—and then he used the word he would never have used with them in Poland—"you've stepped in dog-shit!"

"How dare you say that word!" his grandmother screamed. "Nice little doggies don't produce such a thing as that."

The two women hurried away crossly. Then a moment later, a wagoner whom Amos had know in Lódz came up to him.

"Look," said the wagoner, and he pointed at an open door.

The door opened on to a kitchen, inside which Hannah—'Hannah the Harlot' as she had been known in Lódz—was working at a big table.

"Hello, Amos," Hannah called out warmly. "I'm making you bread."

Her eyes sparkled as she spoke. 'She's in love with me,' Amos thought. He could feel it.

Crowded round the big, pot-bellied stove that stood in the corner of the kitchen—it was a pre-war, Polish kitchen and not a modern London kitchen—there were half-a-dozen tradesmen. They had been drinking vodka and now they were singing patriotic, Polish songs. One or two glanced towards him. Amos felt embarrassed. He didn't want these men to know he was loved by Hannah the harlot, the woman who happily went with every man from the ghetto for a few zlotys. If they gossiped and the story got back to his grandmother and great-aunt at home that Hannah was friendly with him ... No! it didn't even bear thinking about.

Without a word to the wagoner, Amos hurried from the door and away up Clifton Road towards home. But before he could get away, Hannah had begun to hurry after him. Was there no escape from her? Hannah was carrying something wrapped up in a blanket.

"Look!" said Hannah, in an insistent voice, when she finally caught up with him. She showed him the bundle. "I have borne you a son."

Tucked behind the blanket, Amos saw the small, red face of a new born child.

Now, in the dream, Amos started to weep, and when he woke up he was still weeping. His crying woke Katya.

"My darling," she said, "you are crying. Your face is wet. Why are you crying?"

"Katya," he said.

"Yes."

And the words tumbled out:

"Katya, we must face up to it. We were neglectful. We let ourselves behave like old people. For years we knew Jonathan was unhappy. We discussed it often between ourselves. But we did nothing. It's not our business, we said. With this sort of thinking and shirking we let things slide for years. Then look what happened. Yes! I'm afraid we failed to help our son although we knew he was in the deepest trouble ... I'm not excusing myself, Katya—but I never said any of this before, for your benefit. This can't go on. We must face it ... and if we add our strength together—you and I—we will be strong enough."

Katya turned on to her back and sighed in the darkness. Her sighs filled the bedroom, reaching into every corner.

"Is there life after death?" Katya asked.

"Why do you ask?"

"Will we be punished?"

"Don't ask such questions! Of course not! Everyone of us who is alive fails everyday. We fail every minute probably. There isn't a man alive who hasn't sinned in this way. Of course we won't be punished."

Katya turned back to Amos and crept into his arms. And, as they lay there quietly, under the open windows, Amos sensed the city, like themselves, quietly respiring in the summer darkness.

"Katya?"

"Yes."

"Are you all right?"

"Yes." She paused, then she said: "Are you all right?"

"Oh, I am so much better," said Amos, "and in time you will feel much better, I promise. It's as though a millstone has dropped away from my neck. We spend our lives pointing fingers and saying 'He's to blame, she's to blame, they're to blame'. But when you finally say 'I am' such a peaceful feeling comes over you. You don't have to worry anymore. You've confessed. And now you know you will sleep, soundly and sweetly. And to think—for three years I have avoided this. I have made

195

us blindly follow a course. How stupid and pointless it was. At my age, when one's supposed to be wise. It's a bitter thought!"

"Sssshhhh!" said Katya. "You did it for my sake."

Then Katya dozed off, and memories of Hannah came flooding back from well over fifty years ago, before the war, before London.

When he was seventeen, the wagoner had brought Amos to visit Hannah for the first time. Hannah lay in bed under the covers as Amos undressed. When he took off his shirt, she threw back the blankets. Amos nearly fainted. He had never seen a naked woman before, still less one so luxuriously plump. As he unlaced his boots, he wondered if he was going to sink into her flesh, never to return? At the same moment, he noticed a mouse-hole in the wainscoting and he knew he would never forget it.

As he lay on Hannah, all Amos could think about were his grandmother and great-aunt sitting at home. It was late afternoon and he knew they were at their tapestry frames. His grandmother was doing a 'Mill Scene' and his great-aunt was doing 'Mont Blanc'. Mixed in with the smell of Hannah and the feel of her hair on his face, were images of their old nimble fingers, needles and coloured pieces of yarn. If they had known where he was, they would have died. His anxiety prevented Amos from taking any pleasure in what was happening and, when the miracle finally occurred, he experienced nothing more than a mild, tingling sensation of relief. He dressed immediately and left.

Outside Hannah's, Amos found the wagoner waiting for him, a lascivious expression on his face.

"Well," he said, "how does it feel to be a man?"

"Get out of my way, you disgusting man," Amos shouted.

He pushed the flabbergasted wagoner aside and hurried home through a complicated maze of back alleys where he knew he would not be seen.

Two days after his visit to Hannah's, Amos was plunged into torment; he became convinced that he had a small hunch in the middle of his back. What terrified him particularly was the idea that the hunch had been bulging through his jacket the two days before he discovered it was there, and that during all that time he had been marked out, without his knowing it, as one who went with gentile whores. But nobody was saying anything, not even his grandmother and great-aunt. There was a conspiracy of silence.

Every night thereafter, when he went to bed, the seventeen-year-old Amos closed his eyes with a sense of dread. He could feel the hunch pressing through the mattress. But was his punishment to end there? Perhaps he would wake up only to find himself more hideously deformed.

He would have two heads or have turned into a fish. Every morning, when he opened his eyes, Amos expected the worst. But it never happened, and then one morning he woke up and he knew was being ridiculous.

That evening, Amos returned to Hannah's. She was with another customer when he arrived, so he had to wait. When the customer came down, Amos was surprised to see that he was a refined-looking gentleman in his forties, with pointed ears and delicate hands.

Amos went upstairs.

"Come back for more," said Hannah, throwing back the covers. He sat down on the edge of the bed and stroked back the hair from her forehead.

"You are so beautiful, Hannah," he said. The truth of the matter was, he had fallen a little in love.

"Aie! That's what you all say! But you all take little wives, and then you forget about me, and I don't see you for years, not until you're forty and you're feeling lonely. And by that time the best has gone out of you. I get the remains. The carcass ..."

Then she sat up in bed abruptly and kissed him passionately, afraid that she had offended him.

Later, as he lay on Hannah, Amos again thought of his grandmother and his great-aunt. But unlike on his first visit, Amos now felt exhilarated by the idea that he was deceiving them and would get away with it ...

Now he blinked and suddenly, they appeared before him, the two fine women who had brought him up after his mother died, sitting on the end of his London bed.

"Hello, grandmother," he said, "and greetings to you, great-aunt. I've been dreaming about you two, and grandmother, in the dream, you stepped in some dog-shit."

"Amos! Amos, how dare you say such a thing. Go and wash your mouth out and say your prayers ten times over before you go to sleep."

Amos chuckled to himself. They were just the same ... A minute later he fell into a deep dreamless sleep, the first for years, and when he woke up—this was only a few minutes later—he knew exactly what he had to do. He climbed out of bed and went and peered out of the window.

Outside, he saw pale stars twinkling far away. It was still dark. If they left immediately and moved fast, there was a chance no one would see.

"Eh, Katya," he said, touching her on the shoulder, "wake up."

"What is it?" said Katya, sitting up in bed.

"Get dressed. We're going out."

Ten minutes later, Amos and Katya were hurrying down a street towards the Grand Union canal. There was no one around and the big, white houses of Warwick Avenue seemed like the swollen eyelids of a sleeping giant. At the bottom of the road, a dog with a limp passed them.

The way to the canal was through a small gate with sharp spears on top, and then down a narrow set of steps. Amos swung back the gate and Katya went through first. Amos followed, the small plastic carrier bag containing the box swinging at his side.

At the bottom of the steps there was a wide concrete walkway which led to a pool from which different arms of the canal radiated. The still water was the colour of mercury.

"Are we doing the right thing?" Katya asked. "Are you sure?"

"It would be Jonathan's wish. This is right. It's his birthday."

"Will anybody see, do you think?"

"Nobody's about."

"Let's be quick then."

Amos knelt down and took the box from the carrier bag. Sarah had made them take it after the cremation. There were four screws on top, one in each corner. These freed the drawer inside. Trembling slightly—he was anxious about spilling any of the precious contents—Amos slid the drawer out. He didn't quite know what to expect and, in the half-light before dawn, he was surprised to see that the ashes were so pale and so fine.

"Do you have any prayers to say?" he asked.

"I've said them already."

"Let's do it then."

Amos and Katya tipped the drawer forward together. The ashes poured, seemed to hover for a moment in the still air, then landed softly on the water. Amos hoped they would disappear instantly, but instead they formed a dark film on the surface, floated there for a few moments, then finally disappeared.

It was over, but Amos and Katya felt rooted to the spot, unable to move. Then a duck jumped into the water with a loud squawk and ripples started to spread across the stillness.

It was time to go.

They climbed the stairs and began to walk home. A little way up the road they came across a bench. Without speaking—they were both melancholy and sad and tired—they sat down. It was a pleasant spot. There were trees overhead, green and leafy, and in front of them—beyond the black railings and a notice put up by the Waterways Board—lay the canal, with brightly painted barges floating upon it.

Katya shivered.

"It feels like rain, doesn't it?"

Amos looked up into the sky. It wasn't blue as he expected, but grey and darkening.

"You know, I remembered the strangest thing when we were down by the water," said Katya. "I don't know where I learnt it ... 'Who going through the Vale of Misery use it for a well: and the pools are filled with water. They will go from strength to strength ... '"

"What strange things you remember, Katya."

There was a moment of stillness that was almost terrifying, and then it started to rain. The rain fell in large, hard drops. These drops drummed on the wooden roofs of the barges—the noise carried across the street to them—and they formed dark, ragged shapes wherever they fell on the pavement.

"We'll go," said Amos, "but we're going to get wet."

Amos tore open one side of the plastic bag he had used to carry Jonathan's ashes. He put it over Katya's head. She looked as if she was wearing an absurd Dutch hat.

They got up and hurried down Blomfield Road towards home. Thunder rolled. The rain really started to pelt down. Within seconds, the dry patches between the splodges on the paving stones had been made wet— so now the ragged shapes were joined together—and then the whole of the pavement, as well as the road, and even the leaves of the trees, glistened and shone, as if all had been newly varnished.

There was rain running down Amos' collar and goose-pimples were creeping up his arms—but he hardly noticed—for his thoughts were turned towards to the street along which he was going, and the sleeping city which stretched beyond the street, and the sky which stretched above, and the rain—how democratic!—which fell on everywhere, on everyone, on every place.

For the next half-hour or so, while the storm raged, the city would be awash with rain. But then, the rain would stop and the clouds would move on, hurried by the wind, and the rainwater would drain away, along the gutters and down the drains and into the rivers, taking all the heat and the dust of the city along with itself; and the rainwater would flow on, bearing its cargo, until eventually it tumbled out into the sea.

And then, when the people of the city awoke, they would discover their streets were not sticky and dirty, as they had left them the night before; they would discover their streets were clean and cool and as if new; they would find that the air was dry, and that it was possible to breathe again; they would find the sky was blue and clean and open; and they would find that the sun, where it fell, was warming the chilly world with its touch.

And, at more or less this very moment, Amos decided, as the rain stopped and the clouds scrolled away, he would go down to the communal garden. He had planted a rose bush there which Jonathan had given him—this was many years ago. The petals—which were red—would be swollen, and the scent, after so much rain, would be sweet and yet sharp. He would cut two or three blooms. He would smell the smell of the rose sap, leaking from the cut stems. He would lay the flowers in the basket— he would have brought this with him, he would not forget. Then he would carry the red roses back to the flat, to their eyrie as they called it sometimes, and he would present them to Katya, his love.

With this thought, he linked his wife's arm and they hurried towards their home.